Chasing the Demon

Paul Sating

The characters and events portrayed in this book are fictitious. Any situations or similarity to real persons, living or dead, is coincidental and not intended by the author.

ISBN-13: 978-1-7322617-0-9

Cover Art By: Kessi Riliniki

To Madeline: for always believing, encouraging, and
supporting me! GILU & URME

1

The stench of old wood and unwashed people didn't surprise Jared Strong.

Stale beer, peanuts, and people. A lot of the hole-in-the-wall type bars in this western corner of the Olympic Peninsula, his home, smelled like this. His current drinking hole of choice was no different, no better. He smothered a handful of nuts between his palm and fingers, squeezing until he heard the satisfying crack of the shells. Picking out the nuts, he tossed them into his mouth, discarding the shells on the floor. It wasn't something he would do at home, especially not when he and Maria were still together. But, in fairness, this place didn't look like anyone had loved it for at least a generation.

That observation made him wonder how much time had passed since Maria had loved him.

Maria.

Best not to think about her right now. There were other problems he needed to face first. Like the reason for the stack of papers sitting in front of him on the sticky bar top.

This was Olympia, the capital of the state. The gem, right? He laughed to himself, glancing down at the shell-covered floor underneath him. What a dump. He shook his head at how quickly his life had gone off track.

"Great place to start chasing a demon," he mumbled to the stack of papers. They didn't answer.

The drunk seated next to him sneered. "Whatch'da say?"

"Huh?" Jared asked, "Uh, nothing. Sorry. Didn't mean to bother you."

"You ain't no bother," the man said, then returned to his beer.

Jared laughed. "Let me know if that changes, will ya?" *God knows I've already done that to enough people in my life.*

The old man's eyes narrowed as if he was examining Jared's soul. Awkward and uncomfortable, Jared put his attention on the papers, an idle finger tracing their edges.

The drunk squinted at him and laughed, coughing up things that came from deep within his lungs. "Whatcha lookin' at there?"

Nothing. The instinct to protect the knowledge on those pages was strong. It had to be. It was something all hunters of his kind developed early. If they didn't, they didn't stay in the game long. Jared had seen enough of them come and go in his twenty-plus years in the game. He knew what to do and how to do it. And when you hunted the things he did you learned to be careful. "These?" Jared tapped the pile of notes with his finger, looking at them instead of the drunk, "These are my life's work. Child's play to some, but to me … well, to me they're everything I have."

"Mind if I ask what they're about?"

He smiled absently. "I track wild game, I guess you could say, and these," his fingers wrapped around the stack, feeling the texture, an intimate connection, "these are some of the most important things I've spent my adult life on." There was a time when he cared enough to have the notes bound and protected. But they had come loose during all those lost days since his life was turned upside down, becoming nothing more than a frayed and fragile system of knowledge.

"Wild game, you say?" the man leaned toward him like there was an unspoken secret they shared. "Olympics or Cascades?"

Everywhere. "Olympics mostly. I love the peninsula. Spend a lot of time out there."

The drunk nodded as though satisfied. "There's worse places to be if you ask me. Used to do some hunting myself. Stopped when I couldn't get around so easily. Now? Spend most of my days in this dump, drinking away the last of my brain." The bartender scowled from his spot a few feet away, where he busied himself cleaning a few dirty glasses. The old man tipped his glass in the bar keep's direction. "Oh, come now, Jack, you know I love your fine establishment. Just making conversation with … whatcha say yer name was?"

"I didn't, but it's Jared."

"I'd shake your hand but … well, you don't want to know where it's been today, ain't that right, Jack?" The drunk laugh-coughed again. It sounded like water gurgling out from a pipe. Jared wondered how long this man had to live. Would he finish the investigation before this poor soul saw out what was left of his life? Jared wasn't betting on it. "Anyways, nice to meet you, Jared. So, you on your way out to the Olympics for the weekend?"

Jared nodded. "Something like that. I go out for a few days at a time."

"Whatcha do that for?"

What did he do it for? There was nothing to come home to now, not anymore. What was there to stop him from just staying out for a week or two, or until his supplies ran out? It was something he'd never thought about — not until now, and now it seemed so simple. He laughed, "You know,

I don't have a good answer. Habit, I guess? Used to come back every few days when I was married but I don't have that obligation now. Just have a dog at home."

The drunk leaned toward his beer as if he was trying to smell it. Jared guessed it was a ploy to distract, that maybe the man had demons of his own — maybe an unfortunate ex-wife story, maybe something worse that hit too close to the heart. "Some of those habits are hard to break, my friend," he finally said when he spoke again. "Don't mind me if I'm prying too much into your life, but I'm imagining she didn't want to be waiting for you any more than she already was? Prolly supported you the best she could until she couldn't any longer? Somethin' like that?"

Something like that. Now it was Jared's turn to look away.

"Well, listen to me, going on and getting in your business," he said. "My apologies. You look like a nice young man. Life's going to throw you enough stress, don't be letting me add to it. Got to ask. Ain't deer season. Never seen a duck hunter, hell, any hunter, collect notes like you got there. Whatcha after?"

Jared's dead eyes never left his notes even as he replied, "a monster."

2

"There's a monster among us, a monster that's haunted my dreams since I was six years old," Jared hated recording himself. He sounded ridiculous. The fact that his friend was watching him made him even more self-conscious. He stopped to check and make sure the mobile recorder's indicator light was on as an excuse to avoid Lucas' goofy smile. It was. He continued, "A monster that made the Pacific Northwest its home long before Europeans 'found' this continent. I'm Jared Strong, and I'm hunting this monster. These recordings will serve to document this pursuit so I can prove to the world that it exists. I won't stop until it's found."

Lucas Thomson sarcastically clapped his hands. He was a dear friend, the major reason, the only reason, why Jared allowed him to witness what he was doing, but he was still a smartass. "Impressive, buddy. Impressive."

"Stupid, you mean?"

"No, seriously," his friend countered, pointing at Jared with the open mouth of his beer bottle. "I think you're onto something. I mean, this podcast stuff is all the rage with the kids nowadays. There could be something to it."

"I don't know," Jared answered, leaning into the open refrigerator, pulling out two beers. Lucas had stopped by, unannounced, on his way home from Seattle, catching Jared in the middle of launching his first podcast recording. Without a clue what he was doing, this entire thing felt awkward and Lucas' presence heightened that feeling. It was also a great excuse to stop. He hardly ever saw his friend anymore, even though they lived within an hour of each other. "You want another one?"

"Yeah, but just one more," Lucas replied. "I've got to get on the road soon."

"Worried about beating all that traffic back out to Aberdeen, huh? I mean, who knows, you might pass five or even six cars if traffic is crazy." Jared laughed as he slid the bottle across the table.

"Very funny, asshole," Lucas snorted. "Don't hate me because you're stuck in the city life."

"City life? In Olympia? You need to get out more, my friend."

"City enough for me." Lucas' face lost the humor. Jared knew what was coming because Lucas was so predictable. When the comment came, it didn't disappoint. "So you're really going to do this? Going to bring Peter in and formally kick this thing off? Are you sure, bud?" Lucas didn't believe in Bigfoot, didn't believe in Jared's focus or passions. And Jared had to remind himself, even after all these years, that Lucas had his best interests in mind. But the comments still grated from time to time.

Like now.

"Why wouldn't I be?"

Lucas shrugged. "Just asking if this is something you want to do. Once you make all this public, that's it. There's no going back, my friend. You'll be in all the way."

Jared nodded. He wasn't in the mood for Lucas' skepticism. Not now. Not on the eve of embarking on what would hopefully be the end of 20 years of chasing shadows in the emerald kingdom on the Olympic Peninsula. Even recognizing how tired he felt, Jared still considered himself lucky to spend so many hours of his waking life in such a wonderful setting. His office was a gem, a wonderland of enjoyment and exploration, free of bustling cities and crowded roads. Spending the majority of his adult life trekking through that part of the state had changed him in more ways than one. The peninsula was his home away from home. It was a part of him, as much as any location could be a part of someone. And what he was about to do could endanger the region. It was a problem he still needed to solve.

Sometimes he wasn't convinced what he was about to do would be worth it.

But he'd never find peace if he didn't finish this.

God knew, if he needed anything right now, it was that. Peace.

And reconciliation.

If he could finish this last task, if he could give the world what it wanted, then he could focus on her again. And there was nothing more in the world he wanted. Not even this beast he was chasing.

"So what'd he say?" Lucas' comment interrupted his thoughts.

"Huh?"

"Peter?" Lucas' eyes narrowed. "He called you, right? Isn't that what kicked this into high gear?"

Jared couldn't believe it was really happening. Peter Beckingham, a man of science, a respected zoologist, was actually willing to meet him. In public. About the investigation. About ...

Bigfoot.

The smile felt stupid even as it formed. "Yeah, can you believe it? He's willing to talk."

Lucas whistled in amazement. "That's a major coup, my friend."

Peter Beckingham was a couple things to Jared; a friend and a zoologist, and sometimes those statuses flip-flopped in order of importance. A native of the Pacific Northwest and a life-long Washington resident, Peter wasn't convinced about the validity behind the resurgence of Sasquatch lore over the past half-decade. His professional perspective required him to look at Jared's work with the doubt of a Bigfoot-denier, something they had numerous conversations about. More than a few times, those conversations became heated debates. But the thing about Peter, the thing that made him different to just about any other scientific expert Jared called on, was that Peter cared enough to recognize his bias, and more importantly, he was open-minded enough to listen whenever Jared needed assistance. It was something Jared appreciated as much as he appreciated Peter's friendship. You could never be too careful about trusting people and those you could trust were to be valued. Peter was an ally. And Jared needed more of those in his life.

And in his line of work, he couldn't afford to not accept, with gratitude, anyone who was willing to stand beside him. Thousands of conversations with zoologists left an indelible stain on his impression of the profession. He wanted to keep as much distance from those other types as possible, which was pathetic because it was science that would undeniably prove or disprove the existence of the creature he pursued. But the snide remarks and comments, the violations of privacy, and failures to follow through, all served as signals to him that he'd never gain their respect or get their assistance. All of that stopped affecting him a long time ago. The disrespect hurt, but that was when he was blinded by his passion for his work. Time not only healed a broken heart, it also thickened thin skin. The opinions of skeptics, trained scientists or not, no longer mattered to Jared. Especially not now, not when he was this close.

So close.

And Peter?

Peter was on the receiving end of an unfair share of good (and not-so-good) natured ribbing from his peers for his efforts in assisting Jared. Apparently, even those in the scientific field struggled to critically think from time to time. Jared thought the vast majority of intelligent people understood that one of the essential elements of critical thinking was the ability to see and check one's biases. To prevent blind thinking. But what he discovered through the years of sharing his findings with Peter was that wasn't the case.

According to Peter, group-think and careerism were drivers of willful ignorance. A scientist who entertained even the idea of a large ape in the Pacific Northwest found themselves on the short end of opportunities, losing out on enviable assignments and sometimes being shunned in sections of the community.

As far as Jared was concerned, it was damning evidence against the community he'd expected much more from when he started this journey. After all these years, he only expected frustration and disappointment.

What would it be like to drop a Sasquatch in their laps? What would they do when he delivered the irrefutable evidence they demanded? What would their backtracking look like? Would they apologize? Would they even acknowledge their bias?

No, miracles weren't real.

"Yeah," Jared laughed, "it is. Peter is a good guy. One of these days the two of you should meet."

"And hang out with two dorks who think this stuff is real?" Lucas joked. "I'm busy that day."

"Smartass," Jared replied. "You'll regret not hanging out with us. We're pretty cool."

Lucas laughed. "I doubt that."

They finished up with light conversation and then headed their separate ways with promises to not wait so long before getting together again. It was the same thing they said each time they parted. Then months of not seeing each other would pass and they would both try to feel less guilty by checking in through email or quick text messages, usually in the form of Jared giving Lucas shit each time one of his Seattle sports teams lost a critical game. Because Lucas thought every game was critical. Watching Lucas get spun up over stuff that didn't matter was one of life's simple joys; he loved his friend's passionate loyalty. It was something he understood on a deeper level, his just took a different form. Lucas was as passionate about sports as Jared was about finding Bigfoot, as Peter was about his field of study. As passionate as Maria was about —

Maria.

*****

The quiet drive to the restaurant in Tumwater gave Jared plenty of time — too much time — to think about Maria and where they'd gone wrong. Where he'd gone wrong. Having things you were passionate about was commendable, but those very same passions could also be problematic. Too much of anything wasn't a good thing. It was a lesson he hadn't learned until way too late, not until she was already gone.

And he missed her.

The house wasn't the same without her. His life wasn't the same. It was empty, quiet. Food, even lasagna, was blander. The air smelled less fresh. The mornings held less promise. And those times when he did find something in his investigations — not hard, concrete evidence, but the type of evidence that investigators get excited enough about to slog through the rainy and cold autumn days in the Pacific

Northwest, pushing on when there is no other reason to do so — he had no one to share the good news with. Those were the toughest times to come home from. Even when Maria was less than excited about him disappearing for another weekend or an impromptu overnighter in the backcountry, she was still happy for him when he trembled with excitement as he held a possible hair sample or a print. Long ago, on those occasions, her face beamed with happiness at his prideful display. She'd laugh at his childlike sense of wonderment, the way he would talk a thousand miles an hour when he'd discovered something cool, even if it was only remotely linked to a Sasquatch.

Those were the times he missed.

And that was the problem: he missed how she celebrated for him more than the way she smelled, laughed, gave, or loved. He missed the way she supported him more than the chances he had to support her. He missed the way she gave, always gave. Jared's face flushed with the heat of shame. He'd failed Maria; he'd failed their marriage, and he was going to fix it. Fix it all.

As soon as he was done with his work.

As soon as he found Bigfoot.

*****

The restaurant where Peter wanted to meet overlooked the tiny but powerful waterfalls and the abandoned Olympia Beer brewery site. It was an odd place, with the natural beauty of the falls sitting in the foreground of the pale, decaying building that blotted the landscape of this small suburb of Washington's capital, unused since the brewery closed its doors three decades earlier. It was an eyesore, one that Tumwater could ill afford because the town couldn't afford any more eyesores than it already hosted. There were rumors the abandoned brewery had been sold but those rumors were as reliable as the sun in this part of the country.

When you started getting excited about the possibilities it provided, it would disappoint you by fading into obscurity. That building would outlast them all.

The old brewery hovered behind the restaurant, a permanent scar on the horizon, as Jared pulled in and shut off the car, enjoying the peace that came with the relative silence. The only noise was the distant rumble of Tumwater falls, running fast this time of year. With a big sigh and a last thought about how he screwed up everything with Maria, Jared stepped out of the car and took his first step toward the restaurant. Meeting with Peter was, after all, the beginning of the end in his pursuit to find the Pacific Northwest's most famous creature. The host showed him to Peter's table on the balcony, overlooking the falls.

"Hey, old friend," Peter stood and they embraced.

"Hey, bud," Jared smiled, "nice digs. Who do you know to get the prime real estate?"

Peter's bland expression meant his fun jibe missed its mark, as often happened.

Jared laughed. "I've been trying to get a seat out here for three years and they keep telling me it's reserved each time I come. Even on those special date nights I planned for Maria, they couldn't do me any favors. I figured you know someone with pull because I've seen you play the political game before and you could never charm yourself into getting this spot."

Like a switch was flicked, Peter's expression exploded with flavor when he laughed raucously and hugged Jared again. "Oh man, it's good to see you. Who knows? Maybe they think I smell funny after being cooped up in the lab all day so they put me out here where Mother Nature could do her damnedest to hide my funk and not upset the clientele. Ever think of that?"

"I didn't want to say ..." Jared gave his friend a wink as they sat.

"But," Peter indicated the waterfalls, "you've got to admit they provide a nice backdrop to anyone who wants to listen in on our conversation."

"Yeah, I'm going to have a hell of a time cleaning that racket out of my audio," Jared smiled, pulling out the reliable, and only slightly dated, Tascam portable recorder from his jacket. It wasn't the latest model; in fact, it was old enough to enter kindergarten if it were human. But it got the job done. Over and over. Peter eyed it on the table between them as if he was waiting for it to spring to life and pounce on his face at any second. Jared noted his friend's discomfort. "Are you still okay with me recording this?"

Peter blinked. "Oh, sorry. Yeah. I am."

"Are you sure? I don't want to put you out or make you uncomfortable. You gotta feel okay about this, or I don't want to do it."

"No, really," he waved away Jared's comment. "Let's do this. It's my pleasure. This project of yours. It's … interesting. I'm glad you're finally doing it."

Jared smirked. "It's overdue."

The waiter stopped, introduced himself, and took their drink order. Jared asked for two stouts from his favorite brewery, which was located in Oregon. Peter whistled when the waiter walked away. "You know you're not supposed to be supporting our state rivals, especially not in public."

Jared laughed at the very genuine spirit behind Peter's observation. Restricted to a 'Seattle versus Portland' rivalry, tens of thousands of people enjoyed the somewhat friendly combativeness between the states themselves. Washingtonians weren't supposed to like Oregonians and vice versa. It was all rather ridiculous, but since when wasn't that the nature of people? "Yeah, well, when we start making beer as good as this stuff maybe I'll support local," he laughed.

Peter wagged a finger at him. "Tsk, tsk. A public figure, not supporting local businesses? That could be bad for your image."

"Public figure'? I don't think so."

"Not yet," Peter replied. "But by the sound of your voice the last time we talked, I get the impression you're becoming a lot more confident with what you have. You break this investigation wide open with a major find and, sorry, but a celebrity you will be."

Jared hadn't thought about that, didn't want to think about it. Any distractions from what he wanted, including becoming 'the man who found Bigfoot', weren't welcomed.

"What's up, Jared? You seem frustrated? I'd say you're becoming jaded, but I think I know you too well to believe that."

"Ha, yeah. Investigating sightings and gathering evidence for the past twenty years has worn me down a little, I concede that. Which is why I appreciate your help kicking this project off."

The beers arrived. The waiter asked if they were ready to order. "Give us a few, please?" Peter asked. When the waiter walked away, Peter turned his attention back to Jared. "It's not a problem. Honestly. I'm happy to talk about this. You know I geek out about Bigfoot. Plus, if I can help with your project by getting good science behind it, then we all win. There's a story to tell. Plus, you and I both know there aren't enough legitimate influencers talking about Bigfoot in the public forum. That creates a vacuum which has been filled by too many fame-seekers who end up getting the spotlight ... and that's what hurts the legitimacy of your work and my study."

"I'm glad to hear you say that, I really am," Jared smiled as they toasted. "Let's get started. I know you're busy, and I've taken up too much of your time with this over the years. Want to try and wrap up years of conversations in one recording?"

They shared a laugh and Jared tried to transition away from the personal conversation and into something more professional. A podcast audience expected him to sound professional. He just hoped he would be able to fake it well enough. "Can we start by getting your thoughts on why the Pacific Northwest is an area of focus for experts interested in Sasquatch?"

Peter's lips curled down in thought, "Geography and climate. Simple as that. The Pacific Northwest has the perfect combination of four and a half million acres of wilderness, rainforests, and a moderate climate that is preferable to this particular species."

"But that's a sticking point," Jared responded. "How do you answer people who'd have a problem with a fur-covered ape living in a moderate climate?" Careful to cover his internal smirk, Jared clung to the professional tone of the conversation.

"If I bought you the best arctic gear money could buy, would you still live outside in the elements, no matter how moderate they are, or would you spend the winter inside, probably near the fire?" Peter said. "I get it. Hell, I appreciate skepticism, but a species like Sasquatch, of the Hominoidea superfamily, would have evolved for the conditions of their environment. If Sasquatch exists, it is a migratory species. They would have to adapt to their environment, probably by moving."

Peter paused when Jared was in mid-swallow. And before Jared could clear his throat to ask a follow-up question, Peter was off again. "They didn't always live here. Their body hair isn't there to insulate them from the cold but to maintain constant body temperature."

Peter's response didn't surprise or confuse Jared. He knew Peter and he was ready for how the zoologist would respond. The only way anyone would give Jared's work a chance was if he could convince them he was a skeptic-first, Bigfoot enthusiast-second. Otherwise, any potential audience would tune him out before they read a single one of his findings. There was no room to create doubt. "What about the geography? There's plenty of open space all around the country that is temperate. What advantage does this area have over others that skeptics say are similar?"

Peter shrugged. "The forests and waterways. It's an easy land to live off, chock-full of resources for any clever species to take advantage of. Plus, open space in Washington, Oregon, or British Columbia means something completely different than the open spaces of Nebraska or Kansas. No offense to any of your listeners in those places. If Sasquatch ever made it that far, they moved on or died out. An environment like that wouldn't be conducive to their survival for the same reason that history has never shown vast Homo sapien populations in the middle of deserts ... well, not until technological advances allowed for that to happen."

Jared pointed at him. He needed Peter to hit this point accurately. "Would you say having plentiful resources is what keeps Sasquatch here?"

"That and the fact that Sasquatch wouldn't be a stupid animal." Peter made it all sound so obvious. "Few species get the credit they deserve from us humans. Over the course of my studies, and even to this day, I'm amazed at how quick humans are to dismiss the possibility of Sasquatch as an intelligent mammal."

Jared gripped the beer mug handle a little tighter, mumbling, "A cultural leftover."

Peter's raised eyebrow let him know he'd failed in communicating his point.

"I just mean that we're expected to see ourselves as a superior species," Jared clarified, trying to keep the heat out of his voice. "Humans seem to believe everything else, all nature, is part of our dominion, to rule and use how we see fit. When we view the rest of the world that way it's not hard to see why we disregard the intelligence, hell, the sentience, of other creatures."

A family of three walked by toward one of the tables at the end of the balcony. Peter waited for them to pass before speaking again, "You've got a point."

"Sort of one of my frustrations with people," Jared admitted.

Peter chuckled, his cheeks taking on a shine. "I know you've been at this a while. One of these days that stubborn skepticism will jade you into feeling nothing. I promise."

"Hitting too close to home for ya', bud? You can relate?"

"Anyone in this field worth their weight should be able to. Our common area of interest isn't something we parade around, unfortunately. Not if we want to be respected."

Jared grimaced. For a brief second his friend was vulnerable and Jared was reminded that Peter, too, was making sacrifices. For their friendship. For him. "One of these days we need to talk about some of the career problems you've faced because of your interest in Bigfoot."

Peter erased the temporary awkwardness with an unconvincing smile. "And make me relive my shame? How cruel. Mind you, I'm not a careerist so I'm not interested in some manufactured position of power and influence, but it would be nice to have this aspect of who I am taken seriously by my peers. Or at least have it not negatively impact me. That's a rarity. What about you?"

"Same," Jared shrugged. "But I figure I pretty much set myself up for that since I made this my career."

Silence fell. They blamed the natural beauty surrounding them for their distraction. But Jared couldn't deny that Peter got him thinking. He wondered if he had the same effect on his friend. "Well, I don't want to dwell on that," Peter interrupted his thoughts. "Let's change hearts and minds, shall we? At least that's what it sounds like you're attempting to do."

Am I? "You could say that. This project is my big, final push. If I can't convince people of the existence of Sasquatch when I'm done with this ... well, I worry my entire career will have been a waste."

"You must be pretty confident with what you're tracking to say something like that."

"I'm confident. If I'm not, then what's the point?"

Peter stared at Jared for what felt like the longest time. There was suspicion in those eyes. Peter was onto him. "You found tracks, didn't you?"

Jared was smug in response. "Even better."

After twenty years of heartbreaking and frustrating searching, he'd stumbled on a trail of evidence he knew in his heart was going to lead him to prove Bigfoot's existence once and for all. Or he'd prove the skeptics right. Either way, his recent finds were becoming more common and convincing, and now that Maria decided she could do other things with her life besides wait for him, Jared was determined to chase the demon to the end of the trail. As he listed the number of breaks he'd gained over the past few weeks Peter's face lit up. His friend was nearly as excited about the possibilities as he was.

What he had wasn't going to be enough though. It was encouraging without quite reaching convincing. The eternal question he pondered was how solid did the evidence need to be to convince those who refused to accept proof? That was the struggle. That was what led some other investigators down less scrupulous paths to the point of desperation. Creating their own evidence where the world failed to provide it for them. Jared had always been cognizant of that. From the very beginning, he got a full education on how far some people were willing to go to find Bigfoot. Since those early let-downs, he was careful to avoid creating even the perception that he was being fraudulent. There were times he'd dumped decent evidence because he worried it would be perceived as faked and he didn't want that door even cracked for skeptics to step through. Those decisions were always difficult. They hurt.

"Oh, good," Peter leaned back as the waiter carried a large serving tray toward them. "Looks great. Smells great."

Peter loved his food.

It was nice to have a meal with him again. But it wasn't enjoyable when Peter asked about Maria. Jared avoided that topic and hadn't told any of his friends much in the way of details. He didn't want to trouble them, he told himself, but it was a lie, the same lie that all selfish people told themselves to rationalize away their shame. Deep down he didn't want to tell anyone because they knew how much he sacrificed and everyone was amazed how he and Maria did it all without killing their marriage. And now his friends had no idea how dead that marriage was. So he couldn't be upset when Peter asked him about her.

"What's Maria think about this? She has to be so happy for you, being this close to finding Bigfoot?"

He didn't mean to sound rude, but the flat response came before he could think through his response. "We're separated."

"Oh," Peter stopped eating, setting his fork down, "I'm sorry. I—I didn't know."

Jared tried to put on his best reassuring smile. "No, no. It's fine. You couldn't have known. This ... all of it, the investigation, the time, the expense, the professional consequences. It's been ... taxing, to say the least. Maria tried to be patient ... she waited a long time. So, yep, I guess you could say she isn't a fan of what I've done with my life."

"I'm sorry, Jared," Peter said. "There's a heavy price associated with pursuits like these. People don't get it. I've had a lot of friends and colleagues over the years who've paid that same price for conducting their own investigation. That damn thirst for knowledge, it's wrecked too many good homes. It'd be nice to get a break. For all of us."

Jared's laugh was bitter. "I don't know if we ever had a good life, but I get your point. You're preaching to the choir. I hope what I'm doing will be helpful to someone. Maybe I'll save everyone else's marriage, even if I couldn't save mine."

Awkward silence, the type that can only fall between two men suddenly finding themselves in a vulnerable spot, fell again. Peter thumbed the side of his beer mug. Jared moved his pasta around the plate, without design or purpose. Each silently urging the other to make a comment, a remark, to say anything to pull the conversation out of the quagmire.

"A noble aim," Peter nodded at his beer mug before his chest expanded in a deep breath. "So what's next?"

Jared appreciated the abrupt change of direction because his thoughts already spiraled down, chasing the Maria-rabbit down the black hole. He didn't need to be there. Not now. He needed a clear head until this was over. "Headed to Rainier."

"Really? That's not where you've been searching. What's out there?"

"A park ranger called me yesterday," Jared said. "Supposedly there was a sighting. Not sure if he believed it or not, though. It was a strange conversation."

"The National Park?"

Jared nodded. "He sounded ... conflicted. I'm heading out there first thing in the morning. I want to hear what he has to say, see the site before some visitor trips across it and disturbs it. Who knows, it could be legit ... or not. There hasn't been a reported sighting at Rainier in a long while."

"I'd love to hear about it when you get back," Peter said.

"I don't want to abuse our friendship with every sighting."

"Nonsense. Call me when you get back. Even if it's nothing."

Jared conceded to his determined friend. "Alright. You asked for it."

That drew a laugh from Peter. "Let me ask you something, as a friend," he paused. "What's this all about for you? This investigation? Why still do it, especially now that I know what's going on with Maria?"

There it was again: purpose. The most frightening thing he had to face throughout this life-long quest; why he was doing what he was doing, sacrificing everything for ... for what? "Someone has to. Someone has to find the answers ... either way. Either it's out there or it's not and we're never going to know without dogged investigation. So I can either tell people what needs to be done or I can go do it myself. The latter seems ... less hypocritical. And, well, I've got other reasons."

"Got it," Peter smiled regretfully. "Well, I've taken enough of your time. Jared, be careful out there."

"Of course."

Peter's expression turned stern. "I'm serious. The closer you get to finding answers, the more dangerous this is going to get for you. Don't forget that."

"Dangerous? I'm not sure I know what you mean."

"Sasquatch has to be a solitary creature for the most part," Peter answered. "It doesn't want to be found. Tread carefully."

Jared was still confused. It wasn't an insightful reply and Peter wasn't one to dodge or give undue credit to a cryptid. "I will. But ... I feel like you're not saying what you want to say."

Peter laughed off the comment, but Jared pressed him. "No, really. What is it?"

"It's probably just me."

"Please ... tell me," Jared was now very curious. This turn was sudden and so unlike Peter. "Listen, I've already lost almost everything worth having. There's nothing you're going to say that would sound crazy to me."

Peter paused, his eyes flickering at the other tables. "Just don't be naïve about this. Sasquatch are fine when left alone, but they won't like threats and there are plenty of people who don't want you to find them. Plenty of people. You won't be making friends."

3

Ignoring the eyesore of the abandoned brewery building, Jared climbed back into his car and let the air conditioning and satellite radio take him away from his conversation with Peter. It was not a good way to end the meeting. It was disturbing, in fact. Peter wasn't one for hyperbole. What he saw in Peter's eyes was the same thing he'd seen in Maria's eyes for years.

It was the disease of this goddamn investigation, spreading from person to person. Unstoppable.

Words held back. Things unsaid.

Call it a generalization or stereotyping, but Peter was the embodiment of the scientific community—conservative in almost every measure like it was bred into them during their training. Jared hadn't met many in the scientific community who would reach for anything. Ever. Especially not in their words. He had no idea how serious the information was that Peter had. Nor did he know how much truth it held or how reliable Peter's sources were. One thing that was clear; Peter was convinced Jared wasn't alone in his search, enough so to unravel in public. That freaked Jared out.

Peter hadn't given him any more to go on because he hadn't made it safe for Peter to share. There was something there, underneath the layers of the conversation and he was so damn frustrated by not being able to put his finger on it. He wasn't a child; he didn't need protecting. Two decades of investigating Bigfoot taught him that few people were willing to stick their necks out for someone else, even in the safest of circumstances.

He leaned his head back against the headrest. Even if Peter was only partially correct, it meant trouble. He didn't have childish expectations about the Bigfoot community. It was like any other, a compilation of good and bad people, kind and gentle souls mixed with a trace of selfish assholes, ambitious morons mixed with people who'd move out of their tent to give another person cover for the night. It was a microcosm of America. It also had a small segment of people willing to do anything to get ahead, and it was those people who Peter warned Jared about.

But there were things Peter wasn't saying and Jared couldn't understand his friend's silence. Why protect information?

There were no names, no organizations to go with the warning. Peter swore it wasn't that he didn't want to tell Jared but that he couldn't because he didn't know them himself. Message boards spread rumors and half-facts, was all he said. Jared understood. He'd been in the game long enough to know what other Bigfoot hunters could be like. He expected this to happen at some point and was actually surprised it took this long. Why did it have to happen now, though? Was he being talked about because he was making too many waves as he launched this new public project?

He was almost offended it took the darker elements to acknowledge his work — a thought that would have been humorous if the impact on Peter hadn't been so obvious, so significant.

Peter changed. At the end of the conversation, he wasn't the same person he was when they'd started dinner. And Jared couldn't say anything that assured Peter enough. Not to open up. There were layers that Jared would have to pull apart if he ever got the chance. It was frustrating, but he wanted to respect Peter's vulnerability. And he didn't have the time to deal with this childish shit. Not Peter, but envious Bigfoot hunters who were unwilling to make the necessary sacrifices to get where he'd gotten; the people who didn't want to invest the sweat equity to achieve what he'd achieved but who wanted the attention and fame as if they had. Though it was unsaid, Jared felt it. Whatever Peter heard went well beyond the typical sabotage employed by jealous rivals.

Most people had no clue what Bigfoot hunters were actually capable of.

As he drove home through Tumwater he thought about their goodbye. Their departing gestures had lost authenticity. Maybe Peter regretted opening up to Jared about the rumors he'd heard, or maybe he was afraid of how he'd act. There was no way to be sure, but the fact was that Peter was distant and his farewell was practiced, manufactured—the type of farewell someone would give to a boss they wouldn't mind seeing the backside of. The way their conversation ended would give him something to think about all the way out to Rainier tomorrow.

Which was the last thing he felt like doing.

The air blasting his face was a nice distraction from thinking about Peter's sudden change, the way his friend emotionally cut himself off. Jared didn't want to think about how Peter went into protective mode because he felt that he was, at least, partially to blame for it, not Peter. Peter was a dear friend, a confidante, who was often ostracized by the other professionals in his field.

He was a guardian from the very beginning.

Maybe that was why Peter's reluctance to open up bothered him so much. They didn't have the type of friendship where they hid things.

They didn't have the type of friendship filled with things that needed hiding.

*****

Morning coffee and a roadside diner breakfast didn't make Jared feel any better. He would have loved to record for the podcast to tell everyone how great things were, how quickly they'd turned around, or that Peter had called him in the middle of the night to apologize for dumping more information on him than was useful. But none of that happened. Jared started the day the same way he ended it: alone, in a quiet house, with only his Border Collie for company and distraction. Molly was a wonderful dog, but sometimes even the best dogs couldn't balance out the troubles created by humans. Her company was still a release.

Jared tried to think about what his future podcast listeners were going to need to hear, about him, the way the investigation had to progress to make it legitimate, and of Sasquatch. He tried to think about how he could frame it so that even future listeners ignorant of Bigfoot or even unaware that it existed, would be able to understand why Jared spent his life searching for this beast.

But he couldn't wrap his head around anything related to the podcast right now, not when he was consumed with uncovering who was behind what troubled Peter. How did they get so close, so threatening, without Peter being confident of their identity? If Peter could name names, he would, without hesitation. Yet, no names were forthcoming.

It was another pile of worry on top of thinking about how he was going to repair things with Maria. Or even opening the damn door to making up?

But he was a professional. He could pout or he could work. The former wouldn't get him any closer to resolution. Finding Bigfoot was the key; it would allow him to put the rest of this behind him for good. Then he could focus on Maria and begin a normal life again if she'd allow him. But he had to start here to get there.

He had to travel that road, whether he wanted to or not.

And that road began with a park ranger named Andrew Porter and Mount Rainier National Park.

Three hundred and seventy square miles of intense natural beauty in the western half of the Evergreen State, the park is a calling card for the region. The economies of the small dots of townships that surround the national park rely on visitors being drawn to the immensity that is the park's gem, the volcano. Anyone who visits Washington and doesn't make their way to Mount Rainier committed a criminal offense in Jared's mind. It deserves all reverence paid to it.

But he wasn't heading to the volcano to enjoy the splendid natural beauty the park offered throughout the year. He was heading there because Andrew, someone who was unknown to him only two days ago, called to request a meeting. Urgently. What he heard in that call was something he'd heard a thousand times over. An overwhelmed person dealing with something they couldn't understand.

Or he doesn't want to deal with it, Jared thought.

But it didn't make sense. Mount Rainier wasn't a hotbed of Sasquatch activity, at least not the legitimate kind. There were reports from the park, but they were hardly reliable. The vast majority of the videos Jared received claiming to be Bigfoot sightings on the mountain were an outright sham; pathetic attempts to get attention and accolades, all undeserved. The small remainder of claims always fell far short, lacking any substance that would make him even want to think about investing the day-trip. It wasn't a place to waste time or energy. He loved the park, loved being on the mountain, but not to hunt Bigfoot. There were better things he could do with his time.

Jared was making the long drive to see Andrew because, whatever it was that he had, the park ranger made it clear that he had no desire to speak about it over an open phone line. That was exciting.

The archway across the road announced his arrival. Jared eyed the ranger when he handed over the $20 bill for the toll. She smirked as if she knew how painful that was to his wallet and wished him a nice day, releasing him to begin the long trek. Up. Up. Up. It took another hour to reach the summit, if you considered the Henry M. Jackson Visitor Center to be the summit. There were another few thousand feet of mountain to traverse to reach the actual summit, but this was as high as a human could get by vehicle unless you were a park ranger with special privileges. Jared circled the parking lot, looking for a spot, which was nigh-on impossible this time of year. Hell, any time of year it was tough to find a place to park. In the summer, the fair weather sailors came out to enjoy the majestic beauty of Mount Rainier and in the winter twenty feet of snow buried everything except for the small area park services kept plowed, drastically reducing the available spots. He was lucky to find a sliver to squeeze the vehicle into.

He parked and took a moment to enjoy the volcanic mountain for what it was. Even though he acted like an idiot when it came to Maria, he wasn't completely oblivious. How many people lived day in and day out, unable to enjoy beauty like this? How many people would never be able to stand in a parking lot, halfway up the side of a volcano, and contemplate the frailty of being a human being? People thought they were so powerful, sometimes placing themselves on the level of gods and yet, if the volcano decided today would be the day it wouldn't hold its temper any longer, it would send a death cloud spiraling into the atmosphere that would choke out life long after the collapsing mountainside crushed those below it. Whether you lived in Seattle or Los Angeles or any of the filthy cities on the east coast, it was difficult to appreciate how futile the human experience was because life offered too many entertaining distractions in those types of places. Humankind removed itself from nature and lost touch with their own fragility. But Mount Rainier reminded him of that each and every time he saw it.

Regrettably, at least in part, Jared left the beauty of the mountain to its eternal existence and stepped through the long, covered walkway and into the center. A long, low maple counter separated him from the two rangers greeting guests. He asked for Andrew. The female ranger smiled and walked him around the corner of an immense pillar. Darkened offices lined this side of the center. Vertical banners provided other barriers as well as snippets of historical facts about the region. Andrew's office was around the back of one such display. The ranger knocked on the office door and a muffled voice called out from behind it.

"Have fun," she smiled and pushed the handle down, opening the door for Jared.

"Thanks," he mumbled to her back as she turned to walk away, and stepped into the small office that was cluttered with junk. Haphazard stacks of boxes filled one corner. Andrew's desk was layered in loose papers like he was trying to bury some secret underneath their cover. The saying goes that first impressions are lasting impressions and Jared couldn't silence the critical inner voice that told him to run away from Andrew as fast as possible.

But the man looked busy. Very busy. During his time investigating Bigfoot sightings, Jared had come in contact with a number of park personnel. They were like any other profession, but they were also short-staffed a lot of the time, spread across vast areas and responsible for the safety of stupid people who didn't heed posted warnings. He didn't envy them at all.

Andrew looked up at him only after the female ranger left Jared standing alone at the door, unsure what to do. "I take it you're Jared?"

"That's me," he answered, taking a seat after Andrew motioned at it with a distracted gesture. Jared got the sense this ranger wasn't someone who'd be thrilled to have his time wasted, even if it was him who requested the meeting. So Jared had no problem getting down to business. "Thanks for your time. Mind if I record this?"

"I agreed to it."

"I wanted to make sure it was still okay with you. Legalities and all that."

"I get it. I'm sure you've got to be careful with that."

If you only knew, Jared thought, but said, "I have to be careful with everything. Are you a believer?"

Andrew scoffed. "In Bigfoot? Hardly."

It was an interesting response. Andrew wasn't combative. He wasn't antagonistic. Jared felt like he was stopping Andrew from getting to something that needed getting to. But on the other hand, this office gave the impression there was a lot Andrew needed to get to that he wasn't able to. This investigation was probably another task in a long line of tasks that needed to get done at the expense of Andrew's physical and mental health. "But you called me because of something you've got? Something you think I need to see?"

Instead of answering, Andrew asked, "You want anything to drink?"

"Sure," Jared tried to temper his frustration. He didn't have time to dance after spending the last two hours driving all the way out here. "What do you have?"

Andrew gave him a brief shrug as if his mind was already on the next task. "Coffee and water."

"Not much of a selection," Jared grinned. "Tight budget?"

Andrew grimaced, as if Jared had asked something he couldn't possibly understand. "In the park, we survive on coffee. It gets cold and boring out here."

"And the water?"

"To rehydrate," Andrew answered. "We don't have much in the way of medical expertise except what we can do for ourselves. So if we can delay or avoid needing medical help, we do it."

That made sense. "Coffee sounds great," he answered. Andrew rolled the few feet to the coffee maker, poured two cups and placed one in front of Jared without asking if he wanted any creamer or sugar. Deep space looked brighter than the contents of the cup. "So, what needs to happen for someone who doesn't believe in Sasquatch to call someone who is pursuing evidence for its existence?"

"This," Andrew answered, turning and grabbing a stack of papers no less than twelve inches thick. He plopped the stack down right next to the coffee.

Jared looked at the stack through narrowed eyes. "What are those?"

"Reports our stations have taken in over the past few months from around the mountain," Andrew answered.

"All of these?"

"Yep."

Jared flipped through the sheets as quickly as he could, "There have to be nearly a hundred of them in here."

"I know."

For a second, Jared remembered his initial reaction to Andrew; how he wanted to run the instant he saw the disorganized mess of a ranger. He was thrilled he hadn't.

Sitting in front of him was a treasure.

4

"Seventy-five reports ... didn't want you having to count all those," Andrew nodded at the stack Jared now held in his hands.

Seventy-five? Over how long? It didn't make sense. There was no activity on Rainier —not legitimate activity. How had this station collected so many reports and no one in the Bigfoot community was talking about this location as a new hot spot? "I appreciate it," Jared smiled, trying to cover his concern. "This is strange. Sightings have been so rare out here for years."

Andrew pointed at him with the cheap, roller-tip pen. "Well, what you've got in your hands disproves that. I'm not sure why, but these have been held back."

"Held back?"

"Sorry, that's all above my pay grade," the ranger replied. "You should find a lot of information in those. I don't know what you can get out of it, but I figured it'd be something useful to you. Some are sightings, some prints. Some are ... crazier."

"What do you mean?"

Andrew's expression darkened. "Last week some hikers claim they came across a Bigfoot. Like, actually interacted with it."

Jared flipped to the front of the reports. "Which one is that?"

"On top," Andrew answered over Jared's question. "I thought you'd want to see that one first."

Jared took his time reading it. He scanned, read, and re-read what was in front of him in plain black and white. "This is ... remarkable."

"If it's real," Andrew answered.

"You don't believe they saw this?"

Andrew's response made Jared cringe. "I don't believe a large ape stopped to have a conversation with a group of hikers. No."

"This report doesn't say that. It says that--"

"I was being flippant. It's pretty remarkable. Maybe too remarkable."

Jared sighed before he could hold it. He'd heard this so many times. Thanks, YouTube! Because of the idiots who put questionable videos on the internet that were nothing more than pathetic cries for attention, the vast majority of people had become numb to the fascinating beauty of this creature. Any other animal? They laughed it off. Loch Ness monster? Nessie didn't get a tenth of the hate Sasquatch did. As land mammals, humans didn't fear anything that couldn't get to them. Sasquatch was different. Sasquatch could pop out without a moment's notice during a family hike. A camping trip? What was that noise at night? People were much more vulnerable to Sasquatch than some aquatic animal of lore. So it made sense for fragile people to demean the legacy of that which they saw as a threat. The only thing people disliked more than being afraid was admitting they were afraid. It made sense. Someone in Andrew's position couldn't be blamed; he spent the majority of his life in the wilderness and that made him vulnerable. Vulnerability bred fear. Fear bred animosity. It was all tied together. Jared understood that part of human nature enough to not fight Andrew's reaction and reasoning. "How long have you worked the mountain?"

To his credit, Andrew didn't seem thrown off. "Seven years. Started working for the service right after college. Been here ever since."

"It's got to be a great job."

"It's alright," Andrew shrugged. "I mean, the mountain is great, it's beautiful. It's just ..."

"Not what you expected?" Jared finished for him.

Andrew sipped his coffee for longer than a sip should take. "I think I sort of rushed myself into a career decision and figured I could make a bigger impact than I actually am." There was a hint of pain buried in those words.

"I've been hunting Sasquatch for twenty years. I can tell you that park services, rangers, forestry ... all of you, have made a very positive impact on the collective psyche about our natural resources. I don't want to think about where we'd be if it wasn't for people like you doing what you do."

"Thanks," Andrew smiled. "I think I had illusions of grandeur when I decided to follow this path. I don't know what I was thinking, but it is what it is. I can't change that now. But, if I'm able to help others, that's cool. I've made peace with the fact that I'm not going to change the world."

The ambitions of the young, always so boundless. The immensity of promise that people under thirty saw in their world was a beautiful thing. But it was beaten out after a few years in the job market, struggling along to make sure the mortgage was paid on-time every month. Andrew was the type of person he could be around more often; Andrew was good for him. All this investigating, losing almost everything for something he may never achieve, sometimes felt pointless even as the tug of necessity pulled on him.

"Don't lose that dream yet. You're young. Plenty of time to shake the world awake." A thought came to him. "Is that why you're reaching out to me now with these reports even though you don't believe Sasquatch exists?"

"If this thing exists, if these people are telling the truth ... I don't want to stand in the way of that. If something like Sasquatch is out there somewhere, it's my duty to facilitate their study. I did a lot of reading up on you. You're all over the internet and well-respected ... at least by anyone who isn't a scientist."

Jared paused. Could he believe Andrew? The man had called him all the way out to the park for a reason, the stack of papers and Andrew's hushed, conspiratorially-evasive tone told Jared that much. There may or may not be something happening on Mount Rainier but as far as this one park ranger was concerned something was happening and it was being hidden by someone, and he'd decided to do something about it. That was enough for Jared to keep looking, to keep pushing. "Yeah, well, I gave up caring about what they thought a long time ago."

"It's got to be hard ... doing what you do."

"Depends on how you define it," Jared said. "I enjoy it; it's a passion. It drives me, regardless of what doubters and naysayers think. And I appreciate people like you, who put aside personal feelings about Sasquatch in order to help."

"Mind if I ask why you do this? I don't imagine it pays very well."

"Money is the last of my considerations. Trust me. My reasons are silly, to be honest. But ... it is what it is. Childhood trauma has a way of doing that, of taking something that is pretty trivial and marking you in a way that drives you for the rest of your life."

"I get it," Andrew replied. "I mean I didn't dream of being a park ranger when I was a kid. I wanted to be an astronaut. But I can understand what you're saying. I have friends who went through some really messed up stuff when we were kids and it definitely made them the adults they are today. Mind if I ask what happened?" Andrew seemed to catch himself and rushed to fill the silence, "I'm sorry, that's inconsiderate. My supervisor keeps telling me I've got to be less direct with people. My mother used to always say that too, but I thought she was just nitpicking, you know, like mother's can. I don't mean to be rude, I'm sorry."

How many times had well-meaning people asked that question? Enough times to have a well-practiced answer to keep them far enough away without picking up subtle hints that there was more going on. "No, no. You're fine. I don't mind. But you've got to promise you won't laugh."

"Scouts honor," Andrew said, putting his right hand in the air, thumb to pinky finger with the other three fingers extending straight upward.

"I didn't think park rangers were considered—"

"Boy, I thought I had a bad sense of humor," Andrew laughed.

"Oh," Jared caught on, surprised that Andrew felt compelled to joke. He didn't think the ranger had it in him. "Mind if I get a refill? This isn't bad coffee."

"You mean for park rangers?" Andrew winked, getting up and accommodating his guest.

"What makes me do this?" Jared repeated the question. "I'll give you the short version. My family was a camping family. Outdoorsy types. We'd camp all summer long, every other weekend, at least. My father loved getting away from Seattle and back into nature. We used to go to a campsite near Lake Cushman. It was my father's favorite place and it sort of became our home away from home because we went there so often. Are you familiar with it?

"I'm a Cascadia man myself," Andrew gestured beyond the confines of his office to the mountain outside of it. "Can't say I've ever been out to the Olympics."

"Ha, well, at Cushman most of the sites are private, with heavy coverage and undergrowth so you really felt like you're away from the world. Out in the wild," Jared said. "My mother never got used to that isolation. She and dad got into some very interesting discussions, as they would call them, about going out there. But she always went, complaining the whole way only to talk about how much she enjoyed her weekend on the way back to the city. There was one weekend where the forecast wasn't looking promising but Dad said he needed to get away, needed to unplug. So we went and the campground was nearly empty. Funny thing about Americans, isn't it? Even when we want to rough it we need to perfect conditions to do so."

Andrew's booming laugh filled the small office. "That's so true."

"Yeah, I guess you would know that," Jared said. "So, we were enjoying the site, enjoying the peace that comes with a vacant camp and unwinding. We woke up Saturday morning and headed down to the lake to do some kayaking and swimming and when we came back to the campsite hours later it was destroyed."

"Destroyed?"

Here it comes. Are you ready to go through this again? Jared already knew the answer. "It looked like a group of drunk teens came through and tore everything up. Our coolers were thrown across the site. The fire pit looked like something had run through it, tossing ash everywhere. One of our tents had been yanked from the ground and was shredded. We salvaged as much of the food as we could and set camp back up again. My father was irate. Mom asked him if we could leave but it was getting late. He'd been up late the night before, enjoying the evening and didn't think we could make it back safely. Dad was sure that it was stupid kids. Mom wasn't too happy about that.

"It was a long night," Jared continued. "We were quiet all evening as we ate and tried to distract ourselves with card games. My dog, a six-year-old Collie, was being ridiculous. His name was Sam and he wouldn't lie down. Just kept pacing. It annoyed the hell out of me. We tried to settle in by watching the fire for hours. As a young kid, I don't remember everything but I do remember just wanting to go to bed and get the night over. So I did, but not before my mother asked to keep the fire hot. They argued a bit because he didn't want to be up late and she didn't want to be without the fire and the safety it provided. It was obvious she was scared. I didn't understand why but I could feel it from her. She was usually so ... steady."

Jared tried to hide the dark feelings starting to rise as he recalled the story. Even now, all these years later, he hated this part of it. "I don't know how long I'd been sleeping when Sam started whining. He always slept with me. It was a three-person tent but with all my gear, clothes, and Sam inside it was pretty tight fit. His fidgeting bugged the hell out of me. I remember telling him to lie down but he kept standing up and whimpering. He was looking towards the tent flap and pacing in any sliver of space he could find. It was late and suddenly Sam started losing his mind, whimpering like I was beating him. Then he laid down, his head between his paws, and got real quiet."

The small office felt like it'd gotten fifteen degrees colder in an instant. "That's when I got scared. You sense things, you know? I had this sudden fear. I didn't want to move. I didn't want to turn my flashlight on. I was frozen, not daring to make a sound. To this day I don't know why I felt like that ... I just did. I laid there and didn't move a muscle except to reach for Sam. I thought I was trying to comfort him but now I know I was trying to comfort me. That's when I heard the growl."

Jared paused to sip his coffee. It wasn't deliberately evasive or for dramatic effect. The memories, hard and confusing, were always blurry at this part of the story. He could see it so clearly yet it was obscured by ... what? Pain? Fear? Loss? Jared had asked himself that question a thousand times if he'd asked it once, never finding the answer. "There was something outside my tent. I could hear it moving, grunting, and tossing our stuff around. My parents unzipped their tent. A flashlight came on and my father started yelling. Years later he told me he was trying to scare the camp invader."

Andrew, for his part, appeared fascinated, not moving, not touching his coffee or even rocking in his chair. He propped up on his elbows, leaning toward Jared. "Did it work?"

"Not at all," Jared shook his head. "The camp exploded into chaos. Whatever was out there ... howled. It was ungodly. That howl. I'll never forget that sound.

"There was so much commotion outside. I couldn't get my tent unzipped quickly enough. The zipper kept getting stuck because I was shaking. My mother ... was screaming. I finally got out and Sam bolted. I reached for him ... but ... well, once he had his mind set on something, that was it. I scrambled after him, not thinking about anything else, but my mother grabbed me before I ran more than a few feet. She was hysterical and I was little ... I wasn't going to break free, she made sure of that. Even as dark as it was I could make out enough of what was going on because my father had his flashlight and a lantern in the dirt that lit up enough of the site ... enough to see it. You never forget the first time you see a Sasquatch."

The word, already mentioned, hung in the air. "You saw one?" Andrew drew out the question as if it would help him not trip over his own words.

Jared's response was dry, the words serving as bitter remnants of a life lost. "Everyone's a skeptic until they see Sasquatch. From that day on, we all believe." His cost had been very real, very traumatic, especially at that age, and he couldn't help but be slightly defensive after all the times he'd told this story only to have people blow it off as folly. "My father was waving his arms wildly; using his tactical flashlight like it was a damn lightsaber. The Sasquatch was on the edge of the site, near where we'd left our cooler. I remember it looking ... bewildered. It must have been trying to figure out what the hell my father was. That's when I noticed Sam. He may have been frightened initially, but he was a completely different dog at that moment. His hackles were raised as he stood between my father and the Sasquatch, crouched down on his front paws, ready to pounce."

Jared smiled at the memory of his Sam's veraciously protective nature. "The Sasquatch was growling but so was Sam. That damn dog wouldn't back down. It didn't matter that the Sasquatch was ten times his size; Sam was not letting that thing harm us. I remember hearing other campers coming complaining about 'stupid college kids', but when a few of the men stomped into our site, ready to give us a piece of their mind, they saw that thing and immediately ... I'd never seen grown men collectively cower. Sam was barking, snarling, maybe feeling emboldened by the presence of a small army of humans. And whether it was Sam's increased aggression or the presence of all these people, I don't know, but the Sasquatch suddenly turned and leaped into the trees ... and that's when Sam went after him. That little bastard had so much fight in him."

Andrew groaned.

"My mother wouldn't let go of me no matter how much I struggled," Jared recalled. "I fought, I cried, but she wouldn't let me go. She knew what my young mind was thinking. My father knelt in front of me and assured me Sam would be back any minute. I could hear his barking becoming more distant as he chased that thing through the forest. And I kept waiting for him to turn around. He didn't, though. Just before his barking completely faded I heard him yelp ... and then ... nothing."

A large sigh welled in his chest. There was so, so much more to this story, so much he couldn't ever see himself sharing. "I was an adult before my father told me the truth about what happened. He said it looked like something had torn Sam in half and discarded him on the forest floor. And that's what set me on this course, believe it or not. I told you it was stupid."

"No, no," Andrew blinked, an unreadable expression on his face. He bit his lip, looking every part of someone bothered by his own thoughts. "I get it. You were young. And, dogs are pretty cool. I'm biased, not much of a cat person because they make for lousy company, but I love dogs. I can understand where you're coming from. Hey, this may be good news for you then, but those reports? They're not all I have for you."

"Oh?"

"Yeah," Andrew pushed back from the desk and stood, grabbing something off the table behind him and laying it on the desk in front of Jared. It was a map of the mountain. "If you'd like I can take you to the site."

"Where these people saw the Sasquatch?"

Andrew shook his head. "No, where I did."

5

Everything changed after that first sighting. His family. Him. Some memories get burned into the mind forever. Unforgotten. Unforgettable. First-hand experience made it easy to understand why people changed after their first encounter with Sasquatch; it was all so consistent and obvious. Andrew had changed too, right in front of Jared's eyes. The park ranger was guarded, but that much could be expected due to his profession. Andrew's position in life meant he had to protect his career options. The smart and practical choice and a reason he respected Andrew even more. Andrew could have buried the reports, he could have never taken the time to look Jared up, and he definitely never had to call him.

Yet he had.

And now they were on their way up the mountain so Andrew could show him the location of a Bigfoot sighting.

As they rode in the small utility vehicle, Jared thought about what all this meant; first Andrew, then his own retelling of a restructured story, and finally a sighting on a mountain where there hadn't been a report in ages. Until there were almost one hundred of them! *Well, if they're legit.* Still, even if a quarter of them aren't some damn bear sighting ...

He thought about Maria.

After she left, he kicked the investigation into high gear because he wanted it done and over with. He wanted to find this damn beast before it tore apart the last shreds of his life. Finding Bigfoot would do so much more than validate him.

So much more.

But it also meant he had grown ever-more protective of his time. Anything that took him off-course, away from that aim of finding evidence of this creature as quickly as he could, he met with harsh resistance. So getting a call and spending an entire day on this mountain when he had sightings in the Olympics he needed to check out was a weird position to be in. Usually, he would have been fine ignoring or even denying a request to meet out here, but from the first seconds of their conversation, there was something different about Andrew's request, something that only solidified as the two shared their experiences. Jared didn't understand why at first, he simply felt it. Sometimes that's all an investigator had. He'd been right to trust his gut.

He hoped, though, that Andrew didn't pick up on his dishonesty in retelling his childhood story. There was little reason to worry about it; they weren't likely to talk after today because having ties with a Bigfoot hunter wasn't something park rangers were known to do and, if he was being honest, Jared would advise Andrew against it anyway. The park ranger wouldn't need the connection to Jared. It would be best; distance would protect Andrew's career and it would keep his secrets blanketed, away from a critical eye or exploration.

Jared wasn't sure if the park ranger bought his story about Sam though. He needed Andrew to trust him if he was to get the unadulterated story about what happened here. He'd recited it enough time over the years, at public gatherings, in Bigfoot enthusiast groups, and even to curious strangers, that it was easy to construct it to sound believable. At least he hoped he had. But some people were very perceptive. Some people inquired, some people pried, and others quietly listened and watched him as he explained his motivations. Those were the ones to watch out for, the quiet ones. But it was a risk he had to take; it was difficult enough to get people to open up about their experiences with Sasquatch so, quite often, he had to open up to get them to. It was part of the game. With Andrew, like thousands of witnesses before him, Jared opened up first. It was a deliberate tactic.

Maybe that was why Andrew shared as much as he did? If he saw through Jared's veneer he was kind enough not to say anything.

For now, at least.

"I appreciate you taking me to see this site," Jared said over the rumble of the truck. "I know you probably have a ton of other things you need to get done."

"Nah. I blocked my entire day for this visit," Andrew said, business-like once more.

Jared didn't think it was possible to get away with abusing the clock to that degree and said as much, "Oh yeah, how'd you get away with that?"

Andrew shrugged, his double-fisted grip never left the steering wheel as they bounced over the uneven ground. "We do these periodic conservation inspections that take up a lot of time. I set one up for today so he's expecting me to be out. They take forever."

"Your boss, won't he know you didn't do it?"

"No, not as long as I don't miss anything egregious. Plus, I'm going back out after we're done."

So, the park ranger was making even bigger sacrifices? All in the name of making sure he involved an expert in whatever it was that happened to him. Non-believers didn't do that. "That's going to be a long day for you."

This time Andrew risked a glance across the small cab. "It's worth it."

The change was palpable. The park ranger he'd met a little over an hour ago was a different person now. Even without Jared connecting the dots, Andrew was screaming for an olive branch that would help him make sense of whatever it was he had gone through on this mountain. It was times like this when Jared considered himself lucky; he'd seen a Sasquatch when he was a young boy and that shaped his entire world. Most people didn't believe because they hadn't seen what he saw. What must that be like for them? To think they knew the world, to think they had a deeper understanding of it, only to discover there are creatures walking the planet, swimming in its oceans that have been undiscovered by humankind? The swirl of thoughts and questions must be swamping Andrew's mind. One thing was for sure, the invisible wall that stood between them back in Andrew's office was gone. Andrew felt less resistant, more approachable ... vulnerable.

They made their way up and up, taking winding roads, which looked more like wide trails than anything drivable, even in this utility truck. It was an uncomfortable ride for Jared, but it didn't seem to affect Andrew in the slightest. The park ranger rode the bumps and holes as if he were relaxing in a kayak on a lazy river while Jared locked his grip on the handhold above his head to stop from being jolted all over the small cab. The benefits of youth.

The ride up the mountain was a difficult climb for the small vehicle, taking far longer than it should. Part of Jared expected it. Mountain driving was like this, no matter where in the world you were; it was always slow-going, even in the best of circumstances. Most mountain areas humans explored were spider-webbed by trails and roads. None of them were ever pleasant to traverse. They were always slower and more painful than driving in city traffic. But that didn't take away from the beauty of the experience. Rainier dominated the landscape here. Rainier was the landscape. It was surreal; the immensity of it all. To have the entire sky filled with this volcanic monstrosity was a reminder of how small and insignificant human beings were. One only needed to visit nature to realize that. Maybe that was why more and more people were moving back into cities, where they could feel important. Relevant. Who knew? Who cared? This was the world he felt comfortable in. Here, everything made sense.

After thirty more minutes, Andrew pulled the pickup off to the side of the trail road and shut it off. He turned to Jared as he opened his door, "This is where we hike."

"Excellent," Jared smiled, enthusiastic, "I've always loved being on this mountain. Where are we headed?"

"Up to Anvil Rock."

Jared left the vehicle and retrieved his backpack from the bed, "Isn't that quite the hike from here? I don't have my bearings."

Andrew smiled, slinging his own pack across his back. "It's nowhere near the summit if that's what you're asking. We're not prepared for that long of a hike. And we're not going to Anvil Rock, just near it."

The pair finished gearing up and started out on their journey up the mountain via a trail that was partially obscured by overgrowth. Like all mountains this size, the higher up you went the less vegetation you had to fight through. Up near Anvil Rock, there was going to be even less of it, probably nothing more than grass and rock. Down here though, the vegetation was robust enough that Jared would have overlooked this trail had Andrew not pulled up to the foot of it.

The ascent was immediate, Jared's thighs burned within the first hundred yards. One of the benefits of investigating Sasquatch was staying in decent shape. Good shape when compared to other people his age. Thousands of miles of hiking across the state would do that for anyone. But the drawback to all that hiking was the wear and tear on joints, especially his knees. Jared learned over the years that staying away from doctors' knives meant changing how he approached hiking altogether, before and after the fact. It didn't eliminate knee and joint pain, but it sure went a long way toward making it all easier. He was going to pay for this.

It's worth it.

They were on a tight schedule now, with a lot of hiking ahead of them, and apparently, Andrew didn't even stop to consider that Jared couldn't go into an all-out sprint up the mountainside. *Just when I thought I was doing pretty good for myself this young buck reminds me I'm on the wrong side of life,* Jared thought while he still had oxygen. But he pressed on, keeping up with Andrew the entire way.

"So, want to tell me about it while we have the time?" Jared said between panting breaths.

For the briefest of seconds, Andrew's shoulders slumped. "I was off-duty at the time I saw the ... the creature," he replied. Jared hid his smirk at Andrew's inability or unwillingness to call what he saw by its name. Sometimes this stuff was so predictable.

He figured it wasn't worth pushing the issue; converts usually did much better when given the time and space to figure it out for themselves. "You usually come up on the mountain even on your days off?"

"When I'm around, yeah," Andrew replied. "In case you missed it on your drive, there isn't a whole lot around Mount Rainier besides Mount Rainier. Plus, I like it out here. Gives me a lot of thinking time."

It was easy to see why as they crept closer to the edge of the tree line. Gaps appeared with more regularity, widening as they retreated. Even the pine needle floor incrementally cleared of nature's litter. Mount Rainier could be considered pretty barren when you got to this elevation, in fairness, providing a lack of obstacles that allowed them to hike more quickly. After an hour that felt more like three, they cleared the tree line, leaving Jared to take in the chaotic beauty of volcanic rock covering the rugged landscape. It didn't make sense, though, not in a Bigfoot sense anyways. This part of Rainier, and up, was too barren, too exposed. It was anything but the natural habitat for Sasquatch. The lack of natural tree cover should have been a huge red flag, warning him away from this ruse, but Andrew didn't come across as that type of witness. Not even remotely. Jared kept quiet; expressing doubt wasn't something he was in the business of doing with any believers, never mind new converts. Balanced skepticism won the day. Plus, any doubt he expressed might discourage Andrew. The lack of natural cover didn't invalidate the ranger's experience.

"There's nothing up here," Jared said between deep breaths. They were still a good distance from Anvil Rock, but its prominence couldn't be argued. A wall of jagged peaks shot up from the mountainside, as if Anvil Rock refused to be part of something bigger, asserting its independence from Mother Rainier.

Andrew smiled, giving no signs he was wearing down from the demands of the hike.

God, how I miss those days.

"Don't worry," Andrew laughed, "we're stopping here."

"Good."

"Man, getting old must suck." It was the first quip Jared had heard from the park ranger since they left his office.

"Oh, you'll see," Jared smiled, emptying what felt like half the water in his water pack into his gut. "It happens to all of us. What are you? 25?"

"Missed it by two years," Andrew smirked. "27."

"I've got a good decade on you," Jared said. "It happens fast, especially in your knees. Enjoy pain-free hikes while you can."

Andrew nodded with a tight smile and then pointed up the hillside. "So, I was about here, taking pictures of the summit," he said, putting an end to their quick bonding session. "It was a beautiful day. There'd been a few days of new snowfall and I wanted to capture it. It was pristine but still traversable, so I covered a little more area than I'd planned. I was all over this face of the mountain. That's when I noticed the footprints. They came from left to right from beyond that rock outcropping over there. I couldn't identify what species left the prints, so I started tracking them. I was curious. Really curious. The size and depth of the prints were impressive. Deep enough to be a bear, so I knew it was a heavy animal, but not even close to the correct shape."

"How so?"

In an instant, Andrew looked like he was going to change his mind on this entire escapade. Jared would tackle him before that happened, if he needed to. "It had toes."

"Toes?"

"Big, fat, round-tipped toes," Andrew nodded. "I was fascinated so I followed them. All the way around that outcropping over there. My curiosity got the better of me and, even though I was feeling uneasy, I was probably fifty yards away from the outcropping when I saw it. Man, it's crazy."

Jared gave him a moment to collect his thoughts. When it was obvious Andrew wasn't going to say anything, Jared did, "I get that. A lot of people still don't understand what they see, even years after an encounter. It was a Sasquatch?"

"I'm not saying that," Andrew replied. "I don't know what it was, but it wasn't a bear or gorilla or something. It was very ... human-like. I don't know how else to describe it. Covered in hair. Had to be seven feet tall. At least. Come on. Let me show you the tracks."

They walked toward the outcropping Andrew set as their target. Today's sunshine gave them the advantage of seeing the tracks. Even from this distance, they were easy to distinguish from Andrew's own earlier tracks. The closer they drew to the site the faster Jared's heart raced. These looked legitimate, but it was difficult to be sure. Time is the enemy of anyone studying Sasquatch; long periods between sightings and evidence collection do not serve anyone and the warm conditions had taken a toll. Tracks always suffered in sunny, warmer conditions and at this elevation, without the protection of trees, they were severely degraded by two days of sun exposure.

Ridgelines in tracks don't survive sun exposure unless they're documented soon after a sighting. Jared was too late for these tracks, which had already begun melting into themselves, distorting size and shape. That didn't make for good science and would only feed the trolls who seemed to live to debunk Sasquatch claims. Jared knew that but didn't want to tell Andrew. The man had taken a huge risk in opening up. The last thing Jared wanted to do was make the park ranger feel foolish. For all he knew Andrew might be calling him again in a month, a week, or even tomorrow, with a new sighting. No, it was best to not say anything about the natural damage that ruined what could have been incredible evidence at this new site.

Jared kneeled next to one of the better prints. Whatever left these tracks was bipedal and large. His own tracks went no deeper than two inches, but of course, the snowpack was harder now than it would have been two days ago. These tracks? The depth was six-to-eight inches.

Whatever left these prints was big.

Jared grabbed his camera and took a few pictures of the prints as well as the site itself before plotting the location on his GPS Tracker. None of his peers had reports of sightings out here so there weren't records anyone could share, even if they were willing. For all he knew this was the start of documented sightings on Mount Rainier. If Andrew ever called again with another sighting Jared would need to have something to start with when that time came; comparative data was essential to a progressive investigation.

Seeing this evidence made the trip worth his time. Plus, if he wrapped this up with grace, he might earn himself another ally. Someone on the inside.

The walk back to the truck didn't take half the time the trek up did. "Thanks a lot for this," Jared said as they loaded their gear into the bed.

"Do you think it'll help?"

Jared noted a hint of desperation in Andrew's voice, like he worried his fears of looking like a fool would be confirmed. "Everything helps," Jared was as diplomatic as possible, disguising his own disappointment. "There's a ton of tracks up there. Something crossed that mountain and if you say you saw something you couldn't identify, I believe you. I'd like you to contact me immediately if something else happens. A park guest, one of your peers, you. If someone sees something, please let me know. I'll drop everything and get back out here as quickly as I can."

When Andrew smiled a tight smile, Jared felt a little less guilty. "I will. Uh," Andrew looked around. "You don't mind not putting my name in any of your reports or anything, right?"

Jared spent the next few minutes calming Andrew's regret, the emotion that springs up right after it's dawned on them that they talked about something that their former selves would laugh at.

If he had a penny for every time he saw what he called 'witness regret'.

*****

The ride back was uncomfortable, and not because of the road conditions. Andrew seemed to be struggling with making his admission. He'd become even tenser, his answers even more abrupt. It hung in the air between them all the way back to the visitor center parking lot. Jared tried to be as friendly as possible as they parted ways, thanking Andrew for his time and his help. He didn't want the park ranger regretting this because there were never enough allies and if Mount Rainier had even a trickle of legitimate sightings it meant things had changed. Jared wanted to be at the front of that new situation.

As he began the long trek back down the mountain road, Jared took one last look in the rearview mirror and saw Andrew, still standing at the now-vacated parking spot, watching him. Was he wishing he could take it all back and pretend the entire experience was a dream? Jared learned a long time ago that you couldn't be too careful or too considerate with new converts. Seeing your first Sasquatch, especially in the career field Andrew worked in, could be traumatic and having to rush off like he did wasn't doing anything for the tinge of guilt that pricked at him.

But it was getting late and he had a long drive to Forks ahead of him.

Another town.

Another sighting.

Another shaken witness.

Did this ever end?

6

The drive to Forks was long. It took two hours to get back to Olympia, forty minutes of which was spent struggling to get cell phone reception. The nice thing about that was it provided Jared with plenty of time to record his track for the podcast and to think. The Tascam had plenty of space, even for his ramblings. In fact, he could talk the entire way out to Forks and not fill a tenth of its storage. There was so much to say. Most of it would never make the show, he knew that, but speaking thoughts out loud was an excellent way for him to process what sightings this far east meant to everything he thought he knew about Bigfoot population centers. Especially the troubled ones.

He never expected to see possible evidence at Mount Rainier.

He appreciated having time to think after meeting a witness. That was even truer when he was on his way to meet another one. Back-to-back interviews were becoming the norm, it seemed.

It hadn't always been like that. At the beginning of his career, he would have considered himself lucky to find two people over the course of an entire month who wanted to share their Sasquatch experience. No one shared evidence back then. Over the years, he built trust and a reputation, or maybe it was the other way around, and witnesses began coming forward. With each passing year more and more of them wanted some of his time. There were frauds and scammers too, but Jared learned to deal with them; it only took a few wasted weekends for him to learn to be a little more skeptical about people and their motivations. Now, rarely a week passed where he didn't have at least one interview with a witness lined up. And, lately, it was almost a daily occurrence.

So he valued his thinking time. A lot.

The quiet gave him time to think about Maria ... and how much he missed her. Her voice. Her smell. Her touch. Her patience.

And a long drive after an exhausting day was the perfect excuse to give her a call.

His heart thudded in his chest as the phone rang. Her flat tone smothered his excitement. "Is everything okay, Jared?"

"Hi to you too."

She sighed through the phone. "Sorry. I'm just ... sort of in the middle of something."

"Oh, what are you doing?"

"Jared, you don't get to ask me that kind of stuff anymore. Remember?"

He was tired from the long day and all the wrong turns he'd taken. He snapped back, "I hadn't realized that a separation entitled us to completely distinct lives."

"Don't be like that." There was hurt in her voice.

"Sorry, I didn't realize how far we'd fallen."

"Why are you calling?" Maria redirected.

Way to go, idiot. The opportunity for a healthy conversation was gone. He'd blown it ... again. The only thing left to do now was to rescue what he could. "Never mind. It's ... I need you to check in on Molly if you could."

"You're going to be out of town again?"

"I left Rainier a while ago, but I need to run out to Forks," he grimaced, knowing what she was already thinking. "Something happened out there."

"I have plans tonight, Jared. You can't drop things on me like this."

Fair enough. "Okay. Could you at least swing by and ask Mike if he could?"

"No, I'll do it," Maria replied. "Just plan better next time."

The retort was on his lips immediately. "Thanks for doing me the favor of taking care of the dog you own too. I'll figure something out for the future so I stop bothering you."

"Okay," her monotone voice told him that he'd crossed the line ... again, "listen, I didn't mean to come off as harsh. I thought I was pretty clear about what I needed."

"It's crystal clear, Maria," Jared whined. "Have a good day."

Ending the phone call still hurt.

Why did he do this to himself? Yes, the void was dark and deep and scary, but life went on, with or without Maria. He couldn't grab for her every time he felt himself slipping. Was it old habits? That or his complete failure to realize she may have shared his excitement in the past without recognizing that the unfortunate thing about the past was that it isn't the present? Maria was supportive of his passion for years. Married for more than ten years, though the last few couldn't be considered much of a marriage, she'd not only tolerated what he did but encouraged him to do it. Early on she even went on expeditions with him, but that changed in the last few years after she completely lost interest. Even now, Jared was unsure where it started going wrong, but once it made that turn from good to bad, it got bad pretty quickly.

If he could just turn back time ... if he could have seen where he started straying off course.

If ...

He sighed. Enough of that. Bigfoot wasn't going to be found by moping like this. And Maria was determined to do whatever it was she was doing for herself. He could dwell on it or he could get back into the investigation and allow it to distract him from the mess he'd created for himself. He could lose himself in the journey to Forks and worry about all of this later.

The decision was easy.

Jared always found Forks to be an interesting town, nestled about as far west as you can go in Washington State without getting wet. The phone call that started this came while Jared was getting ready to meet Andrew. It couldn't have come at a better time, for him and his investigation. There'd been no rain for three days, a weird scenario in western Washington for any time of the year, giving him the chance to interview and explore without wearing layers on top of layers of protective clothing, a survival tactic for smart Washingtonians. He might even be able to go out without a rain jacket! Besides his personal comfort, though, the lack of rain may preserve what this tourist claimed to have. If what the couple found was legitimate, it should be in amazing condition. It was a positive start.

And Jared needed anything positive he could get.

He was meeting the tourists, Frank and Dorothy Hollenbeck, at the Forks' Visitor Center, located right off the 101, at the front edge of the town. There were two small buildings tucked in the corner of the gravel parking lot. The smallest contained every bit of memorabilia of a very popular movie series, Forks' only claim to fame, that could be crammed into 600 square feet. Ironic considering the movies were never filmed here. Jared wasn't sure if he would include that tidbit in his podcast, though, he was pretty sure the economy of the small town depended on the propagation of that bad information and the locals wouldn't appreciate him educating his future listeners on that inconvenient truth.

He pulled through the wide parking lot and noticed an RV, a newer model Tiffin Allegro, parked along the ditch near the edge of the parking lot. It was long, over 25 feet, squared off, but with an aerodynamic curve to its edges. The side panels were retracted, for now, but Jared was sure that the couple he was here to see expanded them as soon as they camped. The red and grey paint shone, announcing the care and attention this monstrosity of a vehicle received from its owners.

The RV belonged to Frank Hollenbeck and it dominated the parking lot. Jared wondered what type of person spent the small fortune necessary to own and fuel a vehicle that size.

He soon found out.

Frank Hollenbeck was a portly man. In his early seventies, Frank had thick arms that still showed signs of muscle men half his age had lost long ago. Only his belly, gray hair, and edged facial creases betrayed the fact that time had caught up and overcome his physical prowess. By all indications, though, Frank wasn't going down without a fight.

He greeted Jared by the steps of the motorhome with a grandfatherly smile and crushing handshake. "Come on in," Frank bellowed, "knees are killing me and I need to sit if I'm gonna be able to talk to ya about this thing. Plus," his voice lowered, "I don't wanna be talking out here."

Jared stepped up into the motorhome, amazed at the effort it required from Frank and wondering how much longer this man had to use the motorhome before his body stopped participating. Frank's wife, Dorothy, buzzed about the cabin making dinner. She paused long enough to greet him as if he was a grandchild they hadn't seen in years before she returned to the stove to 'rescue the meal'. Rescuing wasn't necessary; the smell of the chicken cacciatore she was preparing made Jared's mouth water, even though he'd already grabbed a lousy meal when he passed through Olympia. Few cooks could make him hungry again so shortly after eating so this was an encouraging sign that Dorothy was a master. There could no longer be any mystery behind why Frank appeared to be a healthy man with a comparably healthy stomach.

"You get up here often?" Jared asked as they sat. It took a little bit of time and a lot of effort to squeeze into the booth chair.

"This time of year we make it a point," Frank said. "We come up through Oregon, do the loop around the Olympics and then head 'cross the border."

"Ah, Vancouver?" Jared guessed. Frank nodded. "A beautiful city."

"We thought of living up there about twenty years ago but changed our minds once we experienced a November day," he laughed. "Dorothy said 'if this is what November's like, I don't want any business being in the city during January.' Couldn't blame her, to be honest. I was sort of relieved. My bones don't take too kindly to the cold."

"So spring and summer trips only?"

"Once in a while we'll do a fall trip as well, depending on the weather," Frank motioned to Dorothy that he was thirsty by making a backward 'C' shape with his hands and tipping it towards his mouth. "Want something?"

"No, thanks. I'm good."

Dorothy set a diet soda in front of Frank and he patted her on the rear as she turned back toward the stove. Jared couldn't hide his smile but thankfully Frank didn't make a scene of it, instead pointing at the soda. "I'm not 'sposed to have these. Doc's orders. But, hey, there's only one life and I'll be damned if Dorothy's gonna let me stay around forever. Back to our trips though; it's gorgeous here in the fall too, at least if you catch the weather off the ocean on a good day."

"That can change in an instant," Jared laughed. "So, talk to me about this sighting you had. When my associate called, he said it was urgent, like you had to have this conversation before you left town."

A youthful smile spread on Frank's face. "Is this really going to be on the radio? Never been on the radio."

"Well, sort of. I'm going to publish it on a podcast ... sort of like radio, just over the internet. But, yes, it'll be available around the world."

Frank slapped the table hard, making Jared jump. Dorothy, to her credit, didn't flinch. "Hear that, Dorothy? 'Round the world, he says. My grandkids are going to love this."

"I'm glad to hear you say that," Jared admitted. "Not everyone is as excited about that prospect."

"Bah," Frank gave the unnamed people a wave of dismissal. "Ain't no harm in it. Not quite sure how or where to start with this story, though."

"Wherever you like. I'm interested in knowing what happened. Whatever you've got to tell me is going to be helpful, no matter what it is."

"Alright then," Frank nodded. "We were out by Eaten Creek, just north of the Bogachiel River ... outside town, off the 101. We were doing some day hiking. We can't do as much as we used to anymore but we save up our bad joints for times when we get up here so we can enjoy it. Though we only hike mostly flat terrain. We'll pay for it for weeks afterward, but dammit, you only get one trip on this rock, isn't that right? You might as well enjoy it while you're here.

"As it was, we were a mile or so up the creek and I had to stop to relieve myself," he smirked. "That happens a lot more as you age, trust me. So, Dorothy took the chance to rest her knees and stayed up the bank while I went down to the water to ... well, you get the idea. I was just about done with my business when I heard a splash off to my left. Scared the dickens out of me. Isn't nothing funny about a man in that position getting scared by some animal. Well, I looked up the bank toward where I heard the sound come from and ... I saw it."

"Saw what?"

Frank shook his head as if he was either trying to jar the memories loose or wipe them from his mind completely. "My kids'd say I'm going senile, but I know what I saw. I looked down that river, and I swear as I'm seeing you right now, I saw a large animal running 'cross to that riverbank. Thought it was a man at first. Looked like a man. But it was hairy, every inch of its body."

"And you're positive it wasn't a man? Or a bear?"

"Sir, I wouldn't have gone through the trouble of finding someone like you for a bear and definitely not for some man. I know what I saw."

"Mr. Hollenbeck—"

"Frank. Just Frank, please."

"Okay Frank, please understand, I don't doubt you," Jared said, aware that Dorothy's stirring had slowed. "I've seen things myself that I can't explain. I know what the experience is like. And I know that things aren't always what they appear to be, no matter how convinced we are by them. My goal is to eliminate possibilities so I can focus my investigation. I don't mean to imply more."

"I understand that," Frank sipped his cola and nodded, looking over at his wife, who gave him the tiniest of curved lips, encouraging him to go on. "And let me tell you, it wasn't easy to go around asking for an expert. I'm a proud man. Too proud sometimes. But this ... this shook me. I was glad to have someone in town here point me toward your ... what'd you call him?"

"My associate?" Jared clarified. "Will and I have belonged to the same enthusiast group for ... I don't know, ten, fifteen years. Good guy."

"He was," Frank agreed. "Didn't feel so foolish once we was done talking. As far as what I saw ... I don't know what it was for sure, but I do know that it wasn't a man. Wasn't a bear. A dog. A coyote. A deer. I'm telling you, it was upright. Bigfoot. Funny name, isn't it? Probably doesn't help you much."

"What do you mean?"

"Far as lending any credibility to the beast," Frank replied. "How'd that name come about? Who in their right mind thought that was a good idea?"

"Well, I don't want to bore you with the details of the history of Sasquatch."

The older man adjusted in his seat, getting comfortable. "Consider it just entertaining an old man," Frank flashed that youthful smile again. "I'm interested in hearing about it. You already know I'm not as skeptical as I was a few days ago."

"In that case, I'm happy to answer your questions if I can," Jared said. "The name? Sasquatch goes all the way back to the 1920s. A Canadian journalist, JW Burns, decided there should be a common term of reference for the species. At that time, it had various names across the Native American tribes and he thought one name to reference would facilitate examining its history."

"Seriously? That far?"

"Yeah, but the Bigfoot name is more recent, for what that's worth. Like, around the late 1950s," Jared attempted to suppress his desire to share the lore with the interested tourist. No need to torture such a kind man. "A construction crew in northern California kept coming across tracks all over a site where they were clearing forest land for new roads. They'd work throughout the day without incident and then come back in the mornings to find fresh, unrecognizable prints all around their equipment. The tracks were huge, too. Sixteen inches."

Frank let out a piercing whistle. From the corner of his eye, Jared saw Dorothy plug her ears and mark her face with the type of scowl only long-time partners can make at one another. "So ... Bigfoot because of the size of those footprints? Makes sense. Sixteen inches, though? I tell ya'; I think I found you something close to that."

"Really?" Jared sat up a little straighter, his excitement now loosed. "You measured?"

With a vigorous shake of his head, Frank replied, "Nope. Got out of there as quickly as we could. Crossed 'em when we were scurrying back down the trail. Looked like he came from where we was going. But, I'm telling you, those prints we're going to see? They're huge. I've still got half a mind to avoid that place, to be honest."

His breath caught in his throat. Please, please don't back out now. It happened. It happened a lot. The emotion of the moment, the unsettling nature of realizing you don't know what the hell you witnessed? It's what motivated people to pick up the phone or send an email. But once that wore off, once the endorphins were flushed from the system, people tended to change their minds and become reserved. Conservative. "But you're still willing to take me?"

"I can. Dorothy? She's not going back."

"Not by a long shot," Dorothy mumbled over her food.

"I don't really want to ... but it just doesn't feel right pulling out of town and leaving what I found where I found it. Someone smart, someone like you, needs to see it."

"Why's that?"

Frank paused before answering, with such a slight shrug that Jared wasn't sure if he was meant to see it or not. "It'll be the only way I can convince myself that I'm not going senile."

"Mr. ... Frank," Jared corrected himself, "I can assure you, whatever you saw, you saw. Whatever you're going to show me is going to be evidence of that sighting. I take this very seriously so I won't be serving up any platitudes to you. But, regardless of what you saw, it was very real to you and that's what matters. If we don't find enough evidence to make you comfortable, then you can ask me to scrap this whole visit and pretend it didn't happen."

"And what if we do?"

"Then I'm going to help you tell your story to the world," Jared's smile was warm, genuine, as excitement washed over him. He hoped Frank Hollenbeck felt it too.

7

Jared stood on the soggy bank looking down the length of the narrow river. It was a typical river you'd find all over this part of Washington—narrow, shallow, winding, and choked by emerald-green trees. Washington State is a beautiful place, a glorious place. But the beauty on the western side of the state usually appeals to those with darker dispositions—people who liked things mysterious and who didn't shudder at the world. Those were the types of people who enjoyed this majesty. Those with sunnier dispositions who kept the lights on when they watched horror films, they stuck to the east side of the Cascade mountain range or stayed indoors and pretended this natural beauty didn't surround them. Jared didn't know who he felt sorrier for; those who, like him, couldn't get enough of this natural beauty, or those who refused to experience it. It satisfied his senses. The smell of the moist ground and mossy undergrowth in the trees. The winding of the river and the sharp ripple of the water as it ran over the rocky bed. The way the trees crowded out the sky, only leaving a narrow slit through which to view the gray expanse above. Cities, the east coast, the entire middle of the country? They couldn't provide so much in such a small space.

"So this is where you were standing when you saw it?"

"Right here," Frank answered before turning downstream and pointing. "And it crossed over there."

A hundred yards up the bed, the river took a sharp turn to the right and disappeared behind the narrow peninsula of trees. Jared assessed the situation before heading along the bank. The river was shallow and narrow, but the water moved swiftly downstream. There were two spots where it was no more than ten feet across, traversable by man and beast. If he could get to the other side, he might be able to get better evidence. It made sense. If the creature was ignorant of a human presence when it stepped out of the trees but then got spooked by Frank getting spooked, it would have hurried across the bank, consistent with Frank's report. It probably would have been careless too, more interested in getting away from the human than preserving its habitat ... or cloaking evidence of its own presence.

Across the river from the downstream point, Frank indicated a tree leaning out over the water at a sharp angle, looking ready to tip over. This was where Frank said he saw the creature disappear. "Are you able to cross with me?"

"I'm old, not an invalid."

"Not what I meant, sorry," Jared grabbed his pack and slung it over his shoulder for easy access and retrieval. Every time he was on an investigation he was careful to be responsive. You could never tell what might happen; it wouldn't be the first time something scurried away from his prying eyes when he was collecting evidence or investigating a site. "I'd like to check the bank over there. See if we can see anything."

Frank let loose a booming laugh that still managed to sound nervous. "Oh, we will."

They began to cross together, careful to not twist an ankle or slip. There was nothing worse than sensing you were onto something only to lose the opportunity because of an injury. Jared wasn't worried about himself, but he couldn't say the same about Frank. The problem was, he wasn't going to tell Frank he had those concerns. Frank started the idle chatter as they took their time crossing, even though Jared would have preferred the man concentrate on his footing. "What is it you do? Do you get paid to do this?"

"Not well. This is it. This is my job."

"Really?" The disbelief in Frank's voice was like a shove from behind.

Jared chuckled. "Yep."

"And you can make a living at this?" Frank asked. Jared had a feeling that if Dorothy was there Frank wouldn't have been able to get away with such invasive questions. He didn't mind though. People seemed more curious about how chasing this creature paid the bills than about the creature itself. Maybe he was the grander mystery in this?

"Not a good one but there are ways for you to make money off investigating Sasquatch. Or any cryptids." The bitter taste in his mouth came along with the thoughts over how some Bigfoot investigators and hunters behaved. "Some people make a lot of money doing it, but they tend to be less scrupulous. I prefer to do honest, serious work."

"Why am I not surprised that less-than-scrupulous people would even get involved in this?" Frank questioned. "They'll take advantage of anything, won't they?"

"You bet," Jared said, trying not to be too short but not wanting to travel down that road. Not now. Not in the middle of an investigation.

Suddenly Frank grabbed his arm from behind, almost pulling Jared off-balance. "Over there is where I saw him. See?"

"Jesus!"

"Sir," came the sharp response, "there's nothing holy about those footprints."

Jared couldn't believe what he was seeing. The prints were well-preserved, as he'd hoped when he got the call and had checked the weather, as was his protocol when deciding to visit a site. It didn't appear anyone had traipsed through the area since Frank was here last. Some of the prints were useless because they were too close to the waterline. The pristine ones were further up on the bank. Jared did a quick count. At least six could be cast.

Careful to keep himself and Frank far enough away, he followed the tracks into the tree line where the underbrush slowed his progress. It was so thick that many of the tracks were difficult to find. As he moved deeper it only got worse. Whatever had come through here did so in a hurry, knocking over and trampling the brush, destroying any chance to collect evidence. After about a hundred yards anything usable was long-gone. The trampled vegetation made the tracks below indistinct from the clumped mud. This part of the trail grew cold thanks to the matted flora. That didn't make sense. No matter how big this thing was, it couldn't have disrupted the vegetation this much. The destruction was too expansive.

Maybe it dragged something alongside? A deer? But that couldn't be what happened. Frank didn't mention the Sasquatch carrying or dragging anything and the rest of the tracks didn't show this wide of a berth.

Unless what he was seeing had come from the other direction.

He hurried forward and was discouraged for all his troubles. The matted underbrush spread out even wider just a few feet ahead.

It didn't make sense and time wasn't on his side; he was wasting the precious moments of sunlight he had chasing bad evidence. He'd have to head back into town with Frank soon and that meant he wouldn't be able to come back out tonight. Anything could happen in those hours he was away. Forks rested along the Pacific, which was unfriendly to evidence like this. Another reason Peter should include in his reasons to understand why the Pacific Northwest served as the home of Bigfoot. Animals evolved from their environment and this place handed Sasquatch all the advantages. Bigfoot hunters were playing against a stacked deck.

He was losing time. He had to make a decision quickly. There were still the footprints on the bank. They were few in number, but they'd make excellent casts. He was going to head back there to collect them. It just didn't make sense to—

A wall of tall Pacific wax myrtle stood defiantly in front of him. But that wasn't what caught Jared's trained eye. He couldn't believe what he was seeing. His heart thudded in his chest as he reached around his side to try to unzip the backpack without taking his eyes off what he was witnessing. He didn't want to look away, afraid that this was a dream, that if he blinked it would be gone. No, he needed to absorb this; it needed to be real.

He was looking at the lair of the beast.

*****

Jared squatted, setting the pack on the ground and feeling around inside to dig out his camera. His eyes never left the nest.

That's what this was. It fit all the eyewitness descriptions he'd taken over the years. The experiences his peers reported; this resembled the structures they described. A fucking nest! After all these years, he was finally seeing one for himself. *Thank God I asked Frank to hang back by the river. He'd have a goddamn heart attack.*

This was starting to make sense, as scary as that was to think about. The underbrush he followed looked trampled because it was a well-worn path, probably used daily. He was confident of it because of what he was now looking at.

The home of a monster.

Never in his twenty years of doing this had he stumbled onto one of these. He heard they existed. He'd seen pictures from other investigators, pictures they wouldn't release to the public that purportedly showed and served as evidence for Bigfoot nests. He just couldn't be too careful when it came to believing the claims. Some of them were easy to dismiss; they were as pushy as used car salespeople. But some investigators and hobbyists spoke about witnessing a nest with a sense of awe that Jared didn't understand.

Until now.

Now he did.

He stood on the edge of a clearing of matted deer fern. A circle about fifty feet in diameter was laid flat by traffic and a body ... or bodies. Someone or something walked through here often. More importantly, this was most likely where they ate, slept, and lived. Off to his right, something had spread the remains of what looked like a raccoon across a small area. They looked relatively fresh, killed within the last day or so.

He snapped a thousand pictures if he snapped one. The expanse was wide, too wide to be natural. This place had been deliberately cleared and designed for living. Twigs, branches, and mud were amalgamated into rounded huts. Three of them spread across the back half of the clearing. Homeless people wouldn't be this far out from town and they wouldn't have done this. Stealing tents would have been much easier than constructing these huts. Animals did this.

Intelligent animals.

His heart raced. His pulse thumped. He felt ... nauseous ... dizzy. Nerves maybe? Adrenaline?

And suddenly aware of something ... disturbing.

A sense that he was being watched. It was a feeling he'd sensed before, a feeling many Bigfoot investigators experienced, but not something he went around telling people about. It wasn't something he even recognized until it was over, and even then, the words failed to capture what it felt like in the moment. It was like that moment when you thought you were over a hangover, right on the cusp of being a normal person again, and the irrepressible desire to puke led you to emptying your stomach all over someone else's sidewalk. That wave of immediate nausea when the world tilted and faces blurred; that's what this felt like. It was something he wanted to remove himself from as quickly as possible.

He knew what it was.

And yet he couldn't stop it.

Fleeing meant acting on instinct, not rationality and he wouldn't fault himself for that.

He had to get clear of the influence. His head was fuzzy the entire walk back to the river, clearing only before he reached Frank, for which Jared was thankful. The tourist didn't need to see him like that. The last thing he wanted, the last thing he could afford, was to give Frank a reason to doubt him or his sanity. By the time he reached the river he was able to put on an act of calmness, though he did catch Frank examining him. His act failed.

To avoid any awkward questions or conversations, Jared set about quickly making casts of the tracks he could grab good samples from as Frank looked on and asked questions about the history of Sasquatch. The older man wondered if these footprints looked faked, like all the other examples and stories he'd heard for years. It was a legitimate question; one Jared always kept in the forefront of his mind when going into investigations. Because people always asked.

Sasquatch enthusiasts could be divided into two categories: knowers and believers. Believers entertained the idea of the viability of the species existing. Some even hoped the beast existed. But knowers were different. They proclaimed its existence, even when there wasn't evidence to support their position. They were the unwavering types, the types that made his job that much more difficult. He wasn't a knower by any stretch of the imagination, preferring to keep a healthy balance between blind faith and equally-blind skepticism, though he had no idea how good of a job he was doing with either of those. As long as no one pried into his personal life he could fake it. If they did pry though, giving him a failing grade would be understandable. Maria might have a thing a two to say about his ability to be skeptical.

He shared his perspective about con artists in the community. Frank looked disappointed. "Have you seen some of the stuff on television?" Jared quipped.

"We don't watch much of it," Frank grimaced. "Bought the damn dish for the motorhome but we find ourselves driving and enjoying the places we stop. Dorothy's got her lady shows and I enjoy some of the fishing programs, but there don't seem to be too many of them on nowadays. Imagine you're saying Bigfoot is getting popular enough to have its own show now?"

Jared shrugged as he started cleaning up the site. "I'd risk saying it's becoming less popular."

"Yet it's got shows on TV?"

"That's the thing," Jared replied, "those are the type of people who are hurting investigators like me; people who want to find legitimate evidence through doing legitimate investigations. It's hard enough to get people to want to speak up about this without some of the crap making a mockery of everything we do to find this animal."

"Hmmm," Frank moaned, "might have to check some of this out. I don't know if I'm crazy about being linked with that kind of stuff."

It was an easy sentiment to understand; Jared couldn't fault Frank for being queasy about it, but he also wasn't going to mislead the man. "Like I said, you feel uneasy about any of this at any point, including me, you let me know and we'll shake hands and go our separate ways, even after we've already gone our separate ways. I don't want you to have any regrets about calling me, Frank. But I'm telling you, what you've shown me ... you've propelled me to the front of the line in the community. There's maybe," Jared paused to do a quick count, "a handful of investigators out of the hundreds that I know who can claim to have evidence like what you've given me today. Even so, some of those claims are very, very weak." Jared didn't feel the need to tell Frank about everything he'd uncovered today.

"You seem like a good man," Frank beamed, "you really do. If what I showed you helps, I'm happy. Someone needed to see this. I just don't want to be looking crazy. It's not that I give a damn about what people think, I'm too old for that, but I do care about how it affects my kids and grandkids."

"I'll honor your name, Frank. Hey, I can even send you the files so you can listen to them before I start releasing them."

Frank laughed so loudly it echoed off the surrounding trees. "Sir, you'd have to teach me how to listen to them podcast things first. I'm a radio man. Never even got into those CDs, never mind all that fancy stuff you kids are listening to nowadays."

They joked all the way back to Jared's truck, Frank helping him carry some of the casts. Jared tried to hide the constant smirk that wanted to stretch across his face at the sight of Frank's fascination with the prints. When they got back to the motorhome, Frank got out of the truck but hung by the open door, looking south, back to where they'd come from. "You know, Jared, it takes a special kind of person to do what you're doing. I don't imagine many would take the chances you're taking and, by the looks of this truck, I don't imagine you're doing it for money. Some people never say it, but you're doing good work. May not feel like it some days, probably doesn't on the lousy ones, but if you do find the evidence you're looking for you're going to change the world. That's something to be proud of. That's called living. Don't you let no one take you off course. You'll regret it."

Jared was stunned into silence.

Frank pounded a hand against the side of the door after he closed it, leaning into the cab. "Stay on course, my friend. Don't be sitting in your motorhome someday wishing you'd done things differently, finding yourself too old to do 'em. Listen to me; I know what I'm talkin' about." And with one more booming laugh, he stepped back, away from the truck. "Now, get out of here. Dorothy'll have dessert for me and you made me work up an appetite."

Jared thanked Frank, knowing his words weren't enough to express his gratitude. This phone call, this random exchange that followed his experience at Mount Rainier, changed the course of his investigation. Changed his future course. This wasn't even something he was planning, it fell into his lap, and yet he was now leaving Forks with digital and physical evidence of what could be an actual Bigfoot community. A few hours ago he was on the verge of passing on this request so he could stay home and mope about the slow death of his marriage. Now he had the best evidence of nests he'd ever seen, validating his theory about communities of the species in this region of the state. What today meant, at a minimum, was that Jared would have more trips to Forks in his future.

He pulled away from the visitor center, heading south, back toward Olympia. Frank stood by his motorhome, waving as Jared pulled away.

Funny, isn't it?

A non-believer-turned-convert might have helped him stumble upon something that might change the course of his investigations for good.

8

Michael Shermer of *Skeptics Magazine* once said, "The key to skepticism is to continuously and vigorously apply the methods of science to navigate the treacherous straits between know nothing skepticism and anything goes credulity." Jared thought about Shermer's quote often, but especially at times like this. He could look at the pictures he took a thousand times and still be amazed by what he captured. What started as a pretty ambiguous trip to Forks to meet an elderly tourist might turn his entire investigation upside down. It might end up validating everything he'd been doing for the last twenty years. He didn't want to get ahead of himself, he didn't want to commit what he called investigator fraud by doing bad science, but it could be a sign of what he'd been looking for all along.

A community of Sasquatch.

He paced as he tried to control his runaway thoughts.

Back and forth.

Back and forth.

Pretty soon the carpet under his feet would have a wonderful stress path carved out if he kept it up, but this was what he did when he was in deep thought.

When he was consumed.

It took everything he had, and a previously-scheduled obligation, to not pack up and make the three-hour drive back out to Forks for a longer stay and observation of the nest site. It consumed every ounce of his mental energy since last night. The entire way home, exhausted as he was, and even when he climbed into bed to try to get something that resembled rest; his brain refused to shut off.

It'd been a long time since anything got him this excited. Seeing pictures of Bigfoot nests was promising, but to be standing at the site, trying to steady a shaky camera, that was something else entirely. To see the construction of those three pods, the careful consideration that was given to each to keep them stable, all from a creature most people were sure didn't exist, was transcendent. It was possible, he reminded himself, that humans made those pods but it was still unlikely. They were too far out, too far removed to sustain anyone who wasn't capable of living completely off the land. There wasn't even a fire pit, so if it was humans they were living a completely vegetarian or raw meat diet in pods that didn't protect their hairless bodies all that well.

No, it couldn't be humans.

He'd stayed up way too late on the internet, thanking the Bigfoot gods for his high-speed connection so he could examine aerial maps of the site. The search engine he used had a wonderful mapping system that allowed him to zoom in to an impressive depth but, even at a close distance, the tree coverage was too thick. Hints of the river and the road poked through occasionally but provided little help. The green canopy of trees shielded large portions of the ground from the flying eye of satellites. His tired mind quipped that it couldn't be a human encampment; humans weren't smart enough to be this thoughtful about how to protect their presence from discovery.

At one point he passed out on the keyboard, a sign that he'd given enough of himself to Bigfoot tonight.

Never gonna learn, are ya?

The worst part of getting a shitty night of sleep was the realization that he had to get up and pack for another trip. Weeks ago he'd scheduled a room at a hotel in Quinault for an extended investigation since the area around the town was a hotbed of activity. Today he'd do anything to get out of that trip.

Molly, his Border Collie, whined at his feet. She hadn't been getting the level of love she usually demanded lately. "You're not the only one, girl," Jared rubbed behind her ears. Her eyes narrowed and her tongue flopped out of her mouth as she enjoyed the attention. "I've got to go again, girl. Promise me you're not going to be mad. Please." He pulled his hand away and she lowered her head to the floor, between her paws.

He better find a Sasquatch soon or he wasn't going to be able to afford the dog sitting the kid next door did for him when Maria wasn't in town to help out. "You're more expensive than a baby, you know that?" Molly whined in response before barking once, with attitude. He was going to pay for this, he knew. *Probably by coming home to a nice, big pile of shit in the middle of the rug.*

But Quinault called. His destination. One more place to chase the never-ending trail of recent Sasquatch noise. An unincorporated community in Grays Harbor County, Quinault was bursting at the seams with an impressive population of about 200 sturdy residents. The town was one of those places that could spend the expanse of eternity not existing as far as the rest of the world was concerned. It could go completely unnoticed and no one would care ... well, except for anyone who visited. There was a quaint isolationistic beauty to the area; it was the kind of place where Jared could retire and fade into obscurity if he had Maria by his side. Without her, the slow pace of life here would drive him crazy. He didn't mind investigating in the area surrounding Quinault, but he didn't look forward to it either.

For the next few hours at least, this was the most important place in the world.

This trip was long overdue.

More and more reports were coming in from the Quinault Indian Nation. Sasquatch were being seen on the reservation. Far too many to be ignored. The secret was finding out why. There had to be a reason for so much activity springing up in such a small window of time. If he didn't hurry, the window of opportunity would close on him and the skeptics would happily taint the perception of anything coming out of the reservation. Give them enough time and those who denounced anything to do with Sasquatch would have half the state convinced there was some sort of collective delusion or correspondence bias going on.

He owed it to the people who confided in him to do everything he could to make sure that didn't happen. *Part of the responsibility that comes with doing a job right.* It was what separated him from most of the investigators he knew, even the ones, like him, who were able to do this full-time. Most of his peers. Not that he considered many as peers, more attributable to a lack of integrity on their part than any sense of conceit on his. He didn't think that highly of himself; how could he after everything he'd fucked up in the past year?

He didn't need to remind himself of where he went off-track, every time he looked around the empty house he knew, he understood. The quiet. The motionless realm he only shared with a dog. Jared was thankful for this constant stream of site visits because it got him out of the morgue that the house had become.

Molly got up, moved in front of the sliding glass door, did three circles and plopped down, sighing deeply at the effort of finding a new resting spot.

"Alright girl, be good," Jared ordered. "And don't shit on my floor." He patted her head one more time, convinced she would leave a steaming pile for his dog sitter to find and walked out without much of a protest from Molly. He locked the door, noticing that the black and white Border Collie didn't bother to come to the window to watch him leave.

Quinault was a ninety-minute drive from Olympia so he had to get on the road soon. But he needed to stop and see Peter first to deliver printed copies of his pictures of the Forks prints.

He couldn't wait to see what Peter thought of them.

*****

"Good morning, sunshine," Peter squinted against the rising sun as he opened the screen door covered with the white metal grate. "Getting an early start?"

"I'm sorry for bugging you on a Sunday morning but I thought you'd like to see these."

Peter moved away from the door, forcing Jared to let himself in. The house was dark, the shades all closed. "Jesus, man, it's like a cave in here."

"Call me crazy," Peter said, alternating between scratching his head and his ass, "but I like to sleep in on the weekends. That's the thing about having a real job, they make you tired."

The slight didn't bother Jared. Hell, he'd worry if Peter didn't try to insult him at least once during a conversation.

"Hurry up with the coffee. I've got stuff to show you."

"From the way you sounded on the phone, I don't doubt it."

"You excited to see them?"

"How could I not be? I haven't heard anyone that excited since my kids believed in Santa. Sugar and cream?"

"Yeah, please," Jared laid the pictures on the table, spreading them out so Peter could see everything at once.

Carrying two cups over, Peter set one in front of Jared and slowly squeezed into the chair. While doing all this, Peter's eyes never left the pictures. "Those came from Forks?"

"Yeah, I met a retired couple who were out on a hike along Eaten Creek. The husband saw something cross the creek a few hundred yards from him."

"A 'squatch?"

"I don't like to jump to conclusions, but—"

"It's just us here, Jared. What're you thinking?"

Jared pointed at the pictorial spread in front of his friend. "You tell me."

For a moment, Peter looked overwhelmed. "What do you want me to say? These are great! Did you cast any of them?"

"Yep. They're in the car. Really impressive. I can bring them in later if you want to see them."

"You bet I do," the enthusiastic reply made Jared smile. "What other pictures did you take? I'm sure you aren't this spun up because of prints, no matter how good they are."

Jared had been waiting for this moment. The question that would lead to him showing the last set of pictures.

The pictures of the nest.

Peter didn't reply. He looked through the pictures, a confused expression etched on his face. Jared waited while Peter cycled through the set two more times. "Wow, is ... is this what I think it is?"

Jared beamed with pride. "That's why I wanted you to take a look at them. Is that not a nest?"

His friend whistled, flipping through the pictures again. "Buddy, this is good. You sure they weren't made by people?"

"I can't be completely sure, but those tracks were a direct line from the water to that site."

"Damn," Peter finally set them. "This could change a lot of things. You know that, right? This could—"

He'd already thought of that, already considered it. "Oh, I'm well aware of what it could mean, and don't you dare get started on that again."

"Jared, you can't keep ignoring it. What's it going to take for you to start taking them seriously?"

Them.

He didn't want to think about them.

"I do!" he snapped and then took a deep breath because he was tired of ruining relationships. When was Peter going to let it go? When would his overactive imagination stop constructing the narrative he created for himself? He loved Peter as much as he could love another man who wasn't a relative, but this rubbed him wrong. Jared didn't like hypocrisy in anyone, but least of all in people who should know better, like those who spent their entire lives focused on evidence-based work. "I'm sorry, Peter. I do take their threats seriously. I promise I'm not blowing it off. I would rather focus on this right now. Plus, I need to get out to Quinault." It might be weak, but it was legitimate, and that was what mattered.

Peter, for his part, didn't look like he wanted to escalate the conversation. They'd done this dance before and both knew where the other stood. Peter was much more conservative, but it'd become a point of contention between the two only once the external threats started coming more consistently. More menacingly. "Okay, buddy. Just think about it, okay? Promise me that much?"

But Jared, reminded once again of yet one more thing he 'should be thinking about' but could never seem to get around to taking seriously, nodded. There wasn't evidence for Peter's opinion but that didn't mean Peter wouldn't cling to it for dear life. He wasn't so forgiving when it came to

Jared's work. Jared got it; it wasn't that simple. They were dancing again, but Peter was the only one who could hear the music. Jared respected his friend, but this was getting old. When there was significant evidence of a threat against him he'd listen, but not until then. No matter how much Peter begged, pleaded, or pouted.

"I'll think about it," Jared lied. "But I have to get going. Let me grab you those prints."

Peter walked to his car with him, not bothering to change out of his pajamas. "Not embarrassed?" Jared poked.

"At our age, you have to ask that question?" Peter smiled at his effective retort.

Jared popped the trunk and Peter let loose another whistle when he pulled back the blanket Jared covered the casts with. "These are gorgeous. They are ... huge," he exclaimed.

Jared pointed at the print to the right of Peter's hand. "That one's roughly seventeen."

"Inches?!" Peter shouted.

"No, feet," Jared replied, checking around them to ensure Peter's vociferousness hadn't drawn unwanted attention.

"Sorry, bud, wasn't ready for that."

"You weren't ready to see the nest either," Jared pointed out. "This is why I wanted to see you. I told you it was an extraordinary find. All because some old tourist wanted to get out of his motorhome and stretch his legs."

Peter gripped the ball of Jared's shoulder, almost like a father would. There was a twinge of pain—emotional, not physical. "It's because of your work, Jared. If you didn't bust your balls like you do every single day, that call would never have made it to you. Some jackass would have gotten it instead, gone out there, pissed off this tourist if they did bother going, and wouldn't have been nearly as thorough as you."

"I'm not so sure about all that."

Peter shook his head. "There's no such thing as luck, Jared. This happened because you created the opportunity over the past twenty years. Please stop thinking you've wasted everything or that nothing you did before matters because of what's happening now with Maria."

He could only nod in response, nothing else was appropriate because it would have been disingenuous. "Thanks, man."

"You got it," Peter said, but his eyes bore into Jared as if he were searching for the truth inside his head. Then he gave Jared's shoulder one firm squeeze and moved to pick up the casts.

"Want a hand?"

Peter sneered, a hint of playfulness in his eyes. "Just because I work in a lab doesn't mean I can't hang with you outdoorsmen, alright?"

"Come hiking with me sometime and we'll see if that holds true," Jared needled.

"Can't hear you," Peter yelled over his shoulder as he walked up the path toward his house.

*****

Jared pulled away, giving a wave to the empty front porch, and started the trek across Olympia and out to Quinault.

So Peter wanted him to think? Add him to the list of people who told Jared, directed him, to do some thinking over the past few years. Whatever their reasoning, they all sounded the same. Baseless, full of opinions and bias; none of them got his attention. How could they? Even when Maria was standing next to him all those months ago, holding his hand in hers and looking deep into his eyes as she explained why she was leaving through the tears and the sobs, he hadn't heard. He didn't register the message of concern from her then, so how in the hell was he ever going to hear it from anyone else over anything that wasn't her?

Even his own safety.

There was only so much energy and time he had for those types of things, something he considered as he passed through western Olympia on Highway 101.

Like her.

He was always thinking about her now. Of course.

But it was damn hard to not let his mind slip back to their last conversation. Just when he thought he was managing himself well he realized the entire time he was holding onto a heavy, wet rope.

Like now.

Like when his phone rang and he nearly drove off the shoulder trying to grab it out of the cradle. It was Maria. "Hello?"

"Hi, Jared." There was a hint of hesitation, of apprehension, in her voice.

His day brightened. The highway became less crowded—even though that was imagined, and the sun finally broke through the clouds--it hadn't. "Hey, ba--Maria. Sorry. How are you? Is everything okay?"

She sounded firmer when she answered. "Yeah, I'm fine. Listen, I don't have much time. Did you get the package I left with Brenda? She said she was going to drop it off when she saw you get home last night."

The package?

She couldn't call it what it was. Didn't she have the courage to even do that? Why the fuck not, if she was so sure of herself? Peter's assertions that he needed to be careful in the face of some invisible group of bullies was enough to set him off, but this ... this was not what he needed, not what he wanted. Not now. Not after showing Peter the finds from Forks. Not in the face of a possible robust Bigfoot community in Quinault. This was all about her and it was bullshit.

The package.

"I didn't," he tried to sound as cold as his temper was hot. He knew what the answer was, but he wanted to hear her at least have the courage to say it, "What is it?"

"The agreement," she sounded apprehensive. "Jared, I need you to look at it as soon as you can, please."

He didn't want to deal with this right now. He didn't want to deal with it at all. "Fine. I'll try to get to it this week."

She breathed. Even through the phone, he could tell she was trying to calm herself. "I've been trying to get you to look at it for weeks now. Can you please take a little time tonight to see what you think about it? I think I'm being fair."

Why was she in such a hurry now? She suffered through hundreds upon hundreds of expeditions over the course of their marriage and when things turned dark for them, when they got their worst, she was still there, slugging along beside him. Why was she now in such a damn hurry to finalize everything and move on? Why was she in a rush to close this chapter of their lives when there was possibly more story to tell?

Jared's hand gripped the wheel tightly. "I'm actually on my way to Quinault right now. I'm not sure if I can get to it tonight because I don't know if I'll be home. I might end up doing an overnighter."

"You need me to take care of Molly again ... don't you?"

Now it was his turn for a victory, small as it was. "No. A neighbor is watching her."

"Good," Maria replied softly. Was that disappointment? There was a pause, the type of pause he knew meant the temperature of the conversation was changing. He was ready; he would not get his hopes up this time. "You're a frustrating man, Jared. You know that?"

Her tone made his heart double-time its rhythm. "That's why you fell in love with me in the first place if you'd admit it."

He could hear the smile in her voice. "Among other attributes, yes."

"Too bad I can't seem to remind you those attributes are still in my possession," he tried to not sound like a pathetic, love-struck teen being broken up with at prom. He wasn't sure how it sounded to her though.

"You're a good person. That's not the problem. You know that." Did he? "Anyways, I've got to run. Please take a look at the agreement as soon as you can, okay? I'd like to not drag this out. Be careful tonight, Jared. Bye."

"Bye, Maria," he said, hanging up. Jared stared at the phone, willing her to call him back.

She didn't.

He replaced the phone in its cradle.

The agreement Maria was referring to was something she'd had her brother, a lawyer, draft up. It seemed that the separation was progressing toward an uncontested divorce. At least for Maria. It wasn't for him.

He'd received her email of the draft two weeks ago and ignored it, not wanting to think about it or deal with it. If he gave her time and space it was possible she would change her mind about all this. He had to hope. But with each passing day, with each follow-up request, it was getting harder and harder to stay positive. He'd misjudged how motivated she was to move on with her life. But he couldn't shake the feeling that there was still something there though, some embers glowing. If he could just spark them, give them the oxygen they needed so that she would catch fire for what they had once, what they could have again ...

... for him.

9

Jared stopped to meet a local at the Lake Quinault Lodge, a quaint, rustic monstrosity that overlooked the water. He was more than happy to give Jared information about recent sightings around the famous resort, because, as he said, the nature and amount of information put him out of his depth. What was happening around the lake, sandwiched between the southwest corner of the Olympic National Park and the Quinault Reservation, was more than he was ready for or wanted to deal with.

This kept getting better and better, coming to a head. Evidence leading to more evidence. Everything was moving toward a discovery.

This edge of the lake was eerie, enough that Jared scribbled a note to encourage his future listeners to make it a stop if their travels brought them out to the Pacific Northwest. It served as an excellent example of how even uncomfortable environments could be exquisitely beautiful. Words, written or even recorded for the podcast, failed him. People had to be standing here to understand it, but looking at the tree-covered hillside that ran up and away from the lodge, Jared couldn't think of any other way to describe it. It was the type of place you wanted to be away from as soon as you got there, especially on the days when it rained. But it was also a place whose beauty enraptured, silently urging you to spend eternity in its embrace.

Jared enjoyed his trips out here, even this time when his conversation with Peter went longer than he wanted and the traffic was worse than it should be. The local amateur investigator he met with more than made up for it when he offered up a buffet of information. After the meeting, Jared was glad he came prepared for an overnighter. With everything the man said it was easy for Jared to see himself staying for a few days. Thankfully, Haley the Dog Sitter knew to check in on Molly a few times a day until she got paid by Jared, her signal that he was back in town and her dog sitting services were no longer required.

He followed the South Shore Road to the Colonel Bob Trailhead, just east of where the Quinault River fed the lake. It was the general area where there were a number of mysterious sightings over the past few weeks and, from what the locals told him, it seemed as if the river was the hot spot. So that's where he decided to start.

The creek was a tributary of the Quinault River. Thanks to climate change, the river wasn't exactly bursting at the seams. For the last few years, it was nothing more than a deep creek by every measure. That could be why a Sasquatch, coming down out of the Olympic Mountains, might be getting more sightings, Jared figured. If Merriman Creek flowed more robustly, Sasquatch, if that is what they were dealing with, might have continued to go unnoticed. But with the creek drying up from a disappointing snowfall over the past few winters, depriving it of run-off, it would be understandable that wildlife would have to extend their search for food and water. That would push desperate animals closer to the river and lake, even if that meant risking exposure to humans.

Jared wasn't a fan of trout or any seafood, but he couldn't fault a hungry primate if he or she were. Seeing the conditions in Quinault was critical to understanding, or at least laying the foundations of understanding, of what was going on. You can't conduct investigations over the internet, though there were a number of enthusiasts who tried. The only way to investigate was to get your feet wet and your hands dirty.

Boots on the ground.

He was going to need some time here. If he was lucky, he'd pick something up tonight or in the morning. The feeling was in the air.

*****

A few hours of strenuous hiking later, Jared set up for the night. He took a deep breath of the crispy Washington air. It filled his lungs, refreshed his system. There was no better place in the world to be. People could have their crowded coastal beach towns and their heat in the south. To him, there was nothing attractive about fighting for a spot to throw down a blanket on a beach some kids spent the night getting drunk on, pissing and vomiting where they pleased. And, as for the heat, ask all those people who love the south where they spent most of their time and you'd discover they never saw the outside world, preferring to remain in the realm of air-conditioned homes. So what was the point? So you could sweat on your way to the car, praying its air conditioner would return your body to its pre-sweat state? No thanks. Humans didn't evolve for that type of existence. This was what billions of years of evolution were about. The only way he could possibly be happier than he was at this moment would be to have her by his side.

Like before. Like she used to be.

Jared took a deep, calming breath. His head arched up toward the open, star-filled, sky that promised a cold night.

He had carved out a safe fire pit after getting his tent set up just in case the night turned on him. He was now glad he had. There would be no breaks, no comfortable sixty-degree evening to sleep through. No, tonight would drive home the spirit of doing hike-in camping. Roughing it, in the most comprehensive ways possible. Nights like this were the reason more people weren't interested in hunting or investigating Sasquatch. So few entertained returning to the days of less-than-perfect climate control. It was a shame. He loved the cold. The peaceful cold. It made focusing on your thoughts a simple task, usually because it was warmer inside your head than it was outside it.

He thought about his childhood.

His father.

And about the passions that drove him to lose the very thing he treasured most.

And yet there he sat, in the middle of the woods, on a cold-ass night so he could get up as early as possible and poke around to see what he could find? *Way to change your life, buddy.* If he didn't start changing soon he might start doubting how serious he was about the promises he'd made to Maria.

And myself.

He had to remind himself of that because he also thought about Sasquatch too. Right in the middle of thinking about the early life experiences that shaped the man he was, right in the middle of thinking about the woman he loved like no one else in the world, the woman he'd lost, he was thinking about that damn animal. Born of desperation, the thoughts pried their way into his mind. He was desperate to close this chapter, to prove to himself he wasn't chasing shadows. He was desperate to prove to the world that a grown man sitting in the woods because he believed an ancient upright mammal was also out there, made sense. Goddammit, it makes sense.

It was convenient to never consider that this creature might not exist beyond Hollywood or fringe members of society who spent most of their free time on message boards and discussion forums, talking about inter-dimensional travel and Bigfoot visiting for the family barbecue. It was easy, too easy, for those types of investigators to get attention from the vast majority of people who don't think or care about Sasquatch. People don't care about wildlife that has been proved to exist, he wondered why anyone assumed people would waste any thought on a creature for which substantial evidence simply hadn't been yet uncovered. There were bills to pay, bad economic news every time you turned around and a world that was going to hell on the expressway.

He understood their apathy.

What he didn't get were the people who asserted the non-existence of Sasquatch without understanding the anthropology behind it. Especially problematic were those who made claims but weren't bothered to provide the evidence to support them. Like those who insisted the Patterson-Gimlin film was nothing more than a man in a monkey suit but ignored all the evidence to the contrary. Those deniers acted as if this was some sort of new phenomena and failed to recognize human history was littered with cultural references to strange primates crossing paths with humans.

It perplexed him, the peculiar mix sandwiched between skeptics so incredulous he could drop a living Sasquatch in their kitchen and they'd still deny its existence, all the way to people who didn't believe that Homo sapiens co-existed with Neanderthals. Interbreeding happened between Homo sapiens and them, as well as Denisovans. The evidence was there, waiting for humanity to choose to walk away from its ignorance. Yet millions had no clue or outright refused to acknowledge facts.

Jared used his pack ax to cut up some of the wide branches he found scattered around the campsite and fed them to the fire. He was going to need to keep it hot and going as late into the night as possible. Fire helped keep away unwelcome visitors.

His thoughts drifted back to the naysayers as he watched the orange flames dance. Skeptics should get it. Many of them knew examples of new species finds littered zoology, even large species which were thought to be extinct, like the Tibetan Riwoche horse or the Vietnamese Vu Quang ox. 15,000 new species are discovered each year. But the vast majority of people didn't care to know that. It was depressing.

They were as ignorant to the hominoid evolution, from the Homo erectus fossils in Indonesia that dated back to as early as 27,000 years ago or homo floresiensis, nicknamed 'The Hobbit', who lived as recently as 12,000 years ago. They looked a lot like the people who didn't believe anything humanoid but Homo sapiens ever walked the earth.

The thousands of intersections of the tree of life was a beautiful thing when you understood it.

And so much of the world was ignorant of that fact.

Jared poked at the fire, accidentally knocking over a log. Willful ignorance was so damn infuriating. People were determined to maintain the status-quo at all costs, dismissing native stories as folklore. All the wild-men throughout history, across vastly diverse cultures. All ignored.

Jared got up and went to his bag, retrieving his notepad. He needed to get these thoughts outlined for the podcast. The points needed to be made. They needed to be heard by anyone who happened upon the show when it went to air. The thoughts, like they often did when he got away from Olympia, away from the stresses and strains of life, away from all the things that blocked good thinking, came fast and thick.

He scribbled the next one before he even finished the current thought. How did people not understand that when they dismissed this heritage they were trivializing the culture and history of these people? Why? Because a Sasquatch hasn't fallen on anyone's doorstep yet? He scribbled furiously. Some Amazonian tribes weren't found until years after humankind had already begun traipsing through and destroying that precious rainforest ecosystem. The Hopi, Sioux, Iroquois, Northern Athabascan, Lakota, the Ojibway, the Coliville ... all include a variation of the 'wildman' in their histories. If all were wrong, then why?

Shouldn't skeptics be thinking about that if they were the critical thinkers they claimed to be?

Jared shook his head as he finished his last note. Not very skeptical behavior for self-professed skeptics, was it?

Sometimes it made him want to give up, pack up, slug back down the mountain to his truck and sleep in his bed. His warm bed.

Instead, Jared stayed up for a little while longer but put the notebook away. It was too frustrating. He pulled out the recorder and started talking. He didn't need the notes once he started; the words flowed into the recorder just as they had to the notepad. Twenty years of running into non-believers and bad thinkers did that, it made talking about the discrepancies so easy. Shaking people out of their comfort zones, though; that was, by far, the least enjoyable aspect of the job.

He finished his beer and his recording at about the same time, strolled into the darkness, away from camp to a spot he'd scoped out when the sun was still up to make sure, at times like this, he wouldn't break his neck just trying to relieve himself. He made it back to camp with both legs and his neck intact and began closing up for the night. The recording wasn't planned, it'd just come to him, but it would make a great addition to the podcast. He hoped his passion made the information entertaining enough to listen to.

People had to get smarter about this, they had to! Every day people were becoming more and more ignorant and what kind of legacy would he leave behind if he couldn't at least attempt to stem the flow?

As he laid down, his mind still buzzed with the intoxicating combination of being out in the woods on an expedition and the impassioned plea he'd recorded. His eyes got heavier.

Within minutes, Jared was in his dream-world, where people understood their own history.

*****

Waaaaaaaaaaaaaaaaaaaaaaaaaaaaaaaaaaaaaah!

Jared bolted upright, stretching his already-wide eyes. "What the fuck?"

Waaaaaaaaaaaaaaaaaaaaaaaaaaaaaaaaaaaaaah! The call sounded again.

"What the hell was that?!" He unzipped his sleeping back and quietly searched for the recorder.

Crickets. Silence. Crickets over the top of silence. Seconds passed without a repeat of the sound.

Waaaaaaaaaaaaaaaaaaaaaaaaaaaaaaaaaaaaaah!

"Shit!" There. The small, red light of the recorder stared back at him, the only thing breaking up the blackness of the night. Jared cleared his throat and narrated. This was going on the podcast! "I'm not sure what that was, but I can guess."

Off in the distance, the sound he was waiting for came again.

Waaaaaaaaaaaaaaaaaaaaaaaaaaaaaaaaaaaaaah!

Silent, strained seconds passed. This time the same type of call sounded, but it was a different direction, distance, and voice! "Oh man, there are two of 'em! I can't believe I'm hearing this; a call and answer! I hope this damn recorder is picking them up. They sound far off; far enough for me to step outside and try to get clearer audio."

He unzipped the tent. A slight wind chilled his forehead and the crickets around his camp quieted, using the advantage of the darkness to protect them from this human invader.

Waaaaaaaaaaaaaaaaaaaaaaaaaaaaaaaaaaaaaah!   From   the same direction as the first calls, but farther away.

Jared waited to see if there would be an answer call. There was.

Waaaaaaaaaaaaaaaaaaaaaaaaaaaaaaaaaaaaaah!

Waaaaaaaaaaaaaaaaaaaaaaaaaaaaaaaaaaaaaah! From the left. A thousand yards.

Waaaaaaaaaaaaaaaaaaaaaaaaaaaaaaaaaaaaaaah! From his right, just as far away.

He pulled the recorder close to his mouth so he didn't have to be loud. He wanted nothing to do with anything out there picking up his presence. Who knew if those were the only two Sasquatch in the neighborhood? "Dammit, they're moving away from my location. It's ... it's 3 am. I'm not going out there to look for them. They'd be miles away before I even got my boots laced. But at least now I know where I'll be heading in the morning. Man ... that was awesome! I just hope I can get back to sleep."

But, of course, sleep came only in fits and spurts, reluctant to give him what he desired and what his body needed. *Especially considering what I'm about to do.*

Jared stretched, his joints as reluctant to flex as his brain had been about allowing him to sleep the night before. Things cracked and popped and his shoulder refused to release a full range of motion until it decided it was time to, which wasn't at this moment. But Jared didn't need his body to cooperate; he needed it to do what it should be doing, and right now that meant cooperating with his brain to get the camp packed up. Fifteen minutes later, he finished and the fire pit was filled in; he wouldn't be taking out an entire forest today.

*****

He pulled the recorder out as he hiked. "It's freakin' freezing this morning. I packed up camp about an hour ago and I'm headed deeper into the Olympic National Park to hopefully find the source of those howls last night ... well, at least clues to what they were. I'm pretty confident those were two Sasquatch, but let's see what the evidence says first."

A chill hung in the air. A frozen haze shrouded the mountainside. It wouldn't lift for another few hours, giving the distinct advantage to anything that wanted to make a breakfast out of him. He could see three hundred yards in every direction, enough to keep him comfortably numb to the risks that could be lurking three hundred and one yards away.

Like what I heard last night.

Even as he climbed, step after step, zig-zagging across the face of the terrain to preserve his knees and his stabilizer muscles, the haze refused to lift. It was going to stay this way, limiting his vision. He was sure, though, that it would lift at precisely the moment he was loading up in his truck again.

This part of the mountain wasn't densely populated by trees. A fire had ravaged it years ago and the new growth was struggling to take root for some reason, though he suspected an active Bigfoot population might have something to do with that since junior trees served a multitude of purposes for them.

He couldn't think about anything else because that was the moment he stepped into an area where fire had laid to waste almost all of the adult trees. This part of the mountainside was very new, very renewed.

It was also where he made his most recent find.

The listeners are going to love this! Jared pulled the recorder up again. "So I think I've found a clue to something. I can't be sure if this is the site of my nighttime entertainment or not but I'm standing at the top of a slight rise on the western slope of the mountain. There's heavy underbrush on all sides of me; this part of the mountain is cleared though. It looks like a small fire ravaged it years ago. It's showing signs of recovery but there's no mature growth here, which gives me a great view of my surroundings. I've also got some nice prints here too. Not as nice as the creek bed prints I got the other day in Forks, but there should be one or two I can cast, though I'm not a fan of carrying those back to the truck from all the way out here. I've already taken some pictures and marked them on the GPS. These definitely aren't of the Ray Wallace variety. No one would bother coming this far out into the Olympics to plant tracks they were hoping someone would accidentally come across, especially in a part of the world where those tracks could be washed away in an instant. And I'm not inclined to believe those calls last night were human, owl or coyote. I'll have them analyzed when I get back. The howls and footprints are great, but they're not all I found."

Jared bent closer, sliding the recorder into his jacket pocket and taking a series of pictures from all angles before stowing the camera and grabbing the recorder again. He couldn't stop smiling. "I found hair samples. I'm not sure what they belong to, I'm not attributing it to Sasquatch, though it is consistent with other finds that have proved inconclusive. Peter has a friend I can send this sample to when I get back to Tumwater. Hopefully, she'll be able to tell me something about what it belongs to. I've got a long hike back. I need to get some answers to these things before I continue my investigation. I'm not sure what I'm going to discover, if anything, from these samples, but before I come out again I need to do some clarifying or some eliminating.

There are way too many things lining up here, falling into place alongside my hunch, and I've got to make sure I'm at least on the right course before I convince myself that I am. There's no room to get sloppy here."

Packed up and excited by the wealth of evidence he now possessed, Jared could have floated back down to his truck.

10

The silence was thick, disturbing. Somewhere, maybe two or three offices down the hallway, Jared could hear the stacking of something. Books? He couldn't be sure. But the specifics didn't matter; this place was so quiet he could hear muffled voices through the air ducts. How did people work in environments like this for more than an hour or two? Sure, the forests of the Pacific Northwest could be 'quiet' at times, but they were never silent like this. The forests were brimming with life; this place was a damn morgue.

But even in a place like this that suffered being alive, Jared couldn't help but feel excited. His knee bounced as he sat in the uncomfortable chair. He tapped the stiff, plastic-encrusted chair arm.

He hated waiting.

Waiting was torture. Especially when you didn't know where you stood on something.

Especially when you potentially had evidence that would rock the world.

He decided he could get back to work, the itch to work on the podcast, which he'd neglected for days, needed scratching. But he had a life that needed attention, a dog that wanted loving, and a soon-to-be-ex-wife who was demanding he sign paperwork he didn't want to have anything to do with. While he waited in the stale office he might as well work on something, so he pulled the recorder out of his backpack.

"I haven't recorded for a while and I apologize," he whispered, knowing that the walls of this professional tomb would easily carry his voice. "After my recent finds in Forks and Quinault, I needed to step back a little and let the science catch up. Now is the appropriate time to resume my investigation. I'm currently at the office of a forensic scientist who specializes in trichology, the study of hair, to see if she can help me with the samples I found at the Olympic Park. Peter handed the samples off to her a few days ago and she gave me a call earlier, asking me to come in. She stepped out for a moment to grab the report for me while I set up to record.

"Her name is Nancy Reegan," Jared continued. "She's in her mid-40s and, I've got to admit, she's an intimidating presence. The way she carries herself. From the moment I met her, I felt like I was in trouble for doing something I wasn't supposed to do. We're about the same damn age but there's something about her that makes me feel like a kid again. She may not be the most welcoming person I've ever met, but if she's as good as Peter says she is, that's all that matters. She came with Peter's recommendation and testimonial, and he doesn't give those out lightly. Hell, I don't think he's ever had a good word to say about me to other people."

He paused as the distinct, sharp click-clack of Nancy Reegan's heels announced her approach. He kept the recorder running as she came into the office. Jared hid his smile at her expense; she was everything he imagined someone who worked in this field would be. Her hair was cut short, probably for convenience's sake, her drab olive slacks added some color to her outfit because the unappealing blouse she wore looked picked out at some discount store. This was a woman who sacrificed style for functionality. She walked with mindless ease toward the back of her desk, avoiding Jared and anything in the office that would otherwise serve as a tripping hazard. Her face, buried in the papers she flipped through, was a mixture of excitement and confusion. When she spoke she did so without looking up at him. "Sorry to keep you waiting. It's been a hellacious week. Here," she slid a thin stack of paper across the desk, "that's your copy of the report."

Jared grabbed it and flipped through a few pages. Pages of data assaulted him. Intimidating. This was no simple document. The amount of verbiage was overwhelming and he didn't have a clue what the small charts were trying to communicate. "No worries. I appreciate you taking the time to do this for me." He was trying to buy enough time to translate what it was he was supposed to glean from what he held. "I hope I didn't create too much work for you."

"It wasn't too bad. I did a microscopy and wasn't satisfied so I had to go the mitochondrial route for the DNA since you didn't bring me anything with a root."

"Sorry. Is that bad?"

One corner of her mouth turned upwards. "It is what it is. Nothing I can't overcome. It just takes a few extra tests ... especially for this sample. Listen, where did you get this?"

"Out by Quinault. Up in the mountains, near the Colonel Bob Trail."

"Well, it's interesting."

"How do you mean?"

Nancy responded with a simple 'hmmm'. Jared swallowed. This could be a long meeting. "The bad news is this sample isn't one animal. There's definitely some cross transfer here. One of them definitely belongs to a deer, I'm positive of that."

"Oh, okay. I've got to say, doc ... do I call you doc?

That got a smirk from her. "Nancy is fine."

"Okay, Nancy. I was expecting worse news. If that was the bad news I'll take that as a win."

His ears thumped from the change in blood pressure when she replied, "Then you'll probably be thrilled with my good news."

"Why's that?" Here it was again, the thrill that erased all his worries and woes, all concerns of the very real life he was fucking up.

"It's not the cross transfer that bothers me," she responded. "There's more than deer hair in what you brought me. And it's also more than one other animal. By that, I mean species, of course."

"That's the good news?" He was glad he hadn't picked up a clump of deer hair, but he also couldn't deny his disappointment.

"Our mutual friend said you were investigating Sasquatch, to see if it exists or not. Right?"

It didn't matter if she was Peter's associate or not, he was going to tread carefully. He didn't know her, hadn't even met her in person until today since their previous, brief interaction was done over the phone. "Something like that. Yeah."

Nancy tapped the papers she held. "Mr. Strong, I've looked at hundreds of thousands of samples. I've seen thousands of variations across hundreds of species and this, this sample you brought? I have no idea what it is. I searched the database in the National Center for Biotechnology Information as well, to double check my hunch. Nothing. But, since you may or may not be looking for Sasquatch, I thought you'd be thrilled to know. Even if I can't tell you exactly what it is, I can tell you that it's a primate, Hominidae family, probably in the Homininae subfamily. And that hair ... it shares a 92% homology with humans."

Jared wanted to high-five Nancy, but that would probably unravel this carefully constructed professional he saw before him. He would have hugged her as an alternate, but she already put off every signal possible that screamed unapproachable. Not sure how to share his excitement with someone like her, or without knowing if she knew how to get excited, Jared thanked her for her time.

Nancy Reegan might be more inquisitive and curious about what Jared found than she was excited by it, but he knew someone who would be as excited as him. First, he had to say his farewells to Nancy, which he did, and then get home to Molly. He needed to take care of her and then he needed to give the good news, his full attention, to the woman who made him the man he was.

And he knew how he was going to do it.

He was going to see her.

Jared pulled out the recorder as soon as he got in the car. The podcast listeners were going to need to hear this at some point so why not give it to them while he was still excited? If anyone subscribed to the show they'd laugh if they could see his face now.

"I've still got a high from my conversation this morning with Doct—Nancy. I'm not going to lie," he started. "I left her office about forty minutes ago and my adrenaline is still pumping. She wasn't willing to go beyond calling the sample inconclusive, but I'm used to people in the science fields being inconclusive about a lot of things when it comes to Sasquatch. But, sorry skeptics, I'm not giving you that golden nugget you want. I'm not going to hand-deliver you justification to paint all Sasquatch researchers, investigators, and hunters into a corner. But I am optimistically cautious. And I haven't even heard back from Peter yet about the casts I left with him. No, I won't draw definitive lines until the science of this investigation gives me a good foundation. I imagine that'll disappoint some of you.

"That hair sample belonged to a primate," he continued after downing half the bottle of Mountain Dew. "Of all the fauna in this part of the Olympics, non-human primates aren't one of them, so that means this sample belonged to an animal that isn't supposed to be here. It belongs to the great ape family, close to the subfamily that includes gorillas, bonobos, chimpanzees and us. Nancy has experience with the others and still wasn't confident in identifying what I brought her. That's significant. Not conclusive, but significant. Something is out in the Olympics that isn't supposed to be there."

Jared smiled at his cleverness. That should hook some of them.

He wasn't a car salesman; he wasn't peddling garbage. This creature was out there. He knew that because he'd lived through it, he'd survived it, but he also knew that asking people who didn't share his experience to walk this journey with him was asking a lot. He couldn't overwhelm them with data or he'd lose them. All good people of science, the savants, anyone deeply invested in a field ... they told stories instead of data dumping. He knew the people who listened to podcasts, the ones who would give his tiny show a chance, needed to be entertained first. Once they were invested, once they cared, then he could educate them. And, if he did his job right, they'd learn. And maybe open themselves to the possibilities.

He needed to hook them, especially now that things were accelerating.

But toward what?

*****

Jared thought about it all the way to Port Angeles, a three-hour drive up along the bays and inlets of western Washington. It was one of the best drives he'd had in a long, long time. Outside Olympia, he'd called Maria and asked if she would meet for lunch, that he was willing to talk to her about the divorce and their future. Tinges of guilt swamped him after they hung up. It wasn't as if he'd lied to her, he hadn't, but he hadn't been truthful either. And she deserved nothing but the truth. But at the same time, she wouldn't completely understand why this recent confirmation from Nancy Reegan was so important, not to his career, not for this investigation, but for them. And he wanted, no, he needed her to understand it from his perspective. He needed her to see it on his face. A phone call wouldn't do, it had to be in-person.

And now he was here, ready to share with her.

He pulled the recorder back out of the backpack. He wasn't sure if this was going in the podcast or not, and he didn't care about that at the moment; he wanted to talk out the jumbled mess that was in his brain. He'd worry about the content of it later.

"I'm in a port city in the northern tip of the Olympic region of Washington State," he said. "It's called Port Angeles. I'm actually sitting in the car outside a tiny restaurant called The Corner House, situated on the bottom floor of a three-story building, which is painted one of the most horrendous shades of orange you'll ever see. It's not a common color in this part of the world, especially this part of the state, which is notorious for its dull grayness. The Pacific Ocean tends to not do the region any favors. Olympia's weather is bad enough, but out here ... I don't even want to know how many people are popping pills to fight off depression. I get that feeling each time I come to Port Angeles ... which has been far too often lately."

Now came the hard part. "The entire reason I'm here today is because of Maria. Yes, I've got something I've got to check out later, but ... right now I need to see her. She moved here after our separation. As a successful designer she earned the luxury of being able to work wherever she wants and, since she has family in the area, she decided to move back here for that support network. She's been staying with her parents since we split up. I guess it doesn't hurt that the move also puts three hours of distance between us." He sighed. "I'd better head inside. Can't have her waiting too long; pushing along this divorce seems to be a priority for her."

His heart skipped when he stepped out of the vehicle. It was like being a teenager again. The enigmatic nature of love always twisted his gut. The excruciating desire to love someone else, holding out hope that they would love you in return and not knowing if they did or if the signs you were noticing were nothing more than wishful thinking. The good thing about maturing was that you learned how to figure that stuff out and deal with it, but the rationality of time didn't always eliminate the exuberance of youthful naiveté.

Maria sat at a table in the middle of the dining room. *A perfect setting for a private conversation.* Sarcasm was harder to defeat than a wife's desire to divorce.

Her smile was conservative. "How was the drive?"

Was she unhappy with him being here? Was he being needy? Was she going to tell him to piss off? *Patience buddy,* he chastised himself, *you're not a pup anymore.* "Not bad. Of course, it's not the weekend so there wasn't much traffic coming up the 101."

"I'm sorry," she said. "You didn't have to come out, you know? We could have talked about this over email or Skype or the phone. I feel bad that you drove all this way."

"Don't," he said as the waitress filled his coffee. "I was coming out here anyway. There's a report I need to check out."

Her reaction was immediate. Deflation. "Oh, of course," she said, her smile now just a memory. "Silly me."

"So, everything okay with the job? How's the family?"

"Fine. Everything's fine," Maria said. He wasn't sure why she was pouting like this. "Listen, Jared, I know you aren't crazy about talking about this, but we need to."

"I know. I'm trying to figure out why you're in such a hurry to get to it. I thought we agreed that we were going to take our time?" He was gripping the cup handle so tightly he could see small ripples in the coffee as his hand shook. He let go and interlocked his fingers instead of making a mess of that too.

"We are."

"This isn't taking time, Maria," he threw a hand in the air in frustration. "God, I'm in the middle of an investigation right now, I've actually found something significant. Possibly very significant. Your timing sucks."

She leaned forward over her own coffee. "Believe it or not, I'm not doing this to torture you or screw with you. I've asked you numerous times to sit down with me and talk. I want to keep this amicable while we figure out how we're going to split up our things. You said you were interested in that. You said you were willing to do that and then you keep avoiding it. Avoiding me. I'm trying to be patient, but it's time, Jared. I need you to get serious about this and take some time for me."

Everything flashed before his eyes—the self-talk, deprecating as it always was, the chastising he gave himself over the things he'd done, every sleepless night since she left, the drinking binges like his father's—it all came to him in a flash of disappointment. All those times he told himself that he was going to fix what he broke stared him in the face. All it required was his stopping past behaviors. "But I don't want to Maria. I don't want to split up. I don't want a fucking divorce." He didn't remember picking up the coffee spoon but it was in his hand, pinched between his thumb and his index finger. "I want you. I want us again. I wish you did too."

Maria bit her lower lip. He loved when she did that. "I don't know if I can give you what you need. Not right now."

"Can you at least try?" Jared realized he was close to begging now. "Can you stop being in such a hurry to make

108

this official and give me a chance to prove myself? Give me a chance to show you that I'm serious about us? Can you give me that?"

"You know what I need," she answered. "I've been telling you for years what I want, but you're so goddamn busy with ..." she paused to compose herself, "you're busy with your passions and I don't feel right asking you to give those up. So, where do we go?"

That was the million dollar question, wasn't it? The path was so clear on those lonely nights when all he asked was to have her back in his life. He could see it, without obstruction. He knew what he needed, but like most people, had no idea how to get there. That was the difficult part; how did you navigate to a goal that required so much of you and the people you cared about? He didn't have the words but he did have the desire. So he could sit here and continue to look dumbly at her or he could start walking towards that goal, knowing that if he did it correctly, if he was open and vulnerable, she might just walk along beside him. "I swear to you, I'm done, Maria. I am. Once this investigation is over I want to move on. I really do. I want to focus on you and me and ... and starting that family. I swear I do but I know I can only show you that. Words without actions are meaningless. I'm ready."

The words, his plea, hung in the air between them, a foggy haze of love and pain they were both trying to see through, to see the real person on the other side. He felt that. He felt that she was trying to reach across the divide. It wasn't just him; there was a willingness coming from her as well. "Do you mean that? You're asking me to put my life on hold, you know that, right? I've done that for years, the last five, in fact. It's time for me, Jared. Me. What assurances do I have that you're serious? That you'll follow through this time and that we won't be circling around this two years from now?"

This was the test.

"You'll have to take my word for it, trust me," he said, rushing to justify his perspective before she had a chance to doubt. "I know, I know. I don't have a right to ask that. But I mean it. It's time. And if I'm right about my hunch, and the evidence is starting to show that I am, I'll be able to walk away with the closure I need."

Her eyes narrowed. "That's the problem. This runs deep for you, much deeper than any of your colleagues know. I don't know if you'll find the closure you're looking for. Have you told anyone else the truth? About why you do this?"

At least she was tender when she pried open the wound. "No. It's none of their business."

"I want you to get that closure. I hope you do," her voice held a hint of regret. "I don't know if I can wait for it."

The window was closing.

The path was narrowing.

She might need to step off so he had room to walk it.

Alone.

Jared felt it all slipping away. As quickly as the promise had shown itself, it was fading. "Please give me a chance. I know what I've done. I've seen the impact of giving up everything for this. I'm tired of this damned thing costing me the people I love. I don't want to lose you."

Then he remembered the recorder and shut it off. Future fans of the podcast or not, they didn't need to hear this. If they had any taste they wouldn't want to hear it.

The click of the OFF button felt good. It felt like a step down the path. Toward her.

"I'd do anything for you," his voice cracked. "If that means giving this up tomorrow so that I can show you how serious I am then that's what I'll do. I'll do it in a second, without thought."

"I wouldn't ask that of you," she defended herself, though he didn't ask her to.

He nodded. "And that's why I love you. You've given up so much for me and my passions and this stupid goddamn childish dream. Any other woman in the world would have walked away a long time ago. A long time ago. But you didn't. You stayed and you fought and you sacrificed. And I want to do that for you now."

Maria gave him a tight smile after a few seconds. It wasn't the convincing type of smile that you rushed to tell your friends about or the type that would have your mother's head explode with thoughts of future weddings and grandchildren, but it was one that told him she was hearing him. And that's all he could ask for at the moment. He didn't deserve anything more. Not prone to make rash decisions, Maria wouldn't give him an answer today, he knew that. He didn't want one. He wanted to be as fair to her as she'd been to him throughout this and if that meant he had to sit on idle hands and bide his time then that was exactly what he was going to do.

Whatever the cost.

Whatever the price.

For her.

*****

Jared waved to the back of Maria's car as she pulled away from the restaurant. The gray drizzle of Port Angeles' sky reminded him of his chances with the woman he wanted to spend the rest of his life with. He'd spit back at it if he could.

Instead, Jared climbed into his truck and began the long trek into the mountains. He wished he could be excited about another drive because, under any other conditions, it would be a stunning journey. But that emotion never reached him. He couldn't get excited because he couldn't focus; not on the drive, not on the wondrous emerald beauty that surrounded him, and not even on the lack of traffic. He couldn't think about all the progress he was making in the investigation, what Peter was going to say about the prints he'd left with him. And he couldn't even revel in the validation Nancy Reegan gave him about the unidentifiable hair sample. None of that mattered when he realized things may be falling into place with Maria. Even the investigation, by extension, was a positive indication of where things were headed. Sure, tomorrow it would be all over if that was what she asked. She wouldn't, she wasn't like that. But that was also why she wasn't in his life, because she loved him so dearly that she was willing to give up on them so that they both could be happy. But now, things were coming to a head. If he stayed determined, if he stayed focused, he was going to make the find that would pull Sasquatch out of cryptozoology or he was going to prove, at least for the Pacific Northwest, that it didn't exist. Once he reached that mark then he could walk away and live a life of peace.

It wasn't about finding the damn creature, it was about documenting its existence, proving that it was real, and working with local municipalities and the state to preserve a habitat for it since humankind seemed determined to blacktop the entire surface of the planet. If he could reach that pinnacle, then walking away wouldn't be an act of betrayal to the little boy in him. He would have accomplished what that boy had set out to do.

He would have found Bigfoot.

And then he would be able to devote his life to the wife who gave everything, who was his everything.

Jared was in a mental haze the rest of the drive to camp. The talk with Maria went so much better than he anticipated. After he shut off the recorder they talked for another hour. Some of it was about them and the work they had to do if, and it was a huge 'if' on Maria's part, they were going to try and work through this. But a lot of their conversation was light-hearted; fun, Jared wasn't used to this optimistic perspective. The further he drove from her the more he wished they had another hour together to catch up.

It was almost like they were dating again, with the familiarity that only years of intimacy and vulnerability brought. Some of the things they talked about he'd heard a thousand times over, met the people involved, like her family, a million times and once again, yet it all felt fresh. There was energy in her words, in their interaction, that he hadn't felt in years. Since the beginning. She was the same woman and he hoped he was becoming a different man, but the way they conversed, it was like life-long friends who finally realized there was something more there.

Jared realized that a lot of that was in his head and she may feel differently. He wasn't so tactless as to ask her while they sat at the table, getting the ugly looks from the waitress for taking up a spot without ordering more food to increase their bill and her tip, but he did wonder. Was the spark shared? It was difficult to deny the urge to call her and only the lack of a cell signal stopped him.

Once the camp was set up and the fire breathed to life, Jared sat and thought, tapping a stick against his thigh, reveling in how easy it was to be vulnerable with her at the café.

He grabbed the recorder. "I don't know why it took me so long or took her leaving for me to be able to see things more clearly. I'm sort of encouraged. I mean, I don't know where her head is at right now, but at least I know she's thinking and I can't ask for anything more from her. Maybe there's hope for us. I mean, we didn't even talk about how we were going to split stuff up and that was the entire reason for the lunch. She didn't commit to anything, either way, but the fact that she didn't push to have that conversation is better than I could have hoped for at this point."

He looked up into the night sky. The feeling of transcendence wasn't lost on him. He could reach, stretch out, and touch that luminous blanket of twinkling light; it would be so easy now. She had given him hope.

"Ah man," he exhaled a light cloud of cold breath, "I hope so."

Sudden hope helped him see the beauty of the world once more. To see the end of this path. "I've set up camp near Hurricane Ridge. There have been reports out of this area and it's not hard to understand why. It's isolated, it's elevated, and it can be extreme. But it's very peaceful. I love it out here. I'm going to miss places like this after I'm done."

That wasn't a lie either.

"I got the coordinates of a sighting this past weekend from some local outdoorsman and I'll head out first thing in the morning," he continued. "Their report, plus what I've been getting recently from my sources, leads me to believe there's something strange going on in this specific part of the National Park that might validate my hunch about this species' behavior."

He thought about his last conversation with Peter, the look in his friend's eyes. Peter wasn't easily jostled or bothered. But there was something there, something Peter danced around for whatever reason that he couldn't or wouldn't come out and tell Jared. And Jared, for his part, wasn't naive; he knew about the community of researchers and hunters. He was all-too-aware of the pockets of problem children and the cliques that formed over time.

"I think Peter was right to warn me," he said, the weight of the real threat weighed him down. Jared drew a deep breath and admitted, for the first time, that he was making real enemies. "Before I left Olympia I received another phone call. It wasn't the first, but I haven't been documenting them here because ... I don't know why. I think if I did and Maria knew what was happening; it would be the last straw for her. For us. But I can't hide this stuff any longer."

Once he started, it was impossible to stop. He documented his thoughts about the fraudsters, driven by television money, that tainted the community. Money always did that, didn't it? It felt good to name them.

It was all so disgusting.

"I've always been careful about who I associated and shared information with. Not because of vindictive people, the scammers or the envious investigators, but the legitimate groups as well. It probably sounds crazy to any of you listening who aren't aware of the politics within this subculture, but you've got to figure that it's made up of people. And people are people. Fact is, there's a darker side to all of it."

He stared up into the night, clinging to that sensation of hope, of an ending and a future. "For the past few months, I've been getting harassed. Phone calls in the middle of the night. Threatening notes slipped under my windshield wipers. Letters to the office with bogus return addresses. Voice messages. I can't tell you how many times something like that has happened; far more often than I care to count. This last one though, I've got to say I'm glad I made the decision to release these sessions after I'm all done with this. I wouldn't want anyone knowing how rattled they have me right now. Let me play the call for you."

He made a note to insert the call as a clip in the final audio file and pressed the pause button on the recorder, guilt washing over him. How long was he going to let it go on before he let Maria know? This recording was the first time he'd formally made mention of it and even that wasn't very impressive. He could erase the file tomorrow, right now, and the world would never know what he'd been subjected to over the past few months. On one hand, he was promising Maria a changed man, and on the other, he was doing the same type of stuff that had broken her heart for years.

Trust.

How did you build trust if you hid things from the most important person in your life?

Jared thought about the most recent call. "You need to stop this investigation, Mr. Strong," the high-pitched, raspy male voice on the other end of the phone said. "We're not interested in toying with you. Stop now. You've got other things to concern yourself with, like your marriage. Focus on that. It's in your best interest. Don't make us prove that. Don't compound your regrets."

He'd frustrated them to the point that this man was willing to leave a permanent record via a voicemail. Whoever he was, whether he was working for someone else or working alone, he'd been pushed to the point of aggression. Jared took notice. The wise didn't ignore desperation painted as aggression.

This message unnerved him more than he could even admit to himself. How did the caller know that much about his life? How did they know he even had regrets about what he was doing? How much were they watching and how familiar with him and his life were they? How did they have that much access?

They promised that if he didn't stop he'd have regrets, but what kind? What would he regret more than what he'd already done to himself and his marriage? What did they know about him that they could leverage to get him to do what they wanted? As if he didn't have enough on his mind, this was one more thing he had to give serious consideration to, even if that meant hitting the pause button on his work. He thought he could do both, he could think while in the backcountry, away from all the other distractions, but his situation with Maria clouded it. Thinking about more than Maria right now was a struggle. The messages might be legitimate. They might not be. But what he'd lost with her was. And it wasn't what he wanted at all. There was only so much time in a day and each time he was forced to decide where to invest his efforts, Maria would win out.

She would always win.

So where did that leave him and this mysterious caller who wouldn't let go of this pursuit to scare him away? He had no idea. But if the caller was legitimate, Jared was going to find out soon, very soon.

"You've got a week to make the right decision. If we find out you're still in the game after that, you'll regret it," the caller had said.

One week.

Less now.

Jared picked up the recorder again. "I have no idea who that was or even what organization they're from, if any. But getting that call bothered me. A number of Bigfoot hunters, investigations, whatever you want to call us, have had bad things happen because they were on the trail of a find. Vandalism, threats, harassment, break-ins at their homes. There's no line when it comes to intimidating people. A few investigators have even been assaulted when they refused to give up. Almost every single one of them quits. They drop everything and you never hear from them again. There have been a lot of investigators who've been close to important finds who have suddenly given up the chase and walked away. We would have seen something from this field by now if it weren't for people *in* this field."

He could feel the fire burning in his gut like it did every time he thought about this. "I'm not stopping though. I'm not quitting. I'm going to finish this and then live my life. People like that aren't going to frighten me. I need to do it for ... him."

That was the crux of Maria's pain and frustration. It was all about the one person who wasn't even involved in their marriage and if Jared did what he needed to do then he could understand himself and the reasons why he continued more clearly than ever before. *Like losing your marriage and still plowing ahead when there's obviously someone out there who doesn't want you to.*

Jared switched the recorder off and looked into the night sky. "Dad," he choked back the sudden throat-clenching sob, "why?"

He sat there for another two hours, thinking.

About Maria.

About the threatening phone calls.

And about his father.

11

Sleep came hard. The spot he'd picked to camp was a flat area with plenty of soft moss to provide a thick layer of comfort between him and the hard earth. It wasn't the physical conditions that made it uncomfortable; the night was ideal, seasonably cool with only a slight wind, an odd condition for this part of the Olympic Mountains especially at this time of year.

It wasn't the outside world that kept him awake. Everything that prevented him from sleeping was happening within the confines of his head. One after another, problem following problem, he wondered if he'd ever find the peace he sought. He tried. He pursued it and never gave up, never gave in. It might have taken him a long time to see the problems he'd constructed for himself but he wasn't the type to create problems and then whine to anyone who would listen about how they were powerless to change their situation. He was a fixer. He got things done. And he was trying to get things done for himself but sometimes it felt like no matter what he did he was never going to get ahead. He could skip meals, showering, and sleeping and still not outrace the bitch that was fate, which seemed determined to put another roadblock in his way each time he overcame a challenge.

It was a bitter reality, one that kept him awake far later than he wanted, especially since he had a hike in the morning. Every time something hindered his investigation it was a direct assault on what he wanted for his life. Maria.

It was a long time before the anger and frustration faded enough for him to sleep.

If he ever met the man who was leaving him threatening messages it wouldn't end well for one of them. There was no telling what he might do. It was unfortunate he couldn't say the same about his father.

*****

Waaaaaaaaaaaaaaaaaaaaaaaaaaaaaaaaaaaaaah!

Jared tossed and turned.

Waaaaaaaaaaaaaaaaaaaaaaaaaaaaaaaaaaaaaah!

A dream. Go back to sleep. It's a dream.

Silence.

The wind released a low howl.

Waaaaaaaaaaaaaaaaaaaaaaaaaaaaaaaaaaaaaah!

Much closer.

Jared bolted upright. Much closer! "Jesus Christ!"

Waaaaaaaaaaaaaaaaaaaaaaaaaaaaaaaaaaaaaah!

Jared turned, looking over his shoulder. It wasn't that he thought one of the Sasquatch was in camp with him, the sounds came from too far away for that. The reason for his thudding heart was because the response call came from a different direction. "Damn, there's two of them!"

He fumbled for the recorder, his hands not yet as awake as his brain. The red recording light indicator stared back at him. "Good ... I'm getting these recorded. They're close!"

He listened.

Tunk!

Stilled, he didn't dare move. Had he heard what he thought he did?

Tunk! Tunk!

Yep, exactly what I thought.

Tunk!

From the other direction now.

"Dammit, this is good!" he whispered into the recorder. "Tree knocks. They're communicating. They've got to be no more than a quarter mile off. Those knocks are crystal clear. Closer than I've been to them in a long time."

Waaaaaaaaaaaaaaaaaaaaaaaaaaaaaaaaaaaaaaah! Distant now, the caller was moving away from where he camped.

"Still makes my skin crawl, even after all these years, and I've heard dozens of calls and knocks ... I don't think I'll ever get used to them," he said. "I don't think anyone can. There's something primal, nightmarish, about an unseen animal screaming like that. Something so deeply entrenched in our instinctual psyche that we can only react like an animal."

Waaaaaaaaaaaaaaaaaaaaaaaaaaaaaaaaaaaaaah!

This call was further away still, almost imperceptible.

"Even though I think Sasquatch are passive creatures, that doesn't mean they wouldn't respond violently to something or someone they see as a threat," he said, listening. "I think the Sasquatch have moved on or got bored with each other. Maybe they're busy hooking up. I'm going to try and get some sleep so I can track them in the morning. As if I can sleep after that."

He set the recorder down as silence fell over the mountainside. The Sasquatch never called again as he drifted off into yet another round of restless sleep.

*****

In the morning, the sun was bright and teased a warmness that never quite reached the ground. That was the way of life in the Pacific Northwest; he was pleased to have that glowing orb accompany him on his hike. His favorite place in the world became much more beautiful on days like this, when the sun's rays illuminated the mist rising off the wet earth. The landscape was a mix of bright white and brilliant emerald that rose and fell with the peaks and valleys of the mountains. It made hiking first thing in the morning that much more enjoyable.

Not that he needed the motivation to pack camp and get out early. The calls last night had set him on edge, stimulating and encouraging him. The pair, if it were two of them, were close enough to get a decent vector on from their calls. This part of the mountain range near Hurricane Ridge was open, the sound didn't echo around walls of rock like it would in other parts of the Olympics, allowing Jared to be confident of the direction he needed to hike. It wouldn't be direct. He was already looking for traces of clues to indicate one of them had traipsed through here last night. At least it wasn't going to be an endless search for nothingness because of the misdirection of echoes. He was fortunate that the Sasquatch didn't care or were careless in their previous night's conversation. That sloppiness, that lack of awareness on their part, was going to hopefully lead him to them. The potential of a find was massive, impossible to ignore, especially if what he heard last night was some sort of mating ritual.

It was time to record.

"Man, what a night," he said. "I didn't sleep worth a damn. Actually got up a little earlier than I planned but laying in that sleeping bag wasn't an option. The reports from this area are too consistent and hearing those distinct calls last night leads me to believe there's more than a solitary creature out here. How many, though? That's what I'd like to find out. I'm inclined to believe there are possibly more. Even a community."

There had to be more of them, his nest theory led him to that conclusion. They were primates, social creatures, so they'd depend on one another for survival. And in a world that was crowding them out with new housing tracts, strip malls, and massive discount retailers who put mom-and-pop stores out of business two decades ago, it should be easier to find them and they should almost have been forced to clump together. Expansion of the human domain reduced accessibility of all species except for those born of the air or water. Sasquatch wasn't so lucky.

They would also clump together to protect each other from this voracious species. Two Sasquatch could watch for threats more effectively than one; four would be safer together than two; eight would be able to provide safety and stability in a community much more effectively than four. Jared's thoughts fell back to Frank Hollenbeck and the trip to Forks. In logic, one didn't bother proving a negative proposition; that wasn't how it worked. So he wouldn't bothered attempting to prove the structures he found out there weren't a Bigfoot nest community. He was only interested in finding out what it was. If it wasn't Sasquatch, then what the hell made those structures? The lazy answer was humans and his brain kept circling back to that. He knew he had a bias against thinking that humans would live like that, they would; humans lived in worse conditions across America's cities, so a few individuals living in natural structures shouldn't be outside the scope of possibilities, and it wasn't. But it was damn hard to think humans would choose that when a reliable witness had just seen a Bigfoot no less than four hundred yards from where he found the nest.

Bigfoot wouldn't be so comfortable about hunting that close to a small collection of humans, they were more careful than that, even when they were desperate. The river Frank had taken him to wound all the way back up into the Olympics. The Sasquatch, if it needed to feed on the salmon in the river, could have done so much further upstream, away from the highway and a small encampment of humans.

I'll be damned if that was a human encampment.

He didn't have solid proof yet but it did give him insight into the possibilities of their behaviors, their culture, and way of life. All varieties of primates lived in communities of differing sizes so why wouldn't this one? And if it built nests near Forks, why wouldn't another community do the same here? If that was at least two Sasquatch last night, there was a chance he was going to find another site that would confirm his Forks' finding.

Jared stopped, his breath catching.

A snapped tree branch caught his attention, drawing his eyes, and then he saw them.

Prints.

Everywhere.

He knelt down, his fingers dancing into the crevice created by the creature's foot. It was here. Here! He planned to hike a few miles before he reached the distance he calculated the calls came from last night. Instead, he'd made it a half mile before he stumbled across these.

He hit RECORD.

"It turns out my nighttime concert was more than a couple of Sasquatch calling to each other," he said. "See, the vocal range of a Sasquatch is impressive. Their calls can carry miles in the right conditions. And last night the conditions were perfect, so I figured the animals were maybe a mile or so away. I was wrong. I found their trail about a half mile from camp. I stumbled into an area completely trampled by a Sasquatch, which left hundreds of prints behind. I'll cast one of them. It has nice, distinct ridge lines I want to preserve. They're beautiful. They're genuine."

His fingers danced over the print before he leaned to reach another pair a few feet away. This Sasquatch had hung out here for a while! "You don't fake prints like this with a pair of custom boots. These are legitimate and there are hundreds of them in what is an area no bigger than two hundred square feet! I've never seen so many prints in one area; it's like this particular Sasquatch was hanging out for a while, pacing, a lot. Maybe he was getting impatient waiting for his lady friend."

He squat-walked around the trampled area. Branches broken. Vegetation ripped as if the beast got hungry while waiting. Then he saw it, a trail that led back down the slope. Jared stood and followed it. "There's a clear track, about two hundred yards from the trampled site and ... wait. There's something. Jesus. There's a second track joining this one! This other track is equally as fresh and it's definitely from a different Sasquatch! The shape, the size is different than the one I've been tracking!"

It couldn't be possible, could it? Two Sasquatch this close to his camp? They had joined up. Of course, that's why the calls stopped last night. Whatever they'd been communicating to each other was accomplished when they rendezvoused. But what? What was it that made them so brazen? What made this pair so reckless? It was fascinating. And another reason to not give up.

"Two Sasquatch together!" Jared panted. "This is remarkable. I've never had a multiple-track find! Hang on; I need to take some pictures of this." He ripped his pack off and dug around for his camera. The morning light was perfect, bright enough to mark the distinction between the pair without washing out the dimensions. He wracked his brain to remember if he'd ever seen anything like this online or at a convention. He was the first, again. This was going to set him apart from other investigators. *And draw more attention to you and what you're doing, idiot.*

Not now. He was not going to let those dark thoughts return. Not right now. He had a job to do. He was facing remarkable evidence of a pair of Sasquatch and he had a trail to follow. Who knew what was at the end! Today could be the day everything changed.

Today could be the first day of the rest of his life.

"This is incredible," he exclaimed. "Even though they walked single file it's still easy to pick out two distinct prints. They're both fresh, they have to be from last night. The likelihood that individual Sasquatch would trudge the exact same path at different times is slim, especially when you consider the series of calls last night. I'm going to keep following these and see where they lead. This is incredible."

He forged ahead, carefully proceeding, aware of the noise he was making. He didn't want to pose a threat to anything out here, but least of all he didn't want to go plunging into the middle of a Sasquatch nest, completely unaware of what he would be walking into. Even if it was a pair of them, his chances of fighting them off weren't very high. Not that he wanted to. He was here to observe, to study, not to disturb. He had to be careful. But this was strange.

He didn't expect what happened next.

The trail headed downhill. Sasquatch didn't live in higher elevations because those heights didn't provide adequate tree cover. That was why he was shocked to hear about the report at Mount Rainier. But that Bigfoot had only traversed the mountain, leaving one area for another. It was solitary and there was no evidence of a nest, not where Andrew had shown him the location of the sighting, at least. These two could have been doing anything. Because they walked off together didn't mean they were heading back to a nest. But it was still strange that they'd go off together downhill, increasing the risk to themselves with each step they took. There had to be a reason.

He kept going. The Bigfoot had been walking, not running; he could determine that from their stride lengths. There was no hurry, no rush, no escape or pursuit indicated by these tracks. These prints were left by a pair of calm, composed animals who were acting with purpose. Hunting or scavenging? That would make sense. If they'd found a fellow nocturnal friend who would make a tasty meal it wasn't without reason to posit that was all this was. It would explain the series of calls last night. They would have had to communicate their location and the location of their prey to each other as they tried to flank it. Or, if they were taking the more vegetarian route, one of them could have been calling to the other that they'd found a natural vault of goodies. That would explain the area he tripped across that looked as if a Bigfoot had paced for a considerable time.

But this trail didn't deviate. It was a straight march back down the mountainside, indicating a particular destination. That was the kicker. If they were hunting, their trail would have varied as they pursued their prey. There might even have been evidence of their pace increasing. But there was none of that. The prints led down the mountain in a straight path. And there was no indication that they paused either. No area was carved up with shuffled footprints. No steps off the side of this path to survey the berry inventory of particular bushes.

Just straight ahead. Determined and focused. But why? Trepidation crept into his mind. He could be walking into something he wasn't ready for and he had to be ready for that.

Down.

Down.

Down.

The pair of Sasquatch tracks continued in pretty much a straight path. Trepidation turned to unease. There was something wrong here. Something very wrong. Something that told him he should turn around and give up on this folly. He might have even followed that instinct too if it weren't for the fact that turning around would lead him back up the mountain. He was already heading back to the general direction of the road where he'd parked.

Were there dumpsters down there? There weren't, Jared was confident of that. He hadn't noticed any but he also hadn't thought this would happen. It wasn't ridiculous to think that Sasquatch would notice a possible food source like dumpsters, but dumpsters meant humans and Sasquatch did everything they could to avoid their evolutionary brethren. He didn't eliminate the possibility, but he was so far up the mountain that it didn't pass the common sense filter he tried to employ to make quick decisions when investigating. This could also have nothing to do with food. He smiled devilishly thinking that the pair went off to find a place for another basic need all creatures had. Imagine how awkward that would be for everyone involved, he laughed.

And then he stopped laughing as he reached a plateau.

A familiar plateau.

He couldn't believe what he was seeing. He didn't want to see what he was seeing.

He refused to believe this wasn't some nightmare.

Jared pulled out the recorder, speaking only as loud as necessary. If this was it, if this was the end, he had to leave some sort of record and hope it would be found by a future him, a future investigator. Hell, I'd take a park ranger at this point.

"I followed the tracks," he groaned. "They never separated. The Sasquatch stayed single file until they reached the place where I'm now standing. It's obvious the pair stood side by side, behind a thin row of junior trees. Their prints indicate they didn't move much either." He looked around when he thought he heard something. A branch cracking? He couldn't be sure. His thoughts were a mess. For the first time in his collective adult memory, he had no idea what to do. What do you do when you've found this? He put the recorder to his lips again. "But I can't tell how long they were here. There isn't much evidence of shifting or moving around. It's obvious they were only interested in observing and moving on. The tracks turn back to the thicker foliage, splitting off almost immediately."

He swallowed hard, looking over his shoulder. Was this what paranoia felt like? Infrasound? He swallowed the fear. "I'm standing where they stood last night," the darkness of his own voice wasn't lost on him. But he wasn't going to do a re-take. If this was ever going to be heard by the public it had to be genuine. "I'm ... rattled. I'm not going to lie."

Rattled? Is that what this was? No, not at all. What about traumatized? That might be more appropriate. More genuine. But he couldn't think about semantics or aesthetics. He only cared about getting out of here, about getting back to the truck in one piece, and leaving the Olympics.

He only cared about getting to Maria.

"Not because I can't figure out what happened and why they split back off, but because of what they were doing here," he said, his hand trembling. "I'm looking at what they were looking at hours ago. My camp."

12

Jared sat, staring straight ahead, with both hands wrapped around the steering wheel. What the fuck just happened?

Only yesterday he was sitting at a small, wobbly table in a restaurant in Port Angeles. Across from him was his soon-to-be-ex-wife who had given him hope that they might be able to reconcile. He drove out of that town high on life and full of the overwhelming hope only a promising future begat. He could have been t-boned in an intersection on the way out to Hurricane Ridge and still flopped out of his wrecked truck with a smile on his face after that conversation.

And now?

Now he didn't know what he was. In twenty years of chasing this damn creature around Washington State, British Columbia, Idaho, and even parts of the hated land of Oregon, Jared had never felt a series of emotions swirling through his head and body like the last twenty-four hours had born.

Of course, he also never had a pair of Sasquatch stalk his camp.

How? Why? For what purpose? A tumult of questions, yet he had no answers. The Sasquatch had called each other and then spent a portion of the evening outside his camp. Was their observation designed to decide whether or not he was a threat or was it because they were hungry and deciding if his middle-aged body was the juicy morsel they desired? Had he stumbled too close into their realm? It wasn't possible. Yesterday he'd done all the things he always did on expeditions; he carefully scouted the landscape for signs of habitation. Careful to notice subtle differences in the terrain and the flora, he would have seen something. He couldn't have walked right into their realm. He wasn't that sloppy. He wasn't that careless.

Yet, while he was completely unaware, they found and observed him.

And that was unnerving.

They could have done anything to him. It didn't matter if they couldn't figure out what the tent was, they had the power and intelligence to understand there was a human in their presence. They would have been well aware that he wasn't one of them but one of the kind who always came through the natural world and treated it as their personal dumping ground. The pair would have known that he was the kind that destroyed. Maybe they were intelligent enough to know Jared's kind had pushed their kind into this small corner of the world.

But they hadn't done anything more than watch. He was alive and his camp was completely undisturbed. They hadn't even set foot in it. He'd checked. And they didn't scout it either; he verified that by checking all around the camp. They'd visited him, watched him for whatever reason, and then departed the same way they'd come.

It was possible the visit was born of sheer curiosity and nothing more. Was he assigning malice where there was none to be assigned because he was overthinking all of this, missing the opportunity to revel in the fact that two Sasquatch had come to him? Whatever their motivations and reasons for doing so, they'd still done it, and he was their target. Was that the problem with this? He'd never been the target before. Even during his childhood experience at Lake Cushman, when the Sasquatch tore up their camp, he and his family weren't the targets for the beast. That Sasquatch wanted to eat. That was all. It only killed his boyhood dog because it was being pursued. It acted out of self-defense, not malice. Just as these Sasquatch hadn't hunted him for a meal. They hadn't bothered with him. For all he knew, they'd watched him for a couple of minutes, got bored and hiked into the dark woods for a meal and a round of steamy Bigfoot love.

Jared put the truck in gear and pulled back onto the road. Regardless of the motivations of the pair of nighttime visitors, he was grateful to be in the relative safety of the truck and on his way back towards civilization.

He didn't wear vulnerability well.

But none of that cloaked the larger realization: he'd been found by Sasquatch and not the other way around. It could only mean he was getting close. So very close. The scope was narrowing. They were being pinned in. All those hours of researching and studying sightings, meticulously mapping every detail, confirmed or rumored, was paying off. Whereas so many of his peers were still scrambling across the region hoping for sightings without analyzing the data they collected, he was tripping over evidence at almost every turn. Closer.

Closer to finding Bigfoot.

Closer to being able to focus on Maria again.

Closer to the end.

His phone rang, jolting Jared from his sanguine thinking. Right now he wanted to be alone with his thoughts.

But it was Peter and he couldn't wait to tell his friend what had just happened. "What's up, Peter?"

"Are you alone?" Anxiety edged Peter's voice. Jared's news would have to wait.

"Yeah, I'm driving right now. Why? Everything okay, you sound weird."

"Where are you heading?"

"Shelton," Jared answered. He would love nothing more than to get home, shower, and maybe have a beer—or a million—as he thought over the events of the past day. Peter's tone made him uneasy so he tried to lighten the mood. "I'm also drinking a Starbucks latte, wearing jeans and a hoodie, and doing approximately 63 miles per hour. Jesus, Peter, what's going on? You're starting to freak me out."

But Peter did what he usually did at times like this, times when he was uneasy, he answered questions with questions. "You heading down there for something related to your ... work?"

Jared sighed. "Yeah. Peter, listen, don't dance with me, something's going on, I can tell. You're rattled. Whatever it is, I want to help, but I'm weaving through traffic and I've got a lot on my mind. Things with Maria might be turning around and I had a great find this weekend that scared the shit out of me. I was going to call you about that later, actually."

There was only silence on the other end.

"Peter? You there?

"I'm here," Peter's voice trailed off. "Listen, I need you to not go to Shelton. There's ... you're being watched. You're too hot right now. I need you to think about something."

This was starting to go somewhere Jared didn't want to go. Not again. Not with Peter. They'd just done this dance when he dropped off the prints. The prospect of doing it again wasn't on the agenda. He didn't want to snap, but

Peter was as pig-headed as he was and sometimes two men butting heads was unhealthy. "What?"

"How about laying low for a few weeks?"

"Too hot? Laying low? What are you talking about?"

"You're being watched, dammit! And you're being reckless. You've got to stop. At least for a bit."

Peter's advice always came from the right place. If he needed anything in his world right now it was someone he could depend on, someone like Peter. *Especially when the community finds out what I've discovered.* "Who is watching me?"

Peter's response made Jared's throat close. "You know who."

He had a damn good idea of who Peter was referring to. But there was something about putting names to actions that made it all too real for him, especially right now. It wasn't that he feared them. It wasn't that he wanted to live in a lollipop world where people were always kind and good to each other. That wasn't it at all. But thinking that otherwise rational adults could turn into such malevolent creatures due to their own self-interest was wasted energy. Anything that took his energy away from his pursuit wasn't worth thinking about, and definitely not worth exploring.

The fire returned. He squeezed the phone. "Other enthusiasts? I'm not stopping because they're upset or jealous, or whatever their motives are. I'm way too close right now, Peter. Every single thing I find, it's bringing me closer. My theory is right, bud. Right. Why would I give all that up because some amateur hunters aren't happy that they're not the ones with the findings?"

"It's more than that and you know it. Don't be juvenile." There was a pause and a deep breath on the other end of the line. "Listen, I'm your friend. I'm on your side. That's why I called. If I didn't care about you I wouldn't have bothered. I know you're frustrated but this goes beyond your interests. I'm trying to make you see that, Jared. Other people are being impacted by your actions."

A serving of guilt. Jared had no use for the tactic and no desire for someone to use it on him. He'd already had enough of that throughout his life. Dad and Mom. But Mom? She was good, leveraging it most of the years that followed his childhood incident that sparked this Bigfoot passion. He could give up recalling the times she'd berate his father, cried, begged, pleaded, screamed and yelled. Nothing was below her. At times she'd even use Jared as a tool to get his father to quit his pursuits. It worked, sometimes, but most often those tactics fell on deaf ears. Regardless of her varied success, Jared watched, listened, and learned; and he realized the power guilt had as a manipulative tool.

A short, harsh laugh burst out of him. He never reacted well to manipulation, not from strangers, peers, friends or family. "Other people can kiss my ass," he finally said, drawing the line in the sand. It was up to Peter to cross it or not.

"Would you feel that way if I told you that I'm one of those people?" Peter asked. There was a soft vulnerability in his voice.

"What do you mean?"

"They came today."

Jared swallowed. They came? "What are you talking about, Peter? Who? You're not making any sense."

"In the parking garage," Peter's voice shook. He didn't attempt to hide it from Jared. "After work. They followed me to my car. I didn't even notice them until ... until they had me cornered. Two of them. Middle-aged, white men. Large."

"What happened?"

"I'll be fine," Peter evaded the question. "Listen, I'm serious. I need you to take some time away from this. From everything. Give up this chase. Give up Sasquatch. Go invest your energy in Maria. Give her all of you, instead of this pursuit. It'll suck the soul out of you, Jared. I swear it. You've been doing this for twenty years. Isn't it time to do something else? Think about it, please. Do it for me. Do it for Maria. Do it for your marriage. Hell, do it for you. I know you love doing this. This is your passion. I get all of it ... I do."

What did those bastards do to get to Peter like this? Jared wanted to push; he wanted to know the real story about what happened to his friend while he was up in Port Angeles making progress with Maria and that damned ape. While his world was headed in the right direction, his friend's life was being turned upside down by thugs from the fringes of cryptozoology? Peter didn't have to leverage guilt to get his attention; he needed to tell him the damn truth!

What the hell is wrong with these assholes? Was it assault or simply a scare tactic? And to be so bold, so brazen, as to do it in a parking garage where they had to know there might be witnesses and surveillance cameras? That spoke volumes about their desperation.

But ...

What Peter was asking was impossible. There was no way he could honor it. Not now. Peter had to know that. They'd just seen each other. Peter had the goddamn prints! The only missing piece of the puzzle was what happened last night.

And that didn't even matter. Nothing less than undisputable proof sufficed.

Jared tried to soften the blow. "I'm hearing you, Peter. I am. Please don't think I'm not. What you're asking me to do ... I don't know if I can."

"If you'd been standing there with me, facing those two behemoths, wondering if I was going to be able to crawl away after they were done, the decision might be easier." Another pause. Another deep breath.

Jared bit back his response, sensing his friend was struggling. This wasn't Peter, not the Peter he knew.

"Sorry," Peter moaned. "That's not fair."

"I don't want you threatened. I'm glad you're okay but I'm enraged they think I can be bullied into quitting. I'd love to get my hands on them." He meant it too. Not a violent man by any measure, there were things that set him off. Wasn't everyone like that? Especially men? Wasn't there something in the evolutionary code of ethics that demanded it? You didn't threaten anyone he cared about. Ever.

"That would do nothing for you or your cause."

"I know, but it'd make me feel a whole lot better," Jared laughed tightly, trying to give his friend a sense that it was a half-handed comment, nothing more. Is it?

When Peter laughed Jared relaxed. "You're a passionate man, I'll give you that."

"Peter, I'm sorry," Jared said. "This is crazy. I don't care about them harassing me but I never wanted other people to pay the price for me."

"I know," Peter said. "You're a good man and a great researcher. And I know I'm asking more of you than anyone should. Take your time. Think about it. But don't take forever. I don't know how long you have." The change was as quick as it was unexpected. Had Jared's reaction scared Peter away or talked him off the edge? Or did it remind him that to ask Jared to stop would be to ask him to slit his own wrists? "Who knows? Maybe something will break soon, with the right attention, and all of this will be for naught."

He couldn't waver. He couldn't appear to even consider Peter's demand that he quit. "I guess."

For his part, Peter seemed to understand and stopped pushing. Even the tone of his voice changed. Jared didn't expect him to give up the fight but Peter was smart enough to know that wars weren't won in a single battle. There would be another day to fight; you only had to survive to show up for the formation. Jared secretly pitied his friend who still didn't understand that he wasn't going to quit, he wasn't going to stop looking until he completely walked away. What Peter didn't understand, what a lot of people didn't understand, was that no cost was too high. Sometimes in life, there were just things that needed to be done, things that a person had to accomplish before they spent eternity in a rotting box six feet underground.

Peter reacted in a chipper tone. "I have a feeling it will. Those prints you brought me? They're very impressive."

"Oh, yeah?" Jared tried to not sound too excited after forcing his friend to back off.

"They're legitimate." Jared could almost make out Peter's smile through the phone.

Jared chuckled. "I know that."

"There's no doubt in my mind they are from dynamic compression, not a stomp impact," Peter was putting his scientist hat back on. "So you'll have to break the bad news to skeptics that Ray Pickens didn't come out of retirement to screw with researchers and an unsuspecting public." Jared was impressed at his friend's mention of one of the first, and most famous debunked claims of Bigfoot evidence, one that was over fifty years old and still haunting legitimate researchers to this day.

"You saw the pressure ridges?"

"Yeah."

"Can you imagine how long it would take a hobbyist to individually carve thousands of those into some mold he could slap on a boot?" Peter asked rhetorically. "That'd be dedication. And the toes on the third cast? I'm not sure if you noticed but they aren't like the other two."

"I didn't. What did I miss?" He hadn't had a chance to look at them. He intended to study them more closely when he had a chance to breathe.

"The toes are flexed. It makes sense and it's a good thing you grabbed some pictures of the site so I could understand why. Cast three was the one on the slope that ran up from the river, right?"

"Yeah, I wanted to grab a couple different casts there because once it got into the underbrush the ones I could find were too poor to cast."

"No, no, that's good," Peter's excitement swelled. Something big was coming, Jared knew it. His friend was predictable that way. "Flat ground prints are one thing but prints from inclined or declined slopes are different altogether. This one is good, probably your best. The toes are flexed and deeply impressed like the Sasquatch was trying to gain a foothold. There's a ridge of river mud pushed up into the creature's forefoot, that is absent in the other two prints and the heel is barely noticeable, again unlike the other two. It shows a great degree of midfoot flexibility, greater than what you'll find in humans.

"It clearly shows the midfoot bearing the weight of the animal, consistent with other suspected Sasquatch prints, and even other primates," Peter continued, the pace of his words picking up. "In your cast, the deepest part of the imprint is anterior to the midtarsal joint. As if that wasn't enough, I was able to find sweat pores in the damn prints, Jared. Sweat pores! You cast beauties."

So that was why Peter was so excited. Because of the conditions of Forks, he might have cast the most solid print evidence in history. And all thanks to an out-of-towner who didn't think any of this was real until he saw it for himself. Thank God for Frank Hollenbeck's decision to serve science. "I knew it! You've made my day, Peter."

"Calm down, buddy," Peter laughed. "That's not all I found. Four billion years of evolution makes distinguishing bipedal species from quadrupedal brethren a whole lot easier. I'm confident these cannot be bear tracks. Bear pads taper to a blunt point and are usually separated from the interdigital pad by a distinct crease. Plus, bears carry most of their weight on their forelimbs like most quadrupeds do, so those forward prints will show deeper impressions. Bipedal animals carry their weight towards their rear, so the beauty that is evolution gives us broader heel bones. Apes, humans, maybe Sasquatch, have thicker, broader heel bones than what you'll find in a quadrupedal animal. Just like these prints.

"I don't want to get too geeky on you," Peter said while Jared thought it was too late for that, "but body weight increases to the cube of linear dimensions, and the surface area of the sole of the foot increases to the square. So foot length and breadth increase with the increased height of the animal. These prints are sixteen inches, Jared. Sixteen inches!"

Jared's head swirled. He needed a translator with Peter sometimes. "This is starting to sound promising. What are you getting at?"

"I called on a favor from a forensic analyst friend of mine."

Jared laughed. "Damn, you're connected. I'm glad you're on my side."

"I'm on the side of science," Peter reminded him, a playfulness to his voice that overrode any serious undertones. "You're only getting this intel because you're a decent guy. Anyways, using a superimposition method with a graduated pole, he came to the conclusion that whatever left these prints—"

"Sasquatch," Jared cut him off.

"He's not going to say that, buddy. Sorry. Whatever left these prints was big."

"How big?"

Peter's humor was replaced with awe. "Over seven and a half feet tall and weighing nearly seven hundred pounds."

Jared drove in stunned silence, thinking about what it all meant. He clicked off the recorder. Frank Hollenbeck had unknowingly found a monster. Jared had probably the best prints anyone had ever cast.

The western side of the Olympics was the place to be, the place demanding focus. If Bigfoot was going to be found, it would be there. To steal a rural American colloquialism, 'they grew 'em big out here.'

Jared said his goodbyes to Peter, thanking him for his time and for his concern. He promised he would do a lot of thinking about the quixotic request that started the conversation. Peter got reflective, almost vulnerable when he thanked Jared for that.

*****

After they hung up, Jared drove in silence as he weaved his way back to Olympia.

The moment moved him, the realization that a life's work was coming together.

Peter, threatened.

The print in Forks.

Pushing forward.

Pushing against resistance.

He was going to make this right with everyone who supported him. He needed to finish.

He was so close.

So damn close.

13

The phone rang.

His heart thumped against his chest wall. He swallowed the lump in his throat.

Waiting.

Ring.

Ring.

Ring.

He was about to hang up when she answered. "Hey, Jared," Maria sounded concerned like his call was the last thing she was expecting. "Is everything—"

"I'm sorry," he started, and once he began, the words came out so effortlessly. "I'm sorry for everything I've done, for every single time I put us off to go on an expedition. For every single time, I've asked you to give up something for me. For every single time, you slept alone in that bed because I was out chasing a childhood nightmare. It was unfair and selfish. *I* was unfair and selfish."

"Where's this coming—"

"Please," he interrupted again, gentler, "Please. I need to say this. You've deserved so much better than what I've given you. I don't know where I went wrong. One day we were partying in college, not having a care in the world beyond how many papers we could bullshit our way through and the next we were fighting day in and day out about everything. I don't know when it all changed but I know why it did. It was me and my self-centered fixation. I cannot believe you put up with me as long as you did. I owe you so much."

"You don't owe me anything, Jared," Maria's voice was soft, warm. Welcoming. "There isn't a couple out there whose marriage doesn't have bumps and potholes. We're no different. I put up with your crazy pursuits just like you sacrificed for me."

"Not even close," he countered kindly. "You put your graduate degree on hold. You let promotion opportunities pass because I was constantly gone and someone needed to take care of everything else. I didn't even ask."

"Jared, listen to me. Those things don't matter anymore. We both made mistakes. We both screwed up and did things that harmed our marriage. I'm just as guilty as you."

He shook his head, not that she could see it. "Don't. Don't say that. Please."

There was a pause on the line, a reflective silence. "What's this about? Have you told anyone else what happened? Why you're really doing all of this?" The unspoken confirmation hung in the silence that followed. As he was about to speak, Maria said, "That's what I thought. You're going to have to deal with this before you can move on, Jared. You know that, right? If you're serious about this, if you're serious about us, you're going to have to bury your demons. I hope you can, because if you can't ..."

Jared switched off the recorder. He was sure some people would question his judgment, determining for him what was inappropriate to record for the podcast. But they didn't matter. It was his podcast, his life, his journey that he was documenting. He wasn't doing it for their entertainment and enjoyment. He was doing what he needed to do. And this was part of that, what needed to be done. Capturing the cost of his research was always going to be part of it because it'd always been part of it, ever since that day at camp when Bigfoot traipsed into their world.

And changed his life forever.

Jared thought he was ready but Maria had a way of clinging to things he didn't want her to focus on. He'd called her to apologize for the way he'd wronged her throughout their marriage by putting the investigation first, and she'd taken that opportunity to focus on things that didn't matter anymore. Things that were far in the past. Things that were part of another life ... someone else's life.

*****

He didn't even look at the recorder again.

Not for days.

He didn't want to.

That thing was permanently linked to this. Bigfoot. Peter. Maria. This group of ... what the hell were they? Rival investigators? Big-money thugs? It was the one tangible thing he actually had to point at and say '*there, you see, you fucker? Every goddamn thing that has gone wrong in my life is contained therein. You bastard. You. Fucking. Bastard!*' There was no peace. No resolution and no progress.

He hated himself whenever he looked at the recorder.

So ...

... he didn't.

Instead, he ate; he drank; he watched sports and read parts of a novel he had been meaning to read for a long time.

He didn't leave the house.

He didn't answer the calls when they came.

Someone knocked on the door once; he couldn't remember which day it was. He didn't answer it.

For days he sheltered himself in the house, away from the world and the thoughts it provoked. He sheltered his mind, body, and his soul ...

... before they destroyed him.

14

Jared took a deep breath before pressing RECORD.

Am I ready to start this again?

Such a simple question, yet one with so many implications.

He could say yes, but wasn't that one of his biggest problems with other people? They answered their own personal questions well before they should, not taking the time to assess what those answers would mean. Instead, people acted, reacted, without regard, often times harming themselves in some form or fashion, or harming others in a way that sent them off course. Small decisions, big decisions, it didn't matter. People were busy with life or distracting themselves with things that entertained them, too busy to assess what it was they should be doing when faced with a decision. Cars and houses they couldn't afford? No big deal, we'll spend the rest of our lives paying for them. Do we need a house that large? Well, the school district is nice and we don't have to have every room decorated; plus we can take out a thirty-year mortgage. No, no. we don't need to put anything into savings. 401k? Whose got money for those things? We're not rich. But, yes, I must have this huge house, no cars older than three years, two-hundred-dollar coffee makers. What? The kids need five hundred dollars in dental work? Well, where are we going to get that kind of money?

People's poor choices weren't restricted to money either. Jared wasn't sure if people understood how to live happy lives when he saw so many of them dreading waking up each and every day to head off to jobs they hated. What about the vacation days they wasted traveling for some family obligation they didn't want to attend to appease some relative from an older generation? Drinking and driving. Affairs. Too much porn. Being absorbed by Facebook instead of watching their kid's soccer practice. He could go on and on about humans and their decision-making faults. He was sensitive to it and tried his best to not mimic the questionable tactics and choices of others, to not allow them to influence his own actions.

Which was why he'd holed up for days now, his remote control trading places with that book—which he finished— and his thoughts. A few too many good beers thrown in for good measure. Craft beers, of course.

Everything was getting away from him between what happened in Forks, the visit to Maria, and Peter's phone call about what happened to him.

He didn't press his friend when he got back into town. He didn't even call him. Jared figured that if Peter had something to get off his chest then he would call or visit. He did neither. And Jared was grateful for that. The peace and quiet, the chance to be alone with his thoughts, was something he needed as soon as he got back from the mountains. The fact that at least a pair of Sasquatch had visited his camp was something he still couldn't wrap his head around. Stuff like that didn't happen to anyone, not any reliable investigator. It happened to liars and cheats. It happened to drunk hillbillies who wanted five minutes of fame in their tiny local newspaper. It happened to city people who'd been talked into camping by their friends and only went after a lot of pouting and tantrum-throwing. Deep down they were afraid of being out in the wild, without the protection of lights and walls and the comfort of television to get them through the dark night. They heard things, saw things, that were unfamiliar and their fear painted in the rest of the picture, usually with the most hyperbolic details. Sasquatch walking up to an experienced researcher's camp just didn't happen.

Yet it had.

Because he was getting close. Too close.

Everything was moving forward. Quickly.

And that bothered him.

It took Jared a few days to figure out why.

Fear.

It always came down to fear.

If things kept coming to a head then everything he knew, everything he understood, was going to change. What was, will no longer be. What is now, won't be tomorrow's truth. Things that were merely nebulous, the threats from the other investigators, the possibility of reconciling with Maria, would be defined. Either they would happen or they wouldn't and he'd have to move on from them. From her. The fact was, his entire adult life had been consumed by chasing this goddamn animal and, as he closed in on it, he realized that everything would change once he was successful.

And that was scary.

He wasn't afraid of finding Bigfoot and waking up the next day. If that time came he would have the world at his feet for the rest of his life. Interviews, television appearances, radio spots, books, and maybe movies. It would all be his if he said the magic words. But that future was inconclusive. How did you prepare for something you didn't understand or know was coming? How did you make yourself ready when you didn't know what you were readying yourself for?

But wasn't that what he was doing? Hadn't he made his decision inside the dark confines of his home, his last bastion of safety? He'd already decided. The door was open and he was barging through.

After all, wasn't that why he was on his way to Shelton? The investigation was on again.

There was a witness who'd called him before he'd even headed to Forks to meet Frank Hollenbeck. He'd made this witness wait due to his skepticism. Shelton wasn't exactly known for sightings and this guy claimed to have something Jared found odd for anywhere in the state. The fact that it reportedly happened in Shelton just made it even odder. Warning flares sent skyward, he didn't have the time or the inclination to deal with fraudsters. This new witness straddled the border.

Jared pulled into the parking lot and surveyed his surroundings. Shelton was a small town, a town he found to be very depressing. Why in the world was someone from a place like this calling him about Bigfoot? Plenty of humans had no desire to be in Shelton, why would this animal? Not that he believed this guy, at all. Again, this guy might be very smart and deliberately walking that fine line between believability and downright outlandishness. Jared wouldn't be able to tell until he sat with him. But it would surprise him if there was anything of true value that came out of this meeting. He wasn't getting his hopes up. But, if countered, it's a nice way to ease back into all this before the craziness spins up again.

The coffee shop was small and crowded, with every table occupied. Steamers went off every few seconds as the line of customers patiently waited for their intricate brews to be delivered just how they liked them. The American dream: fine, made-to-order-specialty coffee.

Jared scanned the small room for Kevin Jenkins and found him by almost tripping over him. The room was crowded, the tables packed into the small space as closely as they could. Probably violating some fire code. That's precisely why it was so difficult and so easy to find who he was searching for.

As Jared navigated the tight spaces between tables, Kevin reached out from the booth and grabbed Jared's wrist. Jared instinctively yanked his arm back, almost hitting a patron who was waiting in line. Jared apologized before grimacing at the overweight man who'd grabbed him. "Can I help you?"

"Oh," the big man who'd somehow squeezed into the booth waved both hands rapidly, "I'm sorry. Are ..." he lowered his voice, glancing around at a few of the patrons who had their attention captured by this exchange, "... are you Jared."

Jared nodded. "Kevin?"

The man nodded and smiled. The room seemed to warm. It was an infectious smile, one that immediately lowered Jared's defenses. "Do—do you want a coffee?"

Jared shook his head and sat down on the other side of the booth. "No, I can't have too much caffeine. Makes me jittery."

"Oh, gotcha," Kevin said, looking down at the large coffee sitting in front of him. "I love it. Drink way too much of it, I'm sure. Not like I can afford all the calories but I can't imagine life without it. Plus, we're Washingtonians, right? It's part of our diet from the time we're young."

Jared laughed. "I guess so."

"So, um, how does this stuff work?"

Jared raised an eyebrow. "What do you mean?"

Kevin lifted his arm, extended his index finger down toward the table, and made a circular motion with his hand as if he was drawing invisible circles. "All this. This investigation stuff. How ... how do we ... you know ..."

Jared smiled. He'd seen a thousand nervous people before, this was nothing new and it made him feel better about investing his day in coming out here. "We just talk. That's all. There's no formality to this. If you can have a conversation, you can handle what we're about to do, I promise."

Kevin leaned back, well, he tried to lean back. The man was so large that any movement in the booth couldn't be simple or comfortable for him. "Oh," there was a hint of disappointment in his voice as if he expected a bigger production.

"Are you okay with starting?"

"Hmmm?" Kevin's face was a blank canvas of innocence. "Oh, yes. Sorry. Definitely."

Jared set the recorder in the middle of the table between them. Kevin looked at the device and swallowed. Jared started the interview like he always did with new witnesses. There was a natural flow in his words, coming from deep in his recall. There was something else there, though: coldness. It was the first time he could remember not being overly excited to hear what a witness had to say. He wondered if he was losing it and pushed the thought out of his head. There was a job to do. "Thank you for meeting. Like I said on the phone, I record everything that pertains to these investigations. Are you still okay with that?

"Yes," that infectious, yet less-confident smile was back on Kevin's face. "That's fine. Is this going to be on one of those shows?"

Jared laughed at the comment. He was going to have to review his Facebook page one of these days. He'd built it years ago and then never spent any more time looking at what he'd actually put down for contact and page information. He thought he'd done a good job with it, preferring to use the lack of a horde of nutballs as an indicator, but maybe the page could use a little touch-up so people knew exactly what they were getting with him.

"Something like that. From your message, it sounded like you have something to show me."

"Yeah, it's sort of crazy but I didn't know what to do," Kevin replied. "I did some asking around and found a few groups on Facebook and one of them gave me your number. I hope you don't mind."

Ah, so it wasn't Jared's own Facebook page that misled Kevin? Good, one less thing he needed to worry about. Someone else probably planted that harmless seed in Kevin's brain. "That's not a problem. I get a lot of referrals that way, actually."

"Well, this is something I'm not used to doing," Kevin admitted. "I mean, I didn't even know where to start. I've got to be honest; I think all this stuff is crap." His chubby cheeks reddened. "Sorry, no offense."

The comment didn't bother Jared and he let Kevin know that. "Trust me, I've heard it all. It's fine. Some of the stuff you see being passed off as possible Sasquatch proof makes us look pretty ridiculous. In your message, you said you have a video for me?" When was the last time he sat down with someone claiming to have video evidence? It'd been a long time—months. Jared didn't have the patience for video evidence anymore. There were too many fakers, too many grainy, shaky videos in an age when everything is filmed up-close and in high definition. Yet Bigfoot seemed to still be the one exception. It made everyone involved in the field look stupid and he wanted no part of it. When he first started investigating, shooting video on a cell phone wasn't a thing; cellphones weren't a thing. Camera technology had come a long way but, seemingly, the same couldn't be said about eyewitnesses' abilities to film a half-decent video. When he was younger he used to get excited about video evidence. But after a few years and a few hundred obvious fakes and misidentified animals, he'd all but given up hope anything legitimate would ever be captured. If the content Kevin promised didn't materialize,

Jared was going to give the man another five seconds, then a verbal dismissal and be on his way back to Olympia.

"Yeah, I, uh, I don't mean to be weird or anything, but can we go to my truck?" Kevin's earlier jovial tone was gone, replaced by a flat affect that grabbed Jared's attention.

"Sorry? Your truck?" Had he heard the man correctly?

Kevin glanced around the shop. "I promise this isn't some weird sex thing." A small, tight laugh escape him, his cheeks shaking. "I'm sort of freaked out by the video and, well, I've got friends here. Shelton is a small place. A lot of people know each other. I can't be having them think I'm nuts."

Jared switched off the recorder. "Yeah, we can," he answered, "but I need to be clear with you, I'm not one for games. I've seen a thousand bullshit videos. Had enough people think I'm going to pay them for what is nothing more than them going out into the woods with their friends, getting drunk, and trying to fool everyone with a video that any fifth grader in America could make. Just so we're clear."

He liked this new him.

Kevin was taken aback. "Oh, no. No. I swear, mister. I don't know what it is and I'm not wanting anything out of this. I just want someone who knows what they're doing to see this. As much as I hate to admit it, Shelton is my home. My family is from here. My kids are growing up here. I'm a dad, mister. I have to do this for them. Otherwise, trust me, I'd delete the video soon as I could."

Jared watched the man's face, stared into his eyes, as he spoke. There was no way to tell if this was yet another scam but what Jared saw there, more than anything else, was genuineness. If Kevin was about to hand over fraudulent material, it wasn't deliberate. Ultimately, if this ended up being a fake, Kevin wasn't in on it. The way Kevin reacted convinced Jared the man was worth another ten minutes of his time.

They got up and walked outside to Kevin's truck, an older model Ford F150, red. *If the world never sees me again tell Maria my last free moments were spent in a dual-cab with tinted windows.* Well, that wasn't true; half the tint on the passenger side had peeled off a long time ago. They climbed in and Kevin turned on the iPad he had sitting in the driver's seat, pulled up a video and leaned toward Jared, facing the screen in his direction. Jared tried to ignore the big man's nasally breathing in favor of watching the high school football game on the screen. "This is my kid's game from last month. That's him, there," Kevin beamed.

"Running back, heh?"

"You played?"

Jared nodded. "Tight end. I used to have more quickness than size. You can see that's all changed though."

Kevin laughed, the red tint returning to his cheeks. "Me too. I was never that coordinated though. Played offensive tackle. Oh, here! Watch this part."

Jared watched the wobbly and loud video. The ball was tossed back to Kevin's son on a sweep play. The kid was quick, Jared gave him that. Never would have suspected that by looking at his dad. The kid dodged and weaved, the noise of the crowd seated around Kevin's location rose as, yard after yard, Kevin's son raced down the sideline and, eventually, into the end zone. Eruptions distorted the iPad's small microphone. It was all very impressive, but when the video ended Kevin looked him, waiting for a reaction. Jared didn't have one to offer him. "I don't get it. I know you didn't call to show me a football game, even though that was a pretty sweet play."

"Yeah, it was. But, you're right, that's not why I called you," Kevin agreed with a chuckle. "I didn't see it the first few times I watched the play either. Actually, my wife pointed it out to me. She saw it. Let me replay it." Kevin restarted the video from the beginning. This was a clip and not the full original. Interesting. *I'll be even more skeptical now, thank you very much.* Fraudsters did that. They loved their editing tools. The fact that this wasn't the original video disappointed him. He'd just started believing that meeting with Kevin had been a good use of his time; now he wasn't so sure.

"Now, pay attention as my kid gets the ball from the sweep, especially when he cuts the corner and sprints down the sideline," Kevin directed. "Okay, now look. Right here. See that?"

Jared's throat clenched.

Jared couldn't be positive. There was something in the video, but the distance and the conditions of the night game made it difficult to define what he was looking at. He needed to buy himself some time. "Mmmm, sort of. I mean, I can't make anything out except for the chain link fence and someone on the other side of it."

Kevin smiled. This time it wasn't the smile of a charming man, not at all. This time it was the smile of camaraderie, of belonging. Jared would soon understand why. "Keep watching that spot. Follow that shape." Kevin resumed the video.

Kevin's kid broke around the corner of the defense and raced down the sideline. As he sprinted in one direction the video caught up with the figure on the other side of the chain-link fence. The large figure, too big to be any high school football player or proud, energetic and overly-enthusiastic-father, helping coach from the sideline. Even professional football players and wrestlers weren't that big.

That was a Sasquatch. But not just *a* Sasquatch.

Jared swallowed the lump in his throat. It was a clear, high-definition video. The best he'd ever seen. The Sasquatch was easy to spot now that he knew what to look for. "Oh my god."

"Now you know why I called you." Kevin's soft voice floated in the cloud of thoughts.

"Can I have a copy of this?" he croaked.

"Already put it on this flash drive for you," Kevin reached into the cup holder and pulled out a small thumb drive. "I want to be done with this. I don't even want to go near that stadium again, never mind that thing on video. It's all yours. I hope it helps."

Jared took the thumb drive and slipped it into his jacket pocket, zipping it up to make sure he didn't lose it. This was amazing. Forks. Hurricane Ridge. Now Shelton.

He had to get home.

He had to get to work.

Jared thanked Kevin for his time. Relief washed over the larger man's face. "Don't worry," Jared said, "I'm going to look into this. I won't say anything about you or your family, okay? I'll protect your privacy."

"Thank you," Kevin nodded with a tight smirk. "Mister. Good luck with this ... this ..."

"Thank you," Jared said and walked away, saving Kevin the indignity of failing to put words to what he'd inadvertently recorded.

Jared concentrated on his feet. He was shaking. He was unstable. The last thing he wanted to do was leave Kevin with a bad impression. But his body shook with adrenaline. His chest thumped. His fingers twitched. His knees wobbled as he walked across the blacktop parking lot. When he made it inside his own vehicle he loosed a deep breath. Glancing back, he noticed Kevin had already taken off. Jared yanked the recorder out and jammed down on the RECORD button. This was going to make his podcast blow up!

The moment of truth was coming. This was unbelievable! "I can't believe what I was given," Jared tried to project his heavy breaths away from the mic so as to not distort the recording. "A Sasquatch. On video. In Shelton. But not one. The video shows a second, smaller Sasquatch trailing behind it."

A parent and child.

15

Jared laughed and turned off the truck's radio, trying to focus on not speeding. Highway 12 was always one of his least favorite roads to take, not because he didn't enjoy getting to the ocean or that it somehow made him miss the heavy traffic on I-5 from Olympia to Seattle, but because the scenic drive held dangers for him.

When you were cruising on the interstate, going north or south, you could get away with going with the flow of traffic and pushing your needle towards eighty miles an hour, except when you were going through Tacoma. Tacoma was an exception to almost every opinion about life in Washington State. But out here, where the traffic and towns became sparser, it was hard to 'hide' in traffic from bored cops who were looking to help the township meet budgetary goals. They handed out speeding tickets like pimps handed out escort fliers in the old days on the Vegas strip. Jared was pretty sure he'd funded a small expansion on the sheriff department's break room over the years with as many as he'd collected. Nothing screamed monotony to him like slugging down the open road with no distractions from other drivers or the ugly cities. Plus, flirting with the edges of McCleary, Elma, and Montesano were good reminders that life could be hard and pointless if you let it. He preferred to stay away from those places, just as he preferred to stay out of Aberdeen if he could.

But circumstances forced him to head to the small city. Thanks, Kevin Jenkins.

That video of a parent and its offspring in Shelton was something he never expected to get his hands on. Never expected to see. Just like he never expected to have two Sasquatch outside his tent.

That video was as much a blessing as it was a curse. Jared reached over to the computer bag he carried his notebooks and recording gear in. One copy of the thumb drive was in there, safely tucked away. He made no less than five of them in addition to storing it in his cloud account and overnight mailing one of them to Lucas for analysis.

Jared's hand lingered on the bag. He still didn't have a body. That was the darker side of all this, wasn't it? The public would need that before they would invest a second of interest in thinking about the existence of Sasquatch. In the bigger picture, no matter what he did, no matter what he accomplished, none of it would matter if he didn't have a body to show the uninitiated.

No, don't do that to yourself. Don't let them give you reasons to quit. Not when you're this close.

But it was easier said than done. Those dissenting voices of realism distracted him. Jared knew he could only do what he could do; everything else would be left up to fate or destiny if you believed in those things. The opinions of people who didn't care about anything beyond making their next mortgage payment didn't matter. He reminded himself that he could even deliver that body the world demanded and still have millions of people who'd claim his work a worthless hoax. He reminded himself of that because that was reality and the people who mattered, the people who would help those dissenters understand, they would see the value in this wealth of gathered evidence. That's who deserved his attention.

That was why he was headed to Aberdeen on a day he'd rather be anywhere else. He was seeing someone who would put science behind this.

Jared reluctantly moved his hand into the front pocket of the bag and grabbed the recorder. It was painful. "Kurt Cobain was a genius. It doesn't matter what your particular taste in music is, it's pretty hard to deny that claim. The man changed music; something very, very few musicians ever can actually lay claim to, especially nowadays. In Aberdeen, Washington he's much more than that, though. Here, he's a god. In this city you don't question his brilliance or character and, here, Cobain wasn't a victim of suicide either."

Jared let sarcasm taint his words even as he spoke them. "Oh, you didn't know that? Oh yeah, in Aberdeen it was murder, not a suicide. For those of you who enjoy a good conspiracy story, you'd love the atmosphere here. Aberdeen is an interesting city. With sixteen thousand people, living off pretty low annual incomes, it hugs the eastern-most inlet of the North Bay that stretches all the way out to the Pacific Ocean. It's a city struggling to stand up, like a toddler learning to walk and constantly tumbling over. A quick drive through it will show you a city trying to breathe life into itself and hyperventilating. But there's a certain charm to this foundation of grayness. There's a toughness to her people, a determined nature if you will, and I respect that.

"I'm here today to meet an old friend. We go way back," he continued. "To high school, in fact. His name is Lucas Thomson and he's a video analyst and a freelancer to a few of the sports teams in Seattle and some corporate lackeys there too. He's a remote worker so he's earning Seattle wages while living on Aberdeen costs; the man is pretty smart, I will admit, though it pains me to do so. We sort of have had this testosterone-friendly rivalry thing going on since we were kids."

He clicked off the recorder as he pulled into the city limits, meeting her traffic. There weren't many places in Aberdeen to find things to do, and every place that was somewhat interesting was shoehorned right in the same part of town, stifling traffic flow. The vast majority of the city was a sleepy hollow, with half-century old homes silently decaying under gray skies while all the action happened on one, winding strip of gray blacktop where traffic went to die.

Lucas' house was set in one such corner of the sleepier part of town. Jared shook his head as he pulled into the narrow driveway, which was nothing more than two ruts of tire tracks carved out of the lush, green lawn. The ranch home was one story, yellow. Two large windows set low on the front wall exposed the top of his couch. White curtains, laced with flowery design from the previous owner, were parted but not fully pulled to the sides, looping over the top of the couch. A single green, plastic chair, and small hibachi grill sat atop the concrete slab that served as a deck. Lucas made so much money and chose to live like this. Jared was sure he'd never understand his friend's motivations. But the way Lucas chose to live was simple, uncluttered by complications and obligations.

Maybe he is the smart one after all?

He knocked on the screen door, which rattled in its hinges. Within seconds it was flung open by the short, stout man who called Aberdeen home. "Hey, bud!" Lucas exclaimed. "Bring it in! How the hell are you doing?"

"Great, man. Great. How about you?"

"Most excellent. I'm living in heaven. How could I not be? Come on, let's get inside. It's hot out here."

Jared laughed and stepped into the small home. "It's 72 degrees."

Lucas waved off his comment, reaching into the refrigerator. "Beer?"

"One. I'm on the clock."

Lucas stood back up, two cans in hand. Cheap beers, Jared noted. He leaned on the top edge of the lower refrigerator door. "When are you not?"

"I'm working on that." It was an honest answer.

"How are things? You okay?" Lucas' tone switched to serious, as serious as the maze of thousands of dollars' worth of video and computing equipment in the adjoining room. In a normal family, that room would serve as the gathering place to sit and talk, to watch television, or to just spend time together. Not so much with Lucas. For him, it was an office where magic was done. Video might be his first love, but Lucas wasn't oblivious to normal human priorities. His friend knew the toll this separation had taken. Lucas was like that. He didn't have a family of his own so he seemed extra sensitive to the lives of his friends. Jared appreciated that. He appreciated a lot of things about Lucas. Whereas Peter could be compassionate but dry, Lucas wore his emotions on his sleeve. You always knew where you stood with him and him with you. There weren't enough people in the world like that.

"We're actually trying to reconcile," Jared answered.

"No shit?" Lucas knocked the cheap beer cans together, slammed the refrigerator and made his way to the table, sliding one of the cans over to Jared. "Nice, man. When did that happen?"

"Last few weeks; real recent," Jared admitted. "I finally pulled my head out of my ass and realized how much she gave up for me so I could do this. I've been pretty selfish."

"You have."

"Gee, thanks."

Lucas shrugged, wincing as he pried open the beer and was splashed with small, white foam flecks of cheap booze. Jared laughed at the fate his friend created for himself. "That's what friends are for. True friends will tell you how much you suck. Plus, I thought you were above receiving platitudes for the sake of your ego?"

"You're an ass," Jared laughed as they silently toasted each other.

Lucas took a long swig and rolled his lips inward after setting the beer down. "I try," he smiled. "So, this video you sent me. From Shelton, huh?"

"Yeah, a father took it at his kid's game," Jared said. "He didn't see it until weeks later when his wife pointed it out. What do you think?"

"It's an interesting video," Lucas conceded.

"Interesting? That doesn't sound promising."

"Listen, you know where I stand on this stuff," Lucas replied. "We've had these conversations before. And I know you trust me enough to check my biases. This video made it hard to do that."

Whatever he was expecting his friend to say, it wasn't that. It wasn't an encouraging statement and Jared couldn't deny the immediate feeling of regret and disappointment. "What? Why?"

"Well, the environmental factors in the video don't help," Lucas leaned forward. "There's light pollution from the stadium. Too many occluding objects, namely the players on that side of the field and the fence, and, I could argue, even the backdrop. It doesn't help that we're looking across an illuminated sports field into the darkness. I wish he'd shot this during the day."

"Well, he doesn't control the school's football schedule. And, hey, at least there's a video."

"Don't get me wrong. This is good," Lucas stated. "Not perfect, but good. A lot better than almost 100% of all that crap you see on YouTube that claims to be genuine. I went over and over this. Sorry bud, I love ya, but I'm not putting my name on it."

Goddamn it! With one, swift comment Lucas sent waves of disappointment rolling over him. He tried to not let his disappointment show. He didn't want to put unfair weight on Lucas doing exactly what he'd asked him to do. And, to be truthful, he didn't want Lucas giving him shit about it a few months from now when their schedules matched and they finally caught back up with each other again. "So, it's a fake?"

"I used my dynamical model. I used a few variations, actually. I ran a segmentation algorithm. Did detection, looked for variance in intensities. I went over and over this. I'm not going to lie. I even reached out to a friend in Phoenix, another analyst. Sort of my mentor. Thing is, I'm struggling with this, Jared."

Jared leaned back. "Why?"

"Because," Lucas took another long, slow swallow of his horrible domestic beer, his can leaned to the side so he could keep an eye on Jared as he drank. He set it down but, Jared noted, still gripped it tightly, "It's legitimate."

"Ha!" Jared exclaimed, standing and accidentally hitting the recorder, almost knocking it the floor. He picked it up and stopped the recording. He wanted to protect his friend, all of his friends, from now on. After what Peter had been through he didn't want to add Lucas to that list. Friends came before Bigfoot. "Fucking fantastic!"

"You could say that again," Lucas smiled, "and I don't even believe in this shit."

"Well, do you now?"

Lucas shook his head. "Man, I don't know. That was ... crazy. I don't know what to make of it. I'm not supposed to think those things are real. This doesn't sit well with me, Jared."

Now it was Jared's turn to shake his head. "You just can't admit it, can you? You know what that was."

"No I don't, bud," Lucas replied. "Until I know those things are real, all I know is that I have no godly idea what I saw in that video. Don't—" he held up his hand, "I know what you're going to say. And I know you're going to caveat with flowery, non-committal language to make sure you stay as unbiased as possible. And I know you're going to say that's convincing video, and it is, I swear. I'm struggling here."

"Struggling, but not enough to convince you those things are out there though?"

"What things?" he shrugged. "You have to prove to me they exist before you can tell me what I saw in that video, bud. There was something there, no doubt. But I can't be convinced by large shadows. There are a million options as to what that is. Variations."

"Variations?" Jared queried. "Men in suits? Bears walking upright?"

"Could be," Lucas smirked. "I don't know. It freaks me out. I don't know what the fuck those things were and I doubt they were kids or moronic adults trying to get 'YouTube famous'. They're likely to get shot in Shelton walking around in gorilla suits. No, those things were animals. That's all I'm conceding right now. Isn't that enough progress for you?"

"That's it," Jared lifted his beer, extending a finger at Lucas, "I'm taking your ass on an expedition."

"No thanks," Lucas waved him away.

"Why not?"

"Why in the world would I want to go out there? There's mosquitoes and it gets cold, and all sorts of shit crawls around in the underbrush that can see me but I can't see it. No thanks."

"You're afraid that if you go out with me and we hear something, you're going to come over to my side of the argument. You're going to become a dirty believer!"

They shared a laugh and the conversation turned to other things, lighter things. It was good to be with him again. It'd been a long time, too long of a time, but it was always like that with Lucas. Any time that passed between visits felt like ages, even if it was only a month or two. But that was life, wasn't it? As you got older, life tended to become more private. Running with your social circles became less and less important and even dear friends faded away. Lucas had never faded, but Jared was gone so often and Aberdeen was such a pain to get to that they had every excuse real life provided about why they couldn't get together more often. So times like this, even when there was work to be discussed, were valued. Jared treasured every minute of beer drinking and bullshitting. Because he knew there would never be enough and it could all be taken away tomorrow.

Jared ended up having more than one beer with Lucas, but not so many that he couldn't drive a few hours later. Lucas stood in his driveway, in the drizzle that rolled in off the ocean, watching Jared back out of the path that acted as a driveway, waving like a protective poppa sending his kids off to college. Jared waved back at the figure in the rearview mirror, laughing at the silliness of the shared gesture, and mourning the fact that he knew it might be months before they saw each other again unless something came up.

Or if he could grow a pair and come out on an expedition.

It wasn't a fruitless venture though; Lucas warmed to the idea throughout their afternoon beer chat to the point where he almost got Lucas to commit to going. That was saying something. Lucas hated being out in the elements; he hated being wet, hated being cold. Jared was shocked his friend even did yard work, and why he chose to live in Aberdeen, with its perpetual grayness, was something he swore he'd never understand. Lucas was strange like that, and Jared loved his friend's quirkiness.

He wanted to protect Lucas too. Peter's recent troubles were very real; Jared had no doubt, so he had to be careful about every word, written and spoken, from now on. No one else needed to carry the weight of his troubles.

None of them.

Jared scratched his chin. Behind the joy, there was worry, with a little confusion spritz for good measure. His thoughts transferred from his friend to his long-time foe. Why was Sasquatch all the way out in Shelton? Had conditions become that bad in the Olympics? Forks, then Quinault, and now a small city like Shelton? Were they going to start being sighted near Olympia next?

"It didn't make sense. The town is way too far from the Olympics and way too populated," Jared reasoned aloud. "It's not a city by any stretch of the definition, but nearly twenty thousand people is still a significant number when you're talking about this species being anywhere in the area. Why in the world would it be this close to town? Especially when it had a youngster with it? What could have made it leave the safety of the mountains?"

The slow death of the planet aside, what other reasons could these wonderful creatures have to come out of the safety of the mountains? Forks, he could understand. It was still an out-of-the-way destination with sparse human population and, in Forks, Frank Hollenbeck had more gone into their world than they had his.

Even the Quinault sightings could be rationalized. A hungry animal coming down to the river outside a very small town? He was okay with that too.

But this? A parent-child pairing in Shelton? Close enough to be caught on video in the background of a high school football game with hundreds of spectators? It didn't matter that Kevin hadn't witnessed it during the game or the first few times he watched what he recorded. That was a good thing, in fact, because it was likely everyone at the game missed the sighting. But it also spoke volumes about Sasquatch's comfort. Or desperation. Maybe it was time for him to be equally assertive with his podcast target audience, which would include people like Lucas, who would need to get drunk with one before they'd believe it existed.

"I guess, as with most things, as soon as one mystery starts to be revealed another takes its place," Jared continued. "Questions leading to more questions. There's so much people don't understand about this creature. So much they don't want to understand. When it comes to Sasquatch, the old adage that ignorance is bliss becomes pertinent."

This needed to go into the podcast. Momentum was building. The future audience had to feel this, it was the only way he could suck them in.

"Why are people so averse to considering the possibility that these creatures might actually exist? From *Gigantopithecus blacki* forward, there's so much evidence to consider. To at least think about." He clutched the recorder, shaking it in front of his face as he spoke. "A giant, upright, bipedal ape existing in North America! We know it lived here. The fossil record, science, shows that. Something Jeff Meldrum calls the 'serendipity of paleontology' when he talked about distinct genetic inter-species identity and what the fossil record shows and doesn't show. So before you get ready to ignore these accounts, take a second to remember the world you see today isn't the world of antiquity. The absence of evidence alone is not evidence of absence.

"This challenges assertions by those who resist considering giant apes migrating, surviving, and even thriving in this region of the world." The fire burned in him. He was so tired of swimming against the tide of ignorance, so tired of people believing every damn word their favored political party spewed but refusing to even entertain a conversation about a primate. "Yes, a body needs to be found, I get that, but finding fossils will be tough, especially because the Pacific Northwest is especially poor for fossilization due to the moist coniferous forests and volcanic soil. The acidity of the soil here doesn't work well with preservation efforts. Legitimate hair, footprints, and video evidence of something in a very specific region of western Washington State; I'm so damn close to being able to go public with all of this. I'm not sure that right now is the right time. Too early and it might not be taken seriously. I need to have enough to motivate funding for deeper research or all of this was for naught. But I need to do it soon."

He swallowed back the wave of regret washing over him. The darkness he'd tucked away into an emotional box was cracked open. Maria was forcing it open. Still, it was so, so hard. "I need to bury my demons."

16

Jared lay on the couch, the recorder on his chest. He was going to do this, finally.

After his anthropological rant on the way back from Shelton, he'd stopped recording and started thinking. Not that he ran out of material to cover, there was still so much people needed to hear, but because that rant led him straight into thinking about the very thing that was going to put this all behind him, once and for all.

He needed to do this. It only took Maria saying it a few hundred thousand times for it to get through his thick skull. Ignoring it, remaining silent, that wasn't going to help him heal. Ignoring that the lion has escaped its cage wouldn't make him any safer. Unless he dealt with the fact that he was staring at the open maw of a pissed off predator he had no chance of surviving it. For years, too many years, Jared had ignored the loosed lion, even when Maria begged him to deal with it for their sake.

"It's time I'm real with you," his soft tone filled the vacuum of his mind. One arm behind his head, he stared up at the ceiling, focusing on a screw hole where one of Maria's planters used to house her Pelargoniums. *Lose yourself in that, buddy. Get through this. You need to get through this.* "I've been holding off for this long because I needed to be confident of what I was looking at, that I had enough evidence to support my suspicions of the last ten years.

"When I started investigating Sasquatch's existence, I did so for personal reasons. I hinted at those in my earlier recordings. And, shit, I haven't been honest. I'm working on it, I need to if I want to respect Maria; if I want to give her all she's given me and dedicate the rest of my life to her and to us. There's only one way I can do that; I have to prove or disprove my theory.

"See, the thing is, I'm convinced the Olympic National Park is home to this region's Sasquatch population," he continued. "There may be other population centers, far fewer than many claim, but those are the very same people who are in this for the wrong reasons. There are no Bigfoot in Tennessee or North Carolina or West Virginia. No, they're restricted to this part of the country: Washington State, Oregon, and Idaho, stretching into British Columbia. That's where you'll find them. Look at my home state. Almost two-thirds of it is a high desert. Most of Washington State would not be hospitable to them. And even the third of the state that is hospitable is way too overpopulated. The Cascade mountain range is littered with people and outdoor resorts. The only reasonable location left for this species is in the Olympics. But that's not all there is to my theory.

"Even though I believe this is the only area in the state with a Sasquatch population, I also think their numbers are smaller than even the experts claim. Disappointingly small, for some. And I believe they live in tight communities, which I call herds. There are no more than a handful of Sasquatch in each herd, maybe five or less. One male, a female or two, and some offspring. They don't have many offspring, only one or two over the course of their entire lives, so they're not exactly a positive-growth species. But I guess that makes them a lot more earth-friendly than us humans.

"A lot of my peers don't agree with my theory and some in the Bigfoot community have been outright hostile about it. I know the lack of hard evidence doesn't help, but no one else has any either. Nothing legitimate. It's the damning reality of our business. But the evidence I do have is getting better, like what I found at Forks, and it supports my small community theory. None of it stems the negative reactions I receive, but those don't necessarily surprise me. The biggest inhibitor to a Bigfoot investigator are other investigators. I learned that hard lesson early on and it's one of the main factors for my pulling back out of the community and researching on my own, with a relatively small cadre of experts I trust, like Peter and Lucas. There are so many politics in this field. It sucks the energy out of me. Made me start falling out of love with doing this long ago. And, I haven't been honest about that, even to myself."

You've got to do this. Don't quit!

But he was wavering. He was going back into the state he always went to whenever he approached the memories. Even now, with so much on the line, he felt himself turning away. Hiding. The guilt was there, encouraging him to do what he knew he needed to do for himself. Tugging at him. Yanking at his sleeve. But that fork in the road was dangerous, full of potholes and edged with a life-threatening precipice. The safer route, the rough but innocuous route, lay in the other direction. It was the route he'd walked a thousand times already. He was so familiar with it that he could walk it with his eyes closed.

It called to him even as his better judgment screamed a warning to stay off the path. He could feel it fading.

He was giving in.

"I can't wait to be done with this," he said, not caring to hide his self-disgust any longer. He hated himself more than anything right now. "But that's it. I believe Bigfoot exists and they live in herds, in communities, in the Olympic Mountains in Washington. And this, this entire series of recordings, will serve as my evidence. And then, finally, I can walk away and do something else.

"And I can't wait to pick up Molly tomorrow. I miss that damn dog. As much as I've neglected Maria over the years, sometimes I think I've neglected Molly just as much. When I'm done with all this I'm going to cuddle the hell out of her. And Maria? I'll do more than cuddle her."

He switched the recorder off and laid it on the coffee table, fluffing the pillow and setting it underneath his head again.

You're a fucking coward.

He stared at the hanging planter hole. It stared back, unblinking, uncaring.

Jared closed his eyes. It had been such an outstanding day.

Until now.

He couldn't deal with himself anymore tonight.

*****

The ringing of the doorbell woke Jared. He flipped over, almost falling off the couch. "Wha-what the hell?"

The doorbell rang again, and once more before the tone faded.

He shot to his feet, making sure the recorder was on. Just in case.

He flipped over his phone to check the time. 2:07 AM.

"Jesus!" If this was some nut bag bothering him, someone was getting their ass kicked! "I'm coming!"

Urgent pounding on the door, rattling its hinges.

"I swear I'm going to kill somebody." Jared moved around the couch to the window, pulling the blinds aside. Maria's car was in the driveway.

He pulled the door open. "Maria?"

He couldn't get the rest of the sentence out. She looked distraught. Her hair was yanked into a ponytail, frizzled, loose strands she hadn't taken the time to grab dangled from the side. Her eyes were swollen and red. She'd been crying. Her chest heaved when he opened the door and she fell against him. He wrapped his arms around her and held her, looking out into the dark night to see if someone else was in the car. Or the cops. Or an ambulance. Nothing. No one else. What the fuck is going on?

"Oh God, Jared," she sobbed into his chest.

He stroked her hair. She always liked when he comforted her that way. "Maria, are you okay? What's wrong?"

She didn't bother to pull away before answering. "It's—M—Molly, Jared."

"What about her?" Panic tightened his throat. "Oh, Jesus, please don't tell me something happened?"

"Jared, th—they—oh my God. That poor girl!"

Jared pulled Maria inside as he cleared the door, swinging it shut. "Come on inside, I need you to tell me what's going on but I can't understand you."

He walked her over to the couch, the place where he'd confirmed his status as a coward only a few hours before. Maria sat, looking up at him with eyes glossed in hopelessness, sad eyes, sadder than the day she told him that she was leaving. Her mouth moved but only guttural half-words came out. She swallowed, choking back tears, and tried again. "M—men. Some men woke me up. Th—they ... they told me to tell you to stop. Jared, they told me to tell you to st—stop your investigation. And Molly ... oh my God, Jared." She began sobbing again. Jared forced down his rising terror, pushed aside his panic and need to know what happened, to not lash out at Maria. She needed time to collect herself enough to finish. "They—they had Molly and ... and—"

Maria sobbed into the palms of her hands.

His voice broke at her pain and the knowledge that something terrible had happened to his dog. Their dog. "Maria? What is it, babe? What happened?" He knelt in front of her, rubbing her thigh. *Oh God, please tell me! Don't make me wait. Please.*

"Th-they they had Molly. They t-t-told me to tell you to stop or they would do worse to me. The-then ... they, they shot her! They killed Molly!"

17

There was no way Molly was gone.

No fucking way.

She couldn't be. He'd just dropped her off yesterday! Maria was in town, staying with her girlfriend so she could get to a meeting in Olympia. She'd agreed to watch Molly and Jared left the dog with a quick hug and pat on her gorgeous head. Molly had looked up at him with flickering eyes; her tongue flopped out the side of her mouth, swaying like her entire body, from the momentum of an enthusiastically wagging tail. She was used to him leaving her behind and she still loved him that much more than he deserved.

Had loved me, Jared reminded himself.

Molly. Gone.

"Can you please stop pacing, Jared?" Maria sniffled from the couch she hadn't moved from. "Please, sit down."

Sit down? How could he sit down? Adrenaline coursed through his body. His skin prickled. He tried to not snarl at Maria. "I don't want to."

She nodded. "For me, then? You're scaring me."

Of course, he didn't want that. But he had to move or he'd explode and say something he'd regret. "I—I don't understand. Why the hell would anyone do something like that? Goddamn it! She was such a good dog! Why?!"

"Jared," Maria choked back her tears, "what are you involved in?"

He turned on her. "What do you mean?"

"These men. They wanted me to be sure I told you to stop your work. Why?" Maria leaned forward, her eyebrows arcing downward. "Look at me! Why? What do you know that would cause them to do something like this?"

The crescendo was building. He could feel it calling to him from the darker recesses of his gut. He was going to explode. He wanted to explode. This couldn't have happened at a worse time. Not that any time was a good time for something so tragic to happen, but in his fog of self-hatred, the last thing anyone wanted was to push his buttons. Even Maria. "Does it matter? Molly is dead. Peter's been threatened. You're being threatened." The glass of water he'd left on the coffee table was still there. Within arm's reach. The darkness called. He snagged it and propelled it into the wall without a care. Glass sprayed in a million directions as water dripped to the floor. Dammit! "All of this over some fucking investigation about an animal?"

Maria sighed, placing her hands on her thighs and standing. "I'll clean it up. Sit down."

"No, I've got it," he said, with much less fire in his humiliated gut now.

"No, please," she laid a hand on his forearm. "I need to do something. I can't just sit here."

Jared fell into the couch, covering his face. Molly was gone! "That poor girl! She didn't deserve this."

"Come here," Maria was in front of him again, the shattered glass was forgotten for the time being. Her arms were open and this time it was Jared who fell forward into an ex-lover's embrace, seeking comfort for a pain that only time would erase.

"Thank you, Maria," he cried into her chest.

"For what," she said without pulling away.

"For staying. I don't know if I wouldn't have done something stupid if you weren't here." That was half the truth. The dark place he was in tonight, if she'd called him instead of coming over, being physically and emotionally present, there was no telling exactly what he would have done. There was no one he could blame for Molly's death, not yet, but there were a couple of hidden figures, peers he distrusted, he wouldn't mind having an excuse to get his hands on for twenty years of frustration. Blaming them for Molly's death was a perfect excuse to rip their heads off their shoulders.

"That's what we do for each other, isn't it?" she rubbed his shoulder before sitting next to him, wrapping her hand around his. "Plus, what can you do? I have no idea who these guys were. They didn't give me their names. They didn't say much of anything about themselves. Nothing. You can't go after nameless people and I don't want you to, even if you knew who they were. Promise me that, okay?"

"I need to know who it is," Jared avoided answering her. "Who's threatening everyone I care about and leaving me harassing phone calls. I can't sit by--"

"What do you mean?" Now she did pull back, but their fingers remained intertwined. "You didn't tell me about anything like that."

Are you going to keep being a coward or are you finally going to take control of your life? The life that's starting to spin out of control? You're going to lose it forever if you don't step up.

"It's been happening for a while now," he answered. "The last time was a few days ago. I didn't tell you about it because I don't take them seriously. I figured it was just some jealous peers. Not something to lose sleep over. Then I started getting more calls, more hostile calls."

"What did they say?" she pressed. "In the calls? What is going on, Jared?" She gave him a silent stare, waiting for him to fill her in. When he didn't answer, the calm control began to unravel. "This isn't like with your father, okay? You can't keep burying these things!"

No. Not tonight. Please don't go there tonight! "Don't. I'm not in the mood for that."

"Jesus, Jared!" she unlocked her hand from his and waved them at some invisible point of reference in exasperation. "Look at everything that's going on and the toll it's taken! Friendships, your career, our marriage, having children? When is enough going to be enough?"

"That's not fair," he warned. "You can't do that."

She looked at him and then he watched as her face caved to the inevitable disappointment of living a life with him. "It's never fair with you. Anything you can do to avoid having to talk about it or even think about it, right?"

Jared slammed his hand on the coffee table, making Maria jump. "I don't need to think about it." It hurt to look in her eyes. *Coward.* "I'm sorry. I'm—I'm stressed about all this shit. I didn't mean to yell. But, please, don't. This has nothing to do with him."

"It has everything to do with your father. How long are you going to deny that? Are you going to keep pretending that what he did to your family had no impact on you or are you going to finally be honest?"

"What he did…what happened—" he started to say, but she wasn't going to allow him to get away with it.

"Destroyed your family," she shouted over top of his stuttering response. "It destroyed your parents' marriage and it destroyed his life."

If she could yell, then he could too. "No, it didn't! We did fine. We all made it out. Mom moved on. I went to school, got an education, met you, I have a career."

He swore she was about to crack a smile at his response. "A career that you hate, that has worn you out, and has led our marriage in the same direction as their marriage went."

"That's not fair. You're—"

Her voice was so soft he could have completely missed her comment ... if it hadn't been so barbed. So true. "You're walking his path, Jared. How can you not see that?"

But he was ready for it even before she finished her observation. Why? Why didn't she understand that? How many times did they have to go around on this ride? He would deal with it when he could. If she was around now, if she hadn't run out on him, then she would have seen his struggle over the past few weeks. If she'd been here instead of in Port Angeles, staying with her parents, trying to escape her life, she would have seen how much thought and effort he was putting into turning this corner. And if she'd been there to see those behaviors she wouldn't be sitting here on the same night his dog was murdered, trying to push him into exploring what happened with his father. "Are you kidding me?" he raged. "Don't put that on me! And don't talk about him like that. He was a great man; a man I admired."

"Stop defending him," she said in that all-too-calm tone. "You need to recognize what he did and how it impacted you before it's too late. The fact that you can't see that after everything that's happened ..."

Her trailing voice left so much unsaid, but it was all still so clear.

He watched her eyes. A haze of hurt hung behind those crystal mirrors. "What's that supposed to mean?" This time all the heat was gone. Bare. Just him. And her. Exactly as he wanted it to be.

"If you're not going to be honest with yourself then you can't be honest with me. And if you can't be honest with either one of us ... where does that leave our marriage?"

"I love you. Why are you talking like this?"

Her face begun to crumble. "Sometimes love isn't enough."

It sounded like she was giving up. Maybe, this time, for good. "How can you say that? I thought we ... I thought we were going to work on us? I thought you were going to give me a chance?"

"How can I give us a chance if you're not willing to?" Her voice got louder as she spoke. "I told you, Jared, I warned you that this was only going to get worked on if you did your part. Do you honestly think the only thing I wanted from you was for you to stop chasing around this goddamn animal?" She swept her keys up from the coffee table.

He went to grab her arm then pulled back when he realized what he was doing, thankful that she didn't notice. "Wait. Maria. Come on, don't--"

The door slamming was how she ended the conversation. He didn't even get up to watch her back out of the driveway. Her headlights beamed through his front window and across the far wall of the living room. That was enough of a signal to let him know where she was with their marriage.

"You fucking coward," he slumped back into the couch, listening to the sound of her car engine fading into the night.

*****

When he woke a few hours later, he didn't know what to do.

With himself.

With his future.

Everything was in upheaval.

A few hours ago he had more evidence about Bigfoot than anyone in the world. He was on the fast track toward making it all public and then walking away to get on with the rest of his life and reconciling with Maria. Now, his beloved dog was dead and his estranged wife was on her way to a full-fledged divorce. It all fell apart easier than wet paper.

Where do you go when you're already face-down in the gutter? Should he toss a life's work away because of a broken heart, or finally wake up and realize the cost of passion exceeded his capability to pay it?

He rolled over toward the back support of the couch and closed his eyes. He didn't want to deal with a world that didn't include Maria.

Within minutes of waking, Jared was asleep.

18

The rising sun did nothing to lift his spirits. He rolled over and winced at the brightness poking at his eyelids. The flood of memories from last night, immediate. Depressing. Maria was gone. Molly was dead. There were men so serious about him discontinuing his investigation that they were willing to commit violence against an innocent animal and threaten his wife. This was the point he was at now.

Jared rolled over and sat up, scratching his developing beard. When was the last time he shaved? When was the last time he picked up around the house? Or cooked for himself?

Spiraling.

Spiraling.

Spiraling.

Instead of the upward trajectory he should have been on, he was looking to plant his nose firmly in the ground in a spectacular crash. *Well on the path to becoming the non-example in this life, you coward.*

Every marriage had problems. People married for all the wrong reasons—money, convenience, to stave off loneliness, the incredible sex. There were as many bad reasons people got married as there were divorced couples. You could add in another million reasons for all the miserable people who lacked the courage to divorce, preferring to remain in an unhealthy and unrewarding relationship in order to keep up public perceptions, satisfy the will of some god that had nothing better to do with its time, or even because that's what they'd been told they were supposed to do by their culture.

But it wasn't like that with Maria.

She was the type of person he needed in his life because she, out of every single person he knew, made him better. She taught him things about himself he didn't even know. It was Maria who helped him open emotional doors that were sealed his entire life. When he wanted to forgo using the degree he spent four years and tens of thousands of dollars obtaining it was Maria who worked the longer hours at the steady job so they could make the payments on the house and vehicles. She even did it during his early years of schlepping through the backcountry of the Pacific Northwest in pursuit of a monster.

Even when she tired and began asking for things in return, when it was obvious he wasn't smart enough to pick up on those clues himself, she remained faithful and strong. When they fought, she stayed up late talking through to resolution, even though it was her who had to get to the office in the morning. She was the creative one in the relationship, the one who needed as much brain power as she could muster on a daily basis so they could afford to live, but even during the dark times, she continued to sacrifice in order to make them work. She suffered because of him. She gave everything of herself. She loved constantly, even when it felt like the rest of the world wouldn't miss him if he was swallowed by a Bigfoot on one of his expeditions.

And when things started falling apart, she hung in there, came back when he promised change, remained faithful and patient as he stumbled and faltered through committing. In the book of marital excuses, Jared had gone from cover to cover and employed every single tactic more than a few times. He had already given her more than enough excuses to walk away, guilt-free, but she never did.

Until she finally did.

Of course, he'd thought about everything Maria had done for him, for them, and for what they could be. The tacky apologies he would deliver over a poorly prepared meal when he wanted to be romantic, the sacrifice she made when she'd taken on a large job after the separation and he bought them plane tickets to Las Vegas for a getaway. That hotel room became an office as she tried to balance the demands of the job with giving their marriage all the attention she could, even though Jared hadn't even asked her about her schedule when he booked the trip. *Goddamn, you know more about this animal than you do your own wife,* he realized.

He also realized he'd given more to the pursuit of this animal than he had to her.

And he had to change.

For himself, even if it was too late for them.

If he didn't work on himself then he would never be in the place to work on their marriage. She'd been telling him this for years but he avoided it out of selfishness. That's how he saw it; he couldn't apologize for his perspective. The problem was, while he viewed fixing himself as selfish, he didn't have any such reservations about spending a week in the woods looking for large footprints or scat. It was all so ridiculous. She had led him to the water and asked him to take control of his life and drink, yet he'd always turned away to search for his own natural spring.

I've got to fix this. I've got to try.

And it was with that thought that he searched under the small pile of wrinkled and dirty laundry for his recorder. He was going to do this, do it before the courage waned. It didn't matter if Maria would give him another chance or not. It wasn't about that. Plus, she would never come back if he didn't fix himself. His unresolved issues created the separation.

It was now or never.

Drawing a shaking breath, he pressed RECORD.

"I had half a mind to follow her back to her house," he said, trying to block the memory of her disappearing taillights. "It was actually difficult not to. Whoever killed Molly could be still there, waiting for Maria to return. Waiting for me. I should have seen this coming. It's not like things like this haven't happened before. There are divisions within the Bigfoot subculture that are guilty of doing some egregious stuff to other investigators because of their work. My investigations have drawn attention for years but, lately, it seems to have been ratcheted up a few thousand notches. And now everyone but me is paying for it. What I'd do to get my hands on them. I'm afraid of me if I do. There's no telling."

His phone rang. It was Maria!

Jared snapped off the recorder and answered. "Maria? Are you okay?"

Her tone was flat. The three-hour drive gave her plenty of time to put up the wall between them. "Yes," she sounded exhausted, "I wanted you to know that I made it home okay."

"That's, that's good," he stumbled. "Listen, about last night, I—"

She sighed. "Jared, I'm tired. I just got home. I don't want to talk. I want to shower, get something to eat, and sleep."

"Oh." Her words stung. "Okay. Can I call you later?"

"It's probably best if you don't."

"But Maria—"

"I need to go," she said, the firmness in her voice solidifying her stance. "Bye, Jared."

She was gone before he could say anything else.

Jared set the phone down on the coffee table and stared at it like he was willing her to call back by intimidating the small box of electrical circuits, chips, and wires. It didn't ring; he wasn't expecting it to. He couldn't expect her to.

Now or never.

He picked up the recorder again and punched RECORD. "Maria made it home safe. She called me to let me know but didn't want to talk longer than she needed to. I screwed it up this time. I have got to face the facts. My reason for doing this. My real reason.

"I've stuffed it for so long I don't even recognize it anymore. Maybe telling you, sharing it like this, will help. Saying it out loud into a recording that may or may not ever see the light of day, maybe that will be enough practice to someday look her in the eyes and say it to her. She doesn't need that, but she needs me to admit it to myself and start working on it. If it's not too late."

God, please don't let it be too late.

"So I guess this makes it confession time for me," he continued. "Just you and me. Me exposing my darkest secrets to you. So, here it is. Coming clean." He drew a deep breath that did nothing to settle his nerves or the thumping heart in his chest. "In an earlier recording, I shared my childhood story about a Sasquatch invading our camp, traumatizing my mother and, ultimately, killing my dog. I said that was my motivation that launched this career, this passion. Well, that wasn't exactly a lie, but it's not the entire truth either. My dog was killed by a Sasquatch. I saw it with my own eyes. But that's not where that story ended. After that night, nothing was the same for any of us. You know, if I'm going to do this I need a beer."

Jared paused, navigated his way around the clothes on the floor and the box of books that was delivered while he was gone but he hadn't bothered actually opening, and went into the kitchen. It was early, too early for a beer, but extraordinary demands required extraordinary strength, something he lacked. The future podcast audience didn't need to know how early in the morning it was when he popped the top and poured the stout into a frosted mug. If you're gonna do it, do it right.

Jared paused a moment to look out through the narrow slit of a window in the door that led to the backyard. Molly's doghouse sat there, up against the fence, dark and empty. His gut twisted. His eyes burned.

Jared steeled himself. There was no use in getting distracted. If he chased that demon it'd only serve as yet another excuse to not do what needed to be done.

He brought the beer back to the coffee table, setting it down and then immediately pulling it back up, stretching to retrieve a paper coaster to slide under it.

Now or never.

He pressed RECORD and stepped into the demon's lair.

*****

"I'll never forget the sight of that creature. It was terrifying. As much as I want to prove these things exist, I have no desire to come that close to one again. Doesn't make sense, I know, but you're going to have to go with me on this, unless you're itching to get into this line of work. Then you'll understand. I can see that thing as clearly now as I could then, as if the past thirty-plus years have been a blip. Everything I said before was accurate. The Sasquatch invaded our camp until it was chased off by my dog, which it killed. My mother and father fought for days afterward. All of that was real. Every single bit of it.

"But that night, the fallout from what happened, it didn't dissipate when we pulled out of that campground," he choked back the panic trying to convince him to stop. He'd stopped for over twenty years and time was up. "And I'm not talking mourning for a dead dog. Sure, it hurt and I missed him for a few months, but I was a kid, distracted by bikes, and sports, and soon enough, girls. No, it was my father. My dad changed after that night. He started doing a lot of reading, a lot of research. He started buying equipment and going out on expeditions with local cryptozoologists. Then, when they weren't dedicated enough, he started his own organization. It's defunct now. It died away when he did, but he put a lot into it. A lot more than he put into us."

Stop! The world doesn't need to know this. This is private. It's your story, not theirs.

"When things started falling apart, he started drinking."

At least respect your father's legacy!

"Then came the fighting."

You coward. How can you treat him like this?

"Then came the divorce."

Then came you disrespecting your father. The man who gave you life. The man who provided and loved yo—

Enough. Now or never.

"It didn't happen overnight," Jared said, the voice of doubt fading into the recess of his mind. "But it sure seemed to. One day we were a happy family, the next my father was never around, and when he was, he was too distracted by his research, his liquor, or fighting with my mother. He died in 1988. Cirrhosis of the liver. Mom hung around for him, though. Never left his side once he got sick. She was so damn faithful. Better than he deserved. I spent all my teen years without a father. It made me angry and, man, did I give my mother headaches. She put up with a lot. I don't know how she did it if I'm being completely honest. Between his selfish dedication and my rebelliousness, that woman had more than her fair share of struggles.

"It wasn't until Maria came into my life that I even began to take time to think about my father in a different way. Maybe it was because his memory was fading or because I was actually growing up and had my own life to live and adult responsibilities to distract me? I'm not sure. I started being less angry with him for everything he did to destroy our family. It also didn't hurt that I started walking in his steps. I started repeating his mistakes, which made it easier to justify everything he did to pull us apart and to not be mad at his memory. I'm no better than him."

Jared thumbed a droplet of condensation that trickled down the frosted mug.

God, this hurts.

"I'm destroying my life to find a creature that doesn't want to be found."

19

Jared heard the stiff breeze coming long before it swept through the camp. He pulled his hood up, not saying a word to Lucas. Listening to the world helped prepare you for anything it dished out. If you knew what to listen for. Lucas had obviously never learned that lesson. He shivered when the invisible wall of Mother Nature's touch wrapped him in her embrace. Jared smiled as his friend shook like a toddler tasting a lemon for the first time.

Lucas looked at him askance.

"What?" Jared asked.

Lucas shrugged and scooted closer to the fire. "Nothing," he said.

"Oh come on," Jared pried. "Seriously. What's up? What's that look for?"

"Just glad I came out here with you," Lucas replied. "Sort of."

Jared squinted in confusion but didn't reply. He watched the flames dance, almost flickering out under the steady assault of the wind.

It would die down soon. He could hear the silence coming from the west.

"You're not yourself," Lucas commented into the darkness. "I'm worried about you, bud."

"Don't be."

"Not that easy," Lucas countered. "You wear it on your sleeve."

He guessed he had. The past few days had been rough. After recording his confessional about his father, Jared thought he'd feel better, feel relieved of the burden of his family's dark legacy. But he didn't. In fact, hopelessness was his partner now, replacing Maria where she couldn't be bothered. Despair, always the good neighbor, popped in from time to time to see how he was doing. It was the un-invited and unwelcomed guest that pulled the blinds closed and shut off all the lights in your home. It preferred the type of darkness Jared had been sulking in for two days. That's why he was here now, on this cold night, with his best friend. The clearest sign that he advertised his depression was the fact Lucas actually accompanied him on an expedition. If this was all it took to get him out he would have ruined his life ages ago.

But this wasn't a social outing, not completely. It was a much needed mental health break because he'd been slipping and Lucas was attuned enough to recognize a friend in need. And, unlike most people, Lucas cared enough to respond. Funny, they hadn't seen each other more than a handful of times over the past year prior to Jared taking the video footage from the football game to Lucas. And yet Lucas still knew him that well. That spoke volumes about the man's character.

It was good to hang out again. Camping. Lucas is camping! It meant the world to Jared to have his friend here with him during this, his darkest time because he didn't want to be alone anymore.

Jared needed to turn over a new leaf; to start telling people what they meant to him. People weren't strange creatures he couldn't communicate with, that was reserved for Sasquatch. But somewhere in his life, the paradigm had gotten flipped. It was up to him to correct it. Recording his confession about his father was the first step. Now, he had to keep walking. "I appreciate you coming out here."

Lucas crossed his arms, rubbing the opposite arm and shoulder. "Don't mention it. But could you do something about the heat, like turn it up?"

Jared smiled, he couldn't bring himself to laugh; he hadn't in days and was falling out of practice. "I'll get right on that but, sorry, you've got a long night in front of you if you think it's cold now."

"That's what I was afraid of."

"Well, hey, we've got the fire and as long as the wind doesn't whip through tonight we can keep it going for a few more hours."

"Uh," Lucas looked confused, "we're not keeping it burning all night?"

"Are you going to stay up all night feeding it?"

Lucas looked around, shaking his head. "I'm not staying alone out here."

"Awe, you need me as much as I need you."

Lucas chuckled through rattling teeth. "Jesus. You're insufferable. Don't you have some recording to do?"

"Not sure I want to," Jared admitted, noticing that his hand rested on his pack, right over the pocket that stored the recorder.

Lucas stopped. Stopped rubbing himself. He wasn't even moving. Instead, Lucas was looking across the fire at him, unblinkingly. "Get back on the bike, Jared."

"What?"

"You fell down," Lucas reasoned, "and got a boo-boo. It's bleeding. It hurts. The bike is lying on its side and the front tire is spinning, but it ain't broke. You didn't bend the frame. The chain didn't fall off. It works. You can still ride it. So, are you going to walk all the way home or are you going to pick up the bike, dust off your boo-boo, and start riding again?"

"It's not that—"

Lucas held up a hand. "Don't finish that sentence, bud. Do not do that to yourself. You're a hell of an investigator. Everyone close to you knows what you have in your possession and, when you go public, the people who care about this, and even a lot of people who don't, are going to be amazed at your accomplishments."

Jared's bitter laugh made Lucas' eyebrows furl. "Some accomplishment."

"Goddamn, you can be stubborn," Lucas threw his hands up. "Stop doing that to yourself."

"Doing what?"

Lucas' laugh was more of a scoff. "Lying out to serve as a doormat to yourself, bud! Jesus, you fucked up. So what? We all do. It's about what you do afterward that matters."

He was right, of course. Jared knew that. Life didn't stop for adults who felt like pouting. It moved on, constant and unforgiving. You either went with it or you didn't, but there was no fighting it; there was no time for petulance.

Jared reached into the pack and pulled out his recorder, nodding at Lucas. He clicked RECORD. "It's been a few days since I last recorded," he started, slowly. "Maria asked me to give her some space, so we haven't been talking. She's in Port Angeles with her family and I ... said goodbye to Molly. That was hard." Lucas cast his head down on the other side of the fire, nodding. He knew how attached Jared was to the dog. "I haven't been contacted by whoever killed her. They're so interested in convincing me to give up this pursuit yet there's no direct contact with me from their end. I sat around the house for two days before getting nothing done finally drove me crazy. That's when I called Lucas and asked him to go on an overnight expedition with me. He accepted."

"Yeah, but I'm not crazy about this," Lucas piped in from across the fire. "It's freakin' cold."

"It's only going to get colder, buddy," Jared warned. "Wait until about 3 a.m. You'll be ready to sleep in your car with the heater cranked."

"Remind me again why I agreed to this."

"Because you're a friend and you knew I'd need good company."

"Remind me to volunteer someone else next time. Man, it gets creepy out here at night."

"What are you worried about? You don't believe in Bigfoot. You've got nothing to fear." Jared knew things were changing for Lucas in that respect but it was still fun to poke him. It cheered him, a little, to do so and if there was anything he needed in his life at the moment it was reasons to smile. Lucas, for his own good measure, even cracked a smile as he poked at the fire with a long stick. The logs popped, small sparks danced up into the night.

"I am worried about bears and wolves."

"You need to read a little more about the area of the country you live in," Jared cajoled. "There aren't any bears or wolves here."

"I watch and analyze videos all-day, every day. I don't think I even remember how to read."

"That would explain so much." Jared was half-joking; not that Lucas was less of an intellectual because he didn't read everything there was to be read but in general sentiment. If everyone spent a few more minutes reading something that wasn't related to their favorite sports team or Hollywood A-lister maybe the world wouldn't be such a horrible place, filled with horrible people who did horrible things to each other. Like kill dogs because you wanted to intimidate someone? There would be more compassion, more empathy; people would work toward the common goal of understanding instead of asserting their view as the solitary one to consider. They would learn about the very real scientific reasons for things existing instead of thinking there was credence in fairy tales and non-traditional practices. Fewer people would suffer, more people would feel empowered to make new discoveries all the time, enriching the world.

"It's creepy out here," Lucas said, looking into the darkness, breaking Jared's rambling thoughts. "I don't know how you do this."

"You get used to it. Stop talking for a second and just listen." Lucas did as requested and the forest's soundtrack fell over the camp. It was thick. Relaxing. A calming blanket of sounds that cleansed the world of the toxin that was human pollution. "See? Isn't it peaceful? Calming?"

"Being out in the middle of the wilderness, in the dark, where predators can see me and I can't see them, is not calming, you twisted ass," Lucas laughed. "Still, it's good to get away and have a few beers with you. It's been a long time."

"It has," Jared said, his thoughts immediately linking the harmless comment to his own thoughts about how little they spent time with each other. Tomorrow was never guaranteed and you should never take for granted those who are important to you, but damn if that wasn't exactly what he was doing and had been doing for too long. It dawned on Jared that Maria wasn't the only one in his life he'd set as a lower priority than Bigfoot. "Don't worry. There'll be more of that soon, after all this is over."

"Determined to press on, huh?" A playful smile hopped across Lucas' mouth, his eyes danced with youthful exuberance.

Jared knew this game. He wasn't going to commit either way, plus he was supposed to be recording. Hadn't Lucas pushed him to start working again? Now he played the role of distractor? *Ah, Lucas, where would I be without the light you bring into my life?* "Don't know right now. I don't want to think about it tonight, to be honest."

The childish delight faded from Lucas' face. "It's all good, bud. I like hearing the sound of my own voice when I'm freaked out. I probably won't shut up all night."

"I'm going to make a hardened hunter out of you yet," Jared quipped.

"And makes it so—" a noise that came from deep in the night cut Lucas off. "What the hell was that?!"

"Shhh!" Jared ordered. He didn't hear the sound clear enough to make it out. The night was young, the banter with his friend was fun, and he was getting back into the flow of recording. He wasn't expecting any action tonight. That wasn't why he'd taken Lucas out here and he wasn't even sure he wanted any action. He wasn't even sure if dealing with another incident was good for him. "Quiet."

Three rhythmic tree knocks rang out, a few hundred yards away, maybe closer.

"We've got company." The ominous statement hung in the air.

"That's not funny."

"I'm not kidding. Shut the hell up." He needed to gauge the distance and he couldn't risk missing it because Lucas was starting to go into panic mode.

A second set of wood knocks came from a different direction but almost as close. "That's Sasquatch. At least two of them."

Aaaaaaaaaaaaaaaaaaaaaaarrrrrrrwwwwwwooooooooo!

Lucas jumped to his feet, the stick he'd been poking the fire with comically extended in front of him like warriors of old. Jared would have laughed if this wasn't so serious and if it didn't remind him of his last expedition. "Jesus. What the hell was that?"

There was only one answer Jared could give his best friend and it would do nothing to comfort him. "Bigfoot,"

Jared kept his voice low. "That one came from over there; that's not where either of the wood knocks came from."

Lucas' forehead wrinkled with worry. "And? What's that mean?"

At least three Bigfoot, in three different directions, was what it meant. Who knew how many there actually were but it was obvious they weren't stationary. And they weren't moving away. "There's at least three of them out there and ... and I think they're trying to surround us."

His comment elicited the panic he expected. "Man, I— are we safe? I—can't—"

"Sit down and stay by the fire," Jared snarled. He had to get control of Lucas before his friend aggravated whatever was out there. "We're not going anywhere. There's no place safer than where we are right now."

Tree branches, high in the air, cracked.

Thump!

A rock landed in the camp ten feet from where Lucas stood. His friend jumped closer to him.

"Shit!" Jared half-squatted, expecting another stone to follow the first one. "Don't move!"

"Wha—who threw that?" Instead of quieting, instead of sitting still, instead of doing anything that Jared needed him to do, Lucas caved to fear. It was becoming absolute. The crazy realization that he'd never get Lucas back out into the woods after this was over broke his own rising fear. Ridiculous at a time like this, but still very real.

Thump!

This time it was he who was the target of a Sasquatch rock toss. The rock missed him by a good twenty feet but it landed and rolled from the opposite direction of the one that struck near Lucas. Coming from at least two sides.

"Jared, are Bigfoot throwing rocks at us?" Lucas' voice shook with disbelief.

He had to stay calm. If he didn't, Lucas was likely to run off into the night and get himself killed. Or provoke the

Bigfoot. "It's an intimidation behavior. A lot of primates do it. They don't want us here."

"The truck. We can get to the—"

Jared opened his hand and made a shushing gesture. "We're not going anywhere. We can't go on a three-mile hike in the dark! We're blind out there."

Aaaaaaaaaaaaaaaaaaaaaaaaaawwwwwwwwwoooooooooooooo!

Lucas' rapid breaths filled the camp. He was getting louder. *He's on the verge of doing something stupid*, Jared, himself, panicked. The Bigfoot intimidation was working. "Calm down. They're not going to bother us if we don't do anything to threaten them. They're still a good distance away so let's not give them a reason to come closer. We're on their land and they're checking us out, making sure that we don't pose some sort of threat to their herd or nest. They are not going to do--"

Lucas choked, covering his mouth and nose with his sleeved elbow. "Oh my god, what's that?"

"Wha—" Jared smelled it. "Shit!"

Through gags, Lucas said, "Uh, that's horrible! Smells like something died."

Caught. He'd tried to protect Lucas from escalating fear but the threshold was crossed. He couldn't very well protect his friend from a mental break if he was about to enter his own. But how did you protect yourself when you were defenseless and about to meet your tormentor? "He's here," Jared croaked. "Bigfoot is here."

Lucas spun around, the stick extended. Jared didn't move. Didn't speak. Didn't even warn his friend to do the same. He couldn't. He was useless and defenseless. He ran through his memory bank, trying to extract any tip he could remember other supposed Bigfoot enthusiasts used during a face-to-face encounter.

Get big.

Get loud.

Bang things.

Show aggression.

Don't show aggression.

Back away.

Run!

Every tactical thought came at once and none of it was probably right. He couldn't even determine if he was thinking about Bigfoot or bear confrontations. "He's close, Lucas. Don't move. Whatever you do. Do not move."

Jared stared into the trees and thick underbrush. There was no chance of seeing anything move in there but there was no mistaking something big in that covered darkness. Tortuously, branches cracked under heavy feet. This wasn't a deer. No raccoons or possums were that pronounced when they moved around. There weren't bears out there. Bias be damned, the only thing that could be moving around out there was a Sasquatch. Jared couldn't be sure if it was attempting to circle them, scout them, or attack them. The slow, plodding footsteps, each measured, gave him the impression that it was being careful. It was the sign of an animal in a defensive posture. But lions on the Savannah also slowly stalked their prey until they were ready to pounce. Jared didn't want to see what a pouncing Bigfoot looked like.

"What was that?" Lucas backed into Jared after a particularly loud crack cut through the night.

"He's right outside the camp, just beyond the firelight," Jared estimated. "We can smell him because they've got well-developed apocrine sweat glands. They excrete when scared or threatened. Stay right there. Don't move." He crept over to his pack.

Lucas' gaze swerved between Jared's action and that wall of darkened green that hid their stalker. "What are you doing?!"

Jared answered by moving closer to Lucas and disengaging the pistol's safety. "I'm getting ready for him if he comes out of those trees." He doubted an M-9 would do anything to a Sasquatch but he hoped against hope that, if nothing else, the shock of being shot and the sound of the pistol firing would scare the damn thing off. And its friends too. He couldn't forget that there was more than this one here. This was a bad idea, a very bad idea. They had a three-mile hike back to where they'd parked. There was nothing but endless, thick green between them and the safety of the truck. No roads. No park rangers. No other adventurous Washingtonians looking to 'get away' for a few days. Just the two friends and a herd of Bigfoot.

"You're going to shoot it?" Lucas' voice rose in pitch in his panicked state.

"Bigfoot are wild animals," Jared tried to reason with him. "I'm not taking any chances."

"Can't you yell at it or wave fire at it? Doesn't that scare bears?"

"This isn't a damn bear!" Jared's focus never left the trees. The crunching footsteps had ceased. "Sasquatch are intelligent creatures, very intelligent. They don't fall for crude tactics. If he comes through those trees, I'm shooting. Be ready."

"For wha—"

A loud pop sounded. Thick. Probably a dead tree. Branches swayed. It was close. The repugnant smell made him gag. He couldn't worry about that now. He had to hold off throwing up long enough to get a clear shot. Nausea began to swarm his mind and he tried to blink it away. Infrasound. Just like in Forks.

"Oh my God!" Lucas swayed, foot-to-foot.

"Shhhh!" Jared snarled. "Do me a favor. Try to listen for his movements. Help me track him."

Muted grunts wafted from behind the brush. This thing was no more than fifteen feet away. Whatever it was, it was definitely aware of their presence and not afraid to move in for a closer look. Or taste.

"Jesus!" Lucas shouted.

Aaaaaaaaaaaaaaaaaaaaaaaaaaaarrrrrrrrrrrrrrrrrrrrrrrrrrrrrrrrrrrr
rooooooooooooooooooo!

Jared jumped. Lucas cowered in place. The beast hiding in the cover howled into the night. Somewhere, deep in his ear canal, inside his brain, pain exploded. Jared covered his ears with both hands, no longer able to aim the gun. If it came out of the woods now they were as good as dead. Jared pulled his hands away; he had to suffer through this. He had to be ready for that thing when it came at them. More cracking branches, faster, louder, sung out to them.

But they were moving away now! The monster was fleeing!

Jared listened, the pistol still aimed at the branches that no longer swayed. It was gone.

He tapped Lucas on the shoulder and stepped back when his friend jumped up, his eyes wide. "He's leaving. Stay still. Let's give him a chance to go find something else to distract him."

Lucas nodded and they waited as the thundering footsteps faded into the night.

"Oh my God," Lucas exhaled, probably for the first time in minutes, his voice still shaking with the surge in adrenaline. "I ... I can't believe this."

"We're going to need to take turns on watch tonight ... just in case," Jared warned. They weren't going to be clear of the danger until the morning, at least.

"Don't worry about that, I'm not going to be able to sleep at all," Lucas answered, "I don't know how or why you do this. Are you sure we can't make it back to the truck?"

But Jared wasn't paying attention to him, his thoughts were elsewhere. "Hmmm?" he asked, only realizing after a moment what Lucas said. "No. We're not trying that. Too dangerous and, away from the firelight, they may not be so averse to inspecting us a bit more closely. Get some sleep. First light is going to come early and when it does, we're out of here."

They had to get out of there. Not because Jared feared the Sasquatch coming back in the morning with a larger herd. If they were going to do anything it was going to be now. No, they had to get back because he needed to get Lucas home before the man had a breakdown.

And he needed to finish his business.

Now or never.

He didn't even hear Lucas' reply.

His mind was a world away, focused on one goal.

This was going to end.

20

The desire to close this chapter of Jared's life didn't fade with distance from the campsite. The next morning, life arose at a snail's pace, in large part to a night of lousy sleep. Once they started packing the camp they did so with an urgency inspired by trauma. The hike back to the truck was too fast, unsafe. Neither of them spoke so they had plenty of adrenaline-fueled energy to draw from.

Jared had never seen Lucas move as quickly as he did during the trek back to the truck. He was a man on a mission; a mission to save himself from an unseen monster. Conflicted and confused, Jared reflected on the previous night's incident as they hiked. In the heat of the moment of being surrounded by what was probably a small herd of Sasquatch, he had been afraid. There was no doubt, had that thing come out of the underbrush at them, he would have unloaded the entire clip into its body. But it didn't. It didn't even try and it sure as hell didn't give them any indication that it wanted to. What it did do was display an intellectual curiosity. He wasn't going to let its aggressiveness cloud the perception he had in the clear light of day. It could have attacked them if it wanted to, out of fear or predatory instincts, but it didn't.

He saw it now.

Everything that happened on the expedition with Lucas, everything those creatures displayed, was peaceful. The animal was as afraid as he and Lucas had been. And they were as much of a non-threat as the pair of humans camped out in their terrain.

It was time to re-evaluate everything. To step back and analyze; to challenge everything he thought he knew about Sasquatch, their habitat, and their habits. He wasn't the expert he thought he was. But he would be. He would get to the truth of this. And he'd do it before anyone else was able to construct the narrative. Bigfoot's story needed to be told. He knew where to go now; there wouldn't be any more running around the Olympics, scattering to the four winds, hoping to trip across a herd.

The hotspot was his.

He would get the evidence the world demanded.

He needed to do it justice.

*****

Jared spent a few days collecting himself, his thoughts, and evidence and then got to work developing a new plan.

He stood in front of the corkboard in his make-shift office. It had been Maria's, part of her 'creative space', as she called it. When she left, she took only a portion of the things she needed from the office. Without a home of her own yet she had no place to put the desk, chair, drafting table and the such, so the room still felt like her room. It was his least favorite place in the house because it reminded him of her. Over the past four days, though, he spent more time in here than he had in all the months she'd been gone, going over and over his plan, making sure he had the resources to pull it off, along with his personal concerns being appropriately addressed. He was preparing for the big push.

The final push.

Now or never.

Tacked notes of things accomplished and tasks still needing to be done filled the corkboard, all of them just as important as the other. In a very small way, he was grateful Maria was gone; there was a lot he didn't want her to see. The Bigfoot stuff? He wouldn't keep any of that from her. The gear he was going to need to pack, the dates and places he was going to check out and follow up on now that he had the herd's location narrowed down so finely? He'd be more than happy to share that too. But it was the other stuff, the information he noted in a completely separate column on the side of the cork board, that he wouldn't want her to see.

Just in case, he reminded himself. That's all it's there for.

Jared's eyes danced across the information in front of him, trying to think of anything he might have left out. He set the recorder down on the drafting table, satisfied that he'd captured everything he'd need Lucas to do, took out his cell phone and snapped a picture of the board. He swiped through his contacts, finding Lucas' name, and sent the image with the message:

Just in case. Thanks, buddy.

Lucas would know what it was for. After last night, he understood.

Jared stood in front of the board for another few minutes, studying this plan to find Bigfoot or die trying. Then he sighed, his shoulders lifting and falling, almost mechanically. He would trade anything in the world, hand this information over to someone else and let them be the hero who made the discovery of the century if it meant he could have Maria back in his life.

He leaned down and retrieved the recorder, his thumb caressing the RECORD button, and walked out of the room, pausing at the doorway. The corkboard contained all his knowledge, notes and his destiny. He smiled to himself.

Alone.

In this empty house.

That was going to change, one way or another.

And it was time to change in the only way he knew how.

Now or never.

Jared switched off the light and pulled the door closed.

The sound of the deadbolt clicking into place echoed, floating down the empty hallway like the tormenting ghost of a bygone life.

*****

Maria.

Jared closed his eyes, for a second, because he was at a stoplight and could afford the visual break from the world. It could kiss his ass. Cutting off the world made it easier to remember her smell. Here, in the sightless depths of his mind, she became much clearer. Here he could remember the softness of her skin and the smell of her hair when he would nuzzle into her during one of their now-distant cuddling sessions. It was getting harder and harder to recall the little things, important things. Even with the investigation picking up, forcing them to remain involved with each other on some level, the times they did see each other were fewer and fewer. And since Molly, there'd been relatively nothing between them.

She was fading.

He needed her to want him again.

A horn blared. Jared snapped open his eyes. The light was green. He waved an apology to the impatient Olympian behind him and took off. There was still hope. All he needed right now was that, to know that she wasn't gone, that she hadn't closed off her world from him. Maria wasn't that type of person in general. She would let her worst enemy, if she had one; use her for and not bat an eye. Maria's willingness to forgive and forget had been a central point of their arguments over the years when Jared felt like she was being taken advantage of. Maria always told him it didn't matter, that she would give if someone was in need. That was the way she was. It was one of the simple, yet complex, things about her that he'd fallen in love with all those years ago. It was one of her attributes that frustrated and overjoyed him, sometimes at the same time. Maria was a giver and he was grateful for it because he was a failure of a husband. And if husbands like him needed anyone in their lives, it was a spouse who could forgive and a friend who would kick ass when the situation called for it. In Maria, he had both.

His thoughts raced back to the first note card he put on the corkboard after returning from the expedition with Lucas. He was going to make right with Maria, first and foremost. And the only way he could do that was by opening up to her about his father. He led off with an apology, but he'd already apologized a thousand times, and when you apologize that often they start losing their impact. They both knew that and he respected her too much to hope that a simple apology would make everything disappear. He had to do the heavy lifting. She needed to know that he had dealt with his past and she was right to make that demand. For years he'd made excuse after excuse about why he couldn't deal with his father's memory. He could write a book to instruct others on how to rationalize like a pro and not take responsibility for the damage their past could do on their future. He could teach thousands and make millions with his tactics on skirting issues and working in denial. He'd become too good at it; good enough to become numb to the true cost of letting his father's ghost linger.

Jared chuckled. Thinking about the unique feminine huskiness of her voice. The hint of a pleased tone when he admitted to her, over the phone, like a true coward, that he'd made his admission to the world. Even to himself. She'd sounded cautiously pleased to hear he'd recorded it for the podcast. It was a huge step and she knew that, to willingly admit his most vulnerable family secret to whoever bothered to listen to his podcast. But when he broke down and she waited for him to be able to go on, they turned a corner. Jared felt it. It was there in the silence and in her voice when she finally responded. She hurt because he hurt. This wasn't about manipulation, it was the wall finally coming down, crumbling from an adulthood of neglect and painting over cracks instead of patching them up. The wall of shame crumbled and the light of a future shone through when she thanked him for opening himself like that. Thanked him! After everything he'd put her through, she thanked him.

Even now, days later, Jared was stunned. Who was he to deserve her gratitude? Yet, she'd expressed it. Only with great reluctance did he accept it. But in that moment of exchange of vulnerability, unfettered understanding, and compassion, Jared learned what true love was. They made a conscious decision to put off having children. Work, careers, and monsters roaming the Pacific Northwest, consumed them. Kids weren't in the picture from the very beginning, not until they were ready. They wanted them, it just wasn't the time. It was never the time. People often said you don't know love until you become a parent, but Jared could argue he already knew it in Maria's display. It shook him.

A lover. A best friend. And, now, a teacher.

Maria was everything.

And he still had so much to learn.

The chance lingered in the forefront of his mind, encasing every thought. They had a date scheduled for that night. It wasn't to talk about the separation or the terms of the divorce. There was no agenda.

Jared smiled as he took the exit off the highway, feeling the surge of energy coursing through his chest. His heart rate quickened. He was coming to the end of something big, he could feel it, and he had a chance. He still had a chance. The most wonderful woman in the world told him she wasn't going anywhere and that their physical separation wasn't an emotional one. She hadn't even asked about him signing the papers!

He dared not look in the rearview mirror lest he see the goofy man nearing middle age smiling like a teenage boy with his first real love.

Instead, Jared figured he could get some work done. He grabbed the recorder, wanting to capture his thoughts because anything could happen. Peter had left a message about needing to see him. Supposedly he had important news. Jared listened to the message three times. There was something in Peter's voice, something his friend wasn't saying. It was something big.

Jared drove to Peter's reflecting on all he'd put so many people through. Was this what it was like for all those successful people? Did they get there on the backs of hidden figures who sacrificed so much but didn't enjoy any of the rewards that came along with accomplishment, except for the knowledge that they were associated with the person in the limelight? Jared didn't think he'd ever get that kind of status and didn't even want it. The world didn't care that much about an undiscovered primate. But there would be attention if his hunch was right. Talk television appearances. Even a book. And he didn't want any of that if it meant the people he cared about most were hurt, unintentionally or otherwise.

Before he could knock on Peter's door a second time it was yanked open. Jared jumped, stepping back out of instinct and trying to laugh off his fright. "Little excited?"

"Come in, Jared," Peter said. "Hurry."

He stepped in cautiously, half-expecting there to be an intervention on the other side of the door. *Hi Jared, we're all your friends and we love you, but this Bigfoot stuff has gotten out of hand and it's starting to affect us. We care about you so we wanted to ...*

"What's up, man? The message?"

"Huh," Peter moved stacks of paper, searching for something.

"Peter," Jared barked. When his friend looked up, he asked, "Is everything okay?"

"Yes, why?" Peter moved folders, loose papers, searching.

"Jesus, Peter, stop," Jared ordered, surprised by the shock on Peter's face when he turned around, holding a twelve-inch stack of loose papers that threatened to crumble out of his hands.

Peter blinked, once. Slowly. He carefully set the untidy stack on the table he had just pulled it from. "No, everything is fine. Good, in fact."

"So it's been quiet?

"I don't know what happened, but I haven't heard a peep since I asked you to stop the investigation."

That was strange. Unsettling. "Weird," he swallowed back the lurking worry.

"Doesn't mean I'm still not asking you to stop, though. I hope you haven't forgotten that." Before Jared could respond, Peter was on to his next question. "By the way, how are things with Maria?"

Peter was all over the place, as usual. But Jared expected this. Peter wouldn't let it go until Jared gave him what he wanted. He'd have to wait a lifetime and a half for that to happen. "I'll let you know in a few days. We're getting together tonight to talk. I don't want to fill in any blanks when it comes to us."

"Can you blame her?" Peter responded, that evidence-based, scientific mind was always such a counterbalance to

Jared's visceral perspective on life. "It's not like this is normal or easy. Hell, your dog was killed right in front of her. How does anyone process something like that?" He finally sat down, pulling the empty chair next to him a little closer. "I get where she's at. I've only recently started to feel okay again. Getting confronted by those thugs rattled me; I can only imagine how scary it was for her. Someone doesn't want you carrying on your work and, sorry, but it's dangerous to be associated with you right now."

Ouch.

"Then why am I here?" He couldn't hide the hurt but regretted it as soon as it was expressed. The local brewery's coaster sitting in front of him became a focal point. He shifted it around with a finger, sliding it this way and that. "Sorry. I didn't mean to sound like that. I'm a little stressed."

Or am I overwhelmed?

The tease was there again. *Cut yourself free. Let go of all this, of everything. Start fresh, Jared; start fresh. Now or never.*

Peter reached across the table and grabbed Jared's wrist. It was uncharacteristically intimate. "Jared, we're friends. We go way back. I don't give up on friends, even if I have to keep them at a distance from time to time."

He wanted to pull away but thought better of it. For Peter to touch him was a big risk. Peter didn't ever show that level of intimacy with anyone, explaining his bachelor status well into his early forties. Jared didn't want to jar him and send the wrong signals that Peter's warmth was something repulsive. He was rooting for Peter, after all; at some point, the man had to slow down on the science and enjoy the pleasures of having a woman in his life, right? "I know. It's appreciated."

The tender moment didn't last. Peter drew his hand away and stood, slapping his thigh as he did. "Well, I've got something that might excite you. An email. Came in from an organizational box. Some small company out of Port Angeles." He brought his laptop over to the table, spinning it around so Jared could see the screen. Peter opened his email and Jared wasn't shocked to see the inbox filled with unread messages – one thousand one hundred and eighty-three, to be exact. Peter scanned with his finger to help him move through the list. A few days of organization—a few weeks—would do wonders for Peter's schedule if he'd allow someone to take care of the administrative parts of his life. "Looks like they have about fifty employees so there's no telling who sent it without doing some digging ... and that's out of my lane."

"Plus it puts people at unnecessary risk." It wasn't meant to be passive aggressive, he wanted Peter to know that he was cognizant of all the trouble he'd caused. "What did it say?"

Now Peter was sitting up straight, scrolling through the email and attempting to open an attachment. He kept missing the file in his hurry to open it. "That's the thing. It had an attachment, an mp3. Let me play it. You'll like it."

Jared laughed when Peter misclicked another three times before finally launching his computer's media player, punching the VOLUME UP button repeatedly, even though the computer already showed that it was at one-hundred percent. The file began to play and Jared leaned closer. There were natural sounds, crickets forming the sound bed. A slight wind. Jared closed his eyes. Cutting off visual senses helped him concentrate on the auditory. An owl hooted a few times. More wind. The file stopped. When he heard nothing more he opened his eyes and looked at Peter, who was sitting up straight, his eyes wide and a broad smile announcing his thoughts.

"I don't get it. Night sounds?" he said. "Did I miss something?"

Peter winked at him. He actually winked at him. "Let me play the second version for you. I had a friend take the one you just heard and isolate the sound I want you to hear." He closed the email and opened his files window, searched for what seemed like an eternity, and then quadruple-clicked the file.

This time, though, the sound was muted, which Jared didn't understand. It was actually harder to hear whatever it was that Peter wanted him to hear. If this was supposed to be easier, Peter missed the mark. If it was the same exact file it sounded like someone was playing it under water. The audio was horrible. What was he missing?

"Listen here," Peter was smiling." You'll pick it out, no problem."

Jared doubted that. This file was—

Then he heard it. His breath caught and he scooted forward in his chair. Jesus.

A Sasquatch whistle. Not a howl. A nice, clean whistle. Crystal clear. Whoever the friend was who cleaned the file up, they were a master. Somehow all the background sounds were muted, isolating what he hadn't been able to hear before. The whistle of the Sasquatch popped out as clear as if they were standing right there, a few hundred yards from it.

"That's remarkable! Authentic?"

"Yep," Peter nodded. "I trust this guy and he said he has no idea what made that sound, but whatever it is, the file is legit. The signals, pitch, all outside the human scale. It isn't one of us."

Jared already knew that but figured Peter was fascinated by that fact, which made sense with the uber-skeptical view of the world Peter operated under. He didn't want to be a barrier to Peter exploring the possibilities but, he also wasn't going to give Peter room to avoid the obvious. "You and I both know what that was." It was time for Peter to buy in; the evidence was there. Peter had seen it, heard it, and touched it. Jared wasn't asking for him to name the creature, he wanted him to finally admit that there was something out in the Olympics that wasn't on the anthropologic record.

"Did this anonymous emailer happen to mention where they recorded it?"

"Near the Elwha Ranger Station on Olympic Hot Springs Road," Peter answered.

"A ranger?"

Peter grimaced, not out of anger but confusion, and closed the file, turning the computer away and closing the lid. "I doubt it," he answered. "It came from some sales office in a small business. Wouldn't be a ranger, unless they work there part-time or a friend is covering."

"That makes sense," Jared said. Then it hit him. "Wait a second. The Olympic Hot Springs Road? The emailer claimed it came from near there?"

"Yes. Why?"

Another piece of the puzzle! "That's not even five miles from Whiskey Bend. That's where I was with Lucas the other night!" One more conclusive piece of information that was pointing to the pot of gold at the big, hairy end of the primate rainbow! This was where Sasquatch was and Jared was the only one in the world who had so much evidence pointing at the same conclusion! The only one.

Now or never, right?

"I need to get going."

He was up, grabbing his keys and heading to the door, before Peter could finish his sentence, "Wait, Jared! I thought you were going to—"

Jared waved over his shoulder as the door clicked closed.

21

The house was stuffy after being closed up for so long. Jared's fault. That didn't change the fact that it stunk and he was going to have to freshen it up soon. Maria's attachment to the house was strong and he didn't want to give her any thoughts that he was deliberately, or otherwise, neglecting it like he had their relationship.

Jared grabbed a few towels out of the hall closet, laying one on the sill and the other on the carpet underneath the window before cracking it open. It wasn't much, but it would help air out the house without coming home to thousands of dollars of water damage.

The half-packed bag sat on the bed, demanding his attention. The packing was slow going because he tried to record in between trips to the drawers and closet. Jared laughed at his own ridiculousness, before hastily selecting the rest of what he needed and zipping up the suitcase. It needed to be done, he needed to go. The next step needed to come.

The sun was bright and promising. The air was clear of the typical muskiness this part of the world blanketed its inhabitants with. Jared drew a deep breath. He opened the car, the slight warmth drifting out onto his bare arms. Jared threw the bag in the passenger seat. "It's a beautiful day for a drive though. That'll take my mind off sitting through slow—"

He never saw the attack coming. He never noticed the car parked at the edge of his property; the car that didn't belong in this neighborhood. It was too expensive—a black Bentley Continental, with blackened windows. No one in this neighborhood drove something like that. One minute he was throwing his bag into the passenger seat and the next his face was pressed against the warm metal car roof, a forceful hand wrapped in his hair while something small, circular, pressed against the small of his back.

"What the fuck?!" He tried to struggle. The object in his back pressed forcefully against him.

Click.

"Shut up," a gruff voice snarled, close to his ear. "I'm doing the talking."

"Who the hell are you?" Jared asked, his question muffled by having his face pressed against the roof that was beginning to burn his skin. A strange sense of relief rushed through him. This was the coward who threatened Maria and Peter, and who had killed Molly, and this bastard didn't have the balls to square up to him. He had to wait in hiding and attack from behind. *True courage, you fuckers. Let me get loose. Let me get one fucking opportunity. That's all I need.*

"It doesn't matter, does it?" the gruff voice responded. "Uh, uh. The only thing that matters is that you hear me nice and clear. Got it? You're going to stop this little child's play of yours. There are people who aren't happy with your insistence to keep going with your work, even after we've made it very, very clear that it'd be wise to stop. You're making serious enemies, Mr. Strong, enemies that are powerful and have a vested interest in what you're doing. They've been watching you and hoping you were smart enough to stop while you still could, before they needed to stop you. Consider this your last warning."

Jared's back exploded in pain as the man's fist slammed into him. His chin slammed against the roof of the car as he collapsed. He tried to reach for the door frame. If he could get ahold of that he could catch his assaulter unaware. They'd see who was going to get what they wanted out of this after slamming the man's head in the door a few times.

But the chance didn't come. As Jared was still slumping from the first blow, still trying to catch his breath, which had been robbed from him with the unexpected violence, another blow came. He grunted when the fist connected with his side. His focus shifted there. He couldn't think about strategy or about what he could do to defend himself. All he could do was think about how much it hurt. Then the man hit him again and he fell to the ground.

Another kick. Jared curled, trying to cover as many of his vital organs as he could. There was no chance to launch any sort of counter-attack. He had to salvage all that he could now.

Opening his eyes consumed the fleeting energy he had left as his body resisted the blows and kicks. When he did, he saw the underside of the truck, thinking for a second that he could roll under it and buy himself some time. But that didn't work in reality. His attacker had a gun, the awareness, and the lack of pain Jared didn't get to enjoy. Even if he rolled under the truck it would only delay the inevitable. And likely piss off his attacker enough to push the man over the edge and shoot him. But the man wasn't letting him up. This man planned on killing him.

But then, as Jared was sure he was going to die on the concrete slab of his driveway, outside the home he and Maria had shared for a decade, the punches and kicks stopped coming.

"We mean it, Mr. Strong," the voice was distant now. "This is your last chance."

Jared didn't have the strength to roll over to check the location of his attacker. He was going to live! That's what mattered. The fact that the voice sounded more distant wasn't important; drawing another breath was. He had shit to live for!

A car door slammed. An engine revved, pebbles and dirt were kicked up by spinning tires. A car faded into the neighborhood. He only hoped it was the thug's car because he was having trouble breathing and wasn't sure if he was going to be able to stand up and get help if it was just some passer-by. Where the hell is my cellphone? He slowly reached behind him to feel his pocket. Not there. His watery eyes didn't provide enough information. No shadows or movement. Was someone still there, still behind him. His pulse thumped in his ears, depriving him of most of his senses he needed to determine if he was safe or not.

So he waited and tried to catch his breath.

No more punches or kicks or threats rained down on him from the unseen assailant.

Jared risked rolling over and taking a foot square to the face. Relief was the only thing to fall on him when he saw the rising hill of his front yard, the long and neglected grass waving in the wind. He was alone. Now he could get up, regain his composure and see if anything was broken.

Nothing was.

He reached for the armrest on the door and pulled himself up. Everything hurt. Catching his breath was difficult. His cheek burned. And though his ribs weren't broken, drawing deeper breaths was difficult. He stood up, stretching and wincing at the sharp pain that cinched down his side.

The black Bentley was nowhere. Whoever assaulted him was gone, their identity still protected. They still had all the advantages. And now, because he hadn't quit searching for Bigfoot, they were upping their game. Their earlier threats went unheard so they were going to help him understand what was expected of him.

To give up the chase.

He stretched. Drawing another painful breath. At least he was breathing. He needed to get inside. Not having something to lean against made the going difficult, but he was careful, measuring each step. He didn't need to face-plant and crack open his skull, but the way the ground underneath him shifted, rose and fell, made putting one foot in front of the other a challenge. He tried to open the door but the adrenaline surging through his body made it difficult. The key ring caught on a loose thread as he tried to pull them out of his pocket to unlock the door. Even when he achieved freedom for the keys, he couldn't seem to aim it at the lock. His shaking hand missed the key slot for the third time. On a deeper level, his survival instinct forced him to check behind him every few seconds, worried that the scumbag who'd attacked him would come back to finish the job.

But every time he looked he only saw tall grass waving at him, reminding him he was going to get written up by his home owner's association.

He slid the key into the lock.

Click.

Finally.

He went straight to the bathroom to clean up and change, taking in his torn shirt and filthy jeans. A flushed skin stared back at him. Beyond that, there was little other evidence of what he'd just been through. Except for the fire that burned inside him. He was going to find out who that was. His assailant could have been the one threatening him all along, but from what he remembered—it was all so clouded now—Jared didn't think that was the case. The guy who'd treated him like a human piñata was working for someone else, Jared was sure of it. A thug didn't have the pull, the influence, to move and shake a number of distinct players. A thug was the muscle, not the brains. No, there was someone else involved.

But who?

And what did that mysterious person want? Why did they insist on remaining anonymous? What were they protecting?

Once he finished cleaning up, Jared realized he'd left the house while recording and the recorder had been running through the entire assault. He was going to publish this. This wasn't child's play; it had never been for him. The world needed to hear the lengths rival investigators were willing to go to in order to be the first to prove Bigfoot's existence. Or to stop their rivals from doing it.

It wasn't extreme, it was reality.

But he waited to record until he was away from the house. He was vulnerable here and didn't want to be around if they decided to come back. Olympia was well behind him before he put the recorder to his lips again. This was humiliating but necessary.

"I didn't stay in the driveway for long," Jared recorded. "As soon as those thugs pulled away, I got up and got the hell away from the house. I didn't want to be around if they decided to come back and finish what they started. I have no idea who these guys are. I'm not even sure who these people are who have a vested interest in what I'm doing. I'm looking for a goddamn animal! Why would that matter to anyone?" His fists rotated over the hard plastic of the steering wheel, rotating over and back, over and back. "I want to get to Maria."

*****

Three hours later he pulled into Port Angeles.

The winding road between Olympia and his destination was only dotted with traffic and he took full advantage of it, driving it as fast as his truck could handle the curves. Lost in thinking about the assault, in the trail of thought that had him reverse-engineering who could be behind this, Jared lost sense of time and speed limits. As fortune would have it, though, he pulled into Port Angeles without the needless loss of time and hit to the wallet a speeding ticket would have created.

He waited to text Maria until he was already at the restaurant. It might not have been a fair tactic, but he needed some time to compose himself before he saw her. No more lying, no more hiding facts from her. She deserved everything he could give her. That meant not treating her like she couldn't handle the darker side of his work.

Now or never.

"Hi Jared," her smile faded when she saw his face. "What's wrong? What happened?"

How does she constantly do this? She sees everything.

"Babe," he hugged her. When she wrapped her arms around him he felt ... safe, safe enough to risk kissing her on the cheek before sitting down.

She sat opposite of him, her face washed of any emotion as she waited for him to answer. He wasn't going to draw this out. Instead, he recalled the events of the afternoon, starting with Peter and slowly preparing her for what happened at the house. Her lips quivered, her forehead wrinkled, eyes watered, but she listened all the way through. Over and over again, as he quietly shared the details of the strange day, she grabbed his hand, squeezing at the point when he described the assault. When she began to cry he stopped to give her a moment to process everything he was laying at her feet. She dabbed her eyes with a napkin and told him to keep going. And he did.

He told her everything, including how he thought the man who attacked him was intent on killing him. And Maria soldiered on along with him, consuming every detail as he shared it.

"What happens now?" Her question wasn't one he was prepared to answer or for her to ask. There were a million unspoken messages behind it he was attempting to translate. And that was exactly what he wasn't supposed to be doing.

"I don't know," he answered. "I haven't thought that far."

"What?!" she slapped the table. "Jared, this is crazy. Why didn't you call the police?"

He couldn't lie to her. "I—I don't know. I ..."

She grabbed his hand and squeezed, hard. "What?" Her eyes pleaded with him to keep going. He couldn't deny that her encouragement had an effect. It was like she recognized his vulnerability, as meager as it was. Trying to open up was formidable. No longer treating her like an afterthought was imperative.

Because she's not. She never was. You have to prove that to her, you idiot.

"I just wanted to get to you," he croaked. "I needed to see you. It sounds juvenile, I know, but the only thing I could think of was you and I knew if I called the cops I'd be held by them all day. I didn't want that. I wanted to be with you."

"Okay, Jared," her voice lost all heat. The worry was still there in the wavering tones, but so was the kindness and understanding that made Maria the incredible woman she was. "Forget you and me and what we're going through; think about Peter, Molly ... you. These people are serious. This isn't some game of prank callers or kids vandalizing something. These are grown men capable of hurting you."

"I know how serious this is."

"Do you?" she pleaded. "Do you really understand how far this has gone now?"

This was a critical moment for them, not just him as a professional or a man, or even a contributing member of society; it was a critical moment that would define what they were going to be. And, right now, he needed to do what he could to determine that course. He was done letting fate do it for him. "I'm almost done. I'm so close."

Maria let go of his hand. "You've got to be kidding me?" she exclaimed. The couple at the nearby table glanced over, concern mixed with invasive lust for juicy drama. "You're still insisting on pursuing this? You're willing to give up everything for some ... legend?"

He could have exploded. He could have said something hurtful in return. But he didn't. She knew it was more than a legend. She'd walked this path with him for more than half the time he'd been investigating this animal. It was her basement that had been overrun by boxes of gear and evidence. It was her kitchen table that had been taken over on far more than a few occasions by grown men planning a weekend in the woods. She had seen all the evidence he brought back from those expeditions. She knew Bigfoot was so much more than a legend; she was hurt and frustrated and lashing out. He had to understand that and be patient.

Or I could lose her forever.

"Please keep your voice down," he reached for her hand. She let him take it.

"I'd ask you to stop, to stop for us ... but ..."

"Is there even an us to stop for?"

"I love you," she looked down at his hand encasing hers. Then she slid hers away. Before his heart shattered, Maria wrapped her fingers around his this time. "You make it hard, but I love you. None of this changes any of that. You think I don't know that you're struggling right now? You're not doing this for your ego. You're not doing it to get rich or famous. I know that." Her tone lowered and she looked from their intertwined hands to his eyes. "You need closure and this is the only way you're going to get it."

"So you're okay with me finishing?"

"I'm not okay with any of it," Maria admitted tenderly. "Somewhere out there is a normal life waiting for us. I'm rooting against you, but only because I'm being selfish.

You're not the only one struggling with this, you know? If I ask you to stop you'll never get the closure you need and what does that say about me? But if I give up and let you keep going ... I worry what will happen to you."

Tears welled up in her eyes. Jared reached across the small table with his free hand and, with this thumb, wiped the tear. "I'm close, babe," he leaned in and offered her an encouraging smile. "I'm really close."

Maria gripped his hand putting on the same brave smile she did every time something in life upset her but she didn't allow to deter her from whatever course she had set. "I'm sure you are. You've been getting closer, year after year. You've put a lot into your work."

"Lucas and I went on an expedition and had a Sasquatch almost in our camp. It was close enough to smell it."

"What?!"

"It was right outside our camp," he nodded. "There were some wood knocks and a couple of different calls. Then they started throwing rocks at us. There had to be at least three of them. That's when we smelled it. It was ... terrifying. I could hear it walking around outside the firelight like it was scouting us. I know where they are, Maria! I'm so close to getting credible evidence. So close I can taste it. Then ... then I can walk away."

She was silent for a few seconds, making him doubt his assuredness. Was being open with her a bad idea? Could the truth scare her away from something she'd already lived through? But Maria didn't stay silent for long. She nodded once, sharply. "Okay," she smiled. "Okay. I'm here for you, no matter what."

"Here for me but not with me?"

The strong smile faded, like the way a light bulb's glow gives over to a dark room when it's turned off. "I can't promise something I'm not sure I can give you. For all I know you could be doing this for another year or another ten. There's no telling. The reason I left in the first place was that I needed to get on with my life. You know that. And that hasn't changed. I'm sorry."

"Maria, you have nothing to apologize for. The apologies are all mine. I'm going to make this up to you."

"After you've found Bigfoot?"

He couldn't be mad at her for wanting to know what her place in the world was. Resisting that would be a backward step and he was only moving forward from now on. "What do you say? Let's enjoy lunch and talk about something else." It might have been a cowardly way to answer but since when hadn't that been his modus operandi? Change was slow. He could only work on so many things at once.

She's not stupid. She knew the answer before she even asked the question. Was that the point? Had asking just been a test? A test he failed?

"Okay," her voice betrayed her surrender. Her smile was devoid of joy. "It does smell good."

They picked up their menus and took forever to decide what to eat. Jared imagined it was because she was hiding behind hers as much as he used his as a tri-fold barrier. He didn't care about anything he saw on those plastic pages, none of the deliberately-designed pictures did anything for his appetite. He was tired of hurting her.

So tired of all of this.

22

Jared pulled the hotel door closed with a yank. He'd only left the room once during the night, to get ice, and the door wasn't level, making it impossible to close without creating a racket for any of the nearby rooms. He was sure he shook more than a few walls when he pulled hard to get it to lock. The door wasn't the only problem with the hotel; the carpet stank like it'd been drenched in water and the staff left it to air dry. The room he paid for was a non-smoking room but the aroma told him that the room's past occupants, probably stretching back decades, ignored that rule. There were fourteen cable channels, three of which were those over-the-top Christian channels where some charlatan spent ninety percent of the time telling whoever watched that crap that "God" needed them to send money or His work couldn't be done. Jared had a good idea who the true 'Him' was and it had nothing to do with a heavenly spirit.

He checked out and then stopped by a shack situated in the front corner of the hotel parking lot that served as a coffee shop. It was the same formulaic coffee you could buy at any one of the four million coffee houses throughout Washington State. Nothing special, but it sure as hell beat drinking the hotel coffee offering, and it also made the winding drive out to the Elwha Ranger Station more tolerable.

It was a drive he didn't want to make, no matter how gorgeous and inspiring it was. Moreover, he was completely and thoroughly jaded. It never used to be like this. He had the Elwha River on one side and mountainous slopes rising up to touch the sky on the other. He should be happy.

But he wasn't.

Even as he closed in on the person who emailed the mysterious Sasquatch whistle file Peter had shared with him. One of the rangers had to know something about it, even why it was sent from a small business' email account. He had a feeling that was a cover. Someone was protecting themselves, nothing more. And there was damn good reason to be protective; that recording was amazing and there was likely more to the story behind the small sample he heard. Even though this should have excited him, coming out here, being so close to Whiskey Bend and Hurricane Ridge, leaving Maria behind was the last thing he wanted to do at this point.

But to put this entire thing to rest, for the rest of his life, he had to follow his intuition. Coming back out here was the right thing to do because this was where the Sasquatch was. What he didn't tell Maria, what he couldn't tell her, was that he wasn't coming back out of the mountains until he did.

He couldn't break her heart like that.

*****

The Elwha Ranger Station was a tiny building located at the front of the property bordering the Olympic Hot Springs Road. At first, Jared doubted he had the right location. He'd driven by this spot a number of times over the years, even during his recent trips with Lucas and his own trip to Hurricane Ridge, and never noticed the building. It was that irrelevant.

But if it led to more information on who submitted that recording it would end up being the most important visit into irrelevance he'd ever made.

Jared walked up the steps and opened the door, part of him still unsure he wasn't walking into someone's house. There was a small desk inside which looked older than the woman sitting behind it. She was on the good side of thirty, her dark hair pulled back in a tight bun. She offered a warm smile to accompany her surprised expression. "Hi," Jared said, failing to close the door like a respectful human, wincing when it slammed. "Sorry about that. I hope I'm in the right spot."

The ranger smiled, unoffended by his action, and came around the side of the desk, her uniform betraying the fact that she was in excellent shape. Jared hadn't seen a uniform that well maintained and cared for in a long time. This woman took her appearance seriously. "You might be," she still smiled. "How can I help you?"

Jared scratched his head. "This is going to sound strange," he started, "but I'm looking for someone."

"Here?" She couldn't hide her surprise.

Her name tag read McCoy. "Yes, Officer McCoy, I think the person I need to find might be here."

She looked around the small office and then held her hands out to her sides. "As you can see, I'm it, so I hope I can help you or you're in trouble."

Jared laughed when he realized she was being playful. "Trust me, trouble is my closest companion."

"Well," McCoy pointed a finger at him, "leave it out in your vehicle. I've got a walkie-talkie somewhere and I know how to use it."

"They teach you that in ranger school?" Jared teased.

"Yep," she stuck her chest out a little further, "We don't pass unless we can make at least three dangerous weapons out of it." She laughed. It was a light, almost flirtatious, laugh. "But I'm not sure what I can do for you. We don't get many people stopping by here and those who do are usually interested in how much longer they have to go until they get to where they're going. I've got travel times down to a science."

"Well, in that, you have no worries. I know exactly where I'm going, just not sure who I need to speak with before I get there." When she didn't say anything he continued, "A colleague of mine—" with no idea who this woman was or who she was connected with, he wasn't going to name Peter as a friend. No more trusting anyone outside of his small circle "—received something interesting in an email and I'm trying to track down the sender."

That composed, friendly expression flickered but then was gone as soon as it appeared. "Okay, still not a whole lot to go on."

"This is going to sound weird."

"Try me," McCoy crossed her arms before untucking one and indicating the small room with a lateral sweeping gesture. "In case you didn't pick up on it, we don't usually have a lot going on around here."

Jared laughed. "My fr—my colleague received a recording of something the sender claimed came from out here, near Hurricane Ridge." No changes in her expression, not even subtle ones.

"Mister?"

"Jared, please."

"Well, Jared, we're surrounded by national forest. There's all kinds of weird sounds, all the time."

"Yes," he laughed, "I guess that would be true. These sounds, they were from a species I'm investigating."

"Investigating, huh?" she raised her eyebrows and returned to her desk. "Have a seat, Jared. Would you like anything to drink?"

"No thanks," he said, sitting.

"You don't mind if I do, do you?" McCoy was grabbing her thermos even as she was asking for his opinion. "So entertain me. I'm bored and this sounds interesting. What is it you're investigating?"

"You wouldn't believe me."

"Try me." Still polite, but there was a hint to her response that told him she was only going to entertain this conversation for so long.

"Bigfoot," he said, almost apologetically.

McCoy flinched, quickly covering it. "Bigfoot?" she said, very slowly, like she was trying to be careful to annunciate each syllable.

"Yes," he kept his tone light, "Sasquatch. Bigfoot. Ape Man. Yeti. Whatever the name, I investigate it."

Jared noticed McCoy wasn't actually pouring her coffee; instead, she spun the thermos, examining him. "What did you say your name was?" she asked.

"Jared Strong."

"And you're investigating Bigfoot?" a hint of playful skepticism stippled her tone. "Like, the monster on that TV show? Oh hey, are you from that show? Is this for TV?"

It was always the least impressive investigators in any field, whether you were talking about cryptozoology or the paranormal, who got on television. The least qualified, yet they were the investigators everyone knew. They were the standard bearers. So frustrating. "No, sorry, I'm not. I'm an independent investigator. One of the little guys. Thus the lack of a camera crew."

"Oh. Okay. Can I ask you a question?" McCoy actually sounded disappointed.

"Sure."

"Do you really do this as a job?" One eyebrow raised, McCoy was definitely interested in this conversation, though Jared wasn't sure if she was still trying to pass the time. "I don't mean to offend. I didn't know this was a real thing."

"It's okay. A lot of people ask me that," Jared laughed. "Yea, it can be a job. I'm not going to get rich, but that's not why I do it." Sometimes he swore his small personal circle of friends and Maria were the only people in the world who loved what they did. Everyone else seemed fixated on the money aspect of working instead of the fulfillment that comes from doing what you love every day.

Loved.

McCoy looked confused like Jared answered in another language. "Then why? Again, I don't want to be rude, but it's kind of weird for me."

That was it. Now he knew what she was after. He had a sneaking suspicion there was more behind her questions than mere curiosity. He didn't suspect anything malicious from McCoy, not at all, but boredom wasn't what drove this line of questioning. "A grown man, chasing monsters?"

She sat up straight in the chair, her expression wiped clear. She looked like he'd dropped a healthy dose of cuss words right in McCoy's grandma's lap. "I'm sorry. Maybe it's because I'm in these woods all the time. It's kind of strange to think Bigfoot exists. I mean, why haven't they caught one yet? Or even found bones? Or a body?"

Was she this interested in Bigfoot? He was getting a weird vibe from McCoy. Her interest in the topic betrayed her minimal familiarity with Sasquatch history. Every once in a while he came across people like this. They didn't know enough about the subject to have an in-depth conversation, but they also displayed more than a passing interest in the topic. They were like school children who were taking their first lesson in a subject that interested them, sparking their intellect for the first time. It was these people who weren't easily dismissed or engaged on a deeper level. Jared always struggled with not overwhelming the benignly curious.

Stay guarded, dumbass.

"Well, the acidity of the soil here isn't good for preservation," he started. "The deep forest doesn't help either. Plus, it's not unheard of to not find fossils or remains in forested areas. There are 2.3 million square kilometers of forest in the Congo, for example, and six archeological sites, none of which have produced a single chimpanzee fossil, though we know there are huge population centers of them all over that area, right? It's similar here with our forests. And Sasquatch, at best, probably only numbers in the dozens, not the hundreds or thousands."

She clapped her hands and pointed at him. "Needle in a haystack, then?"

"That's a good way to put it. I need to find that needle, even if it's only a Denisovan finger."

"A what?" her mouth twisted as if she'd eaten something repulsive.

"I'm being a wiseass," Jared apologized. "Denisovans are extinct but they existed alongside Homo sapiens, who interbred with them. They were classified after a finger bone segment was found in a cave in Siberia in 2008. Scientists were able to extract DNA thanks to the cave's low temperatures preserving it. That's how they discovered it was a separate species. We don't have that sort of fortune with Bigfoot. Makes it a little more difficult than some people would like to consider. Selective data and all that."

Her eyes grew wide. "Sorry?"

Knock it off, dummy. She doesn't need all this. Way to squash her budding interest in the topic.

"Nothing. I'm a bitter old man." Jared smiled, fidgeting in the uncomfortable plastic chair. *Is it the chair or the fact that you have a sneaking suspicion something else is happening here and you can't figure a way to root it out?*

"No worries," she replied. "So what can I do for you then, if I can't help you find this—"

"Denisovan finger?" he clarified. "Are there a lot of rangers working out of this station?"

"A few of us," McCoy replied. "But there's not usually more than one or two in here at a given time. We spend most of our shifts out in our vehicles, patrolling and stuff."

"Is there a way to get a question to everyone?"

She leaned on the desk. "Why all the weird questions?"

Jared held his hands up in apology. "Yeah, sorry, my interrogation skills suck." He paused, could he trust her? What other options did he have? There was no one else here and time wasn't on his side. He couldn't wait for luck. "I recently received a recording via email of some sounds of what I think might be a Sasquatch. The sender didn't provide any details about who they were but they mentioned being close to this station when they recorded it. I was hoping someone here would know more about that."

"I mean, I could post a note, but you know how people are about reading boards," she smirked and shrugged. "No one will ever bother with it, most likely."

"Are you all on an internal email system? Could someone send an email out to all the rangers here? Have them go through you to contact me if they know something?"

"I could do that."

"Thanks, I'd appreciate it," he said. "I'm going to be camping up here for a few days. There are a couple spots I'd like to check out. So I won't have any cell service, but if you wouldn't mind texting me at this number if anyone has any information, I'd be grateful."

"Sure thing," she said, taking the offered business card.

Jared stood and extended his hand, which she shook warmly. "Thanks. This is something that could be very important, so it would mean a lot if the person who sent that attachment is here and gets that message. Please let them know, anything, and I mean, anything, they want to remain private, stays private."

"I will," she nodded, one side of her jaw jutting out. Then she collected herself with a blink and said, "Well, good luck to you."

Jared regretfully shook her hand and walked out. His gut told him that the ranger knew more than she was leading on. He didn't like failing. But people were people; it was difficult getting information out of anyone who didn't want to play nice. But scared people? They were the most difficult. Every concern you addressed was replaced with something else. The secret was not prying until you found exactly how to make them feel safe. And sometimes you just had to wait.

He was closing the truck door when McCoy burst out of the tiny building. "Jared?"

Jared leaned out to talk through the window. "Yeah?"

McCoy didn't come down to him, preferring to stay up higher on the steps. She shifted her weight from side to side. "Um, this recording you said you had?"

"What about it?" he said in a measured tone, careful to hide his emerging excitement.

"I might know something about it." She rang her hands and then, as if she noticed what she was doing, stuffed them in her pockets.

"Oh?"

Then she dropped the bombshell he'd been waiting for. "I recorded it."

Jared smiled and stepped out of the truck when she indicated the ranger station with a nod, turning to head back inside. He followed her. She was holding the door for him and, when he stepped inside, she closed and locked it. Jared gave her a quizzical look and she shrugged, moving behind the desk and closing the door to the back office. "Prying ears," a youthful smile spread across her face.

"Aren't we alone?"

McCoy nodded. "We are and will be for hours, but ... I don't know ... I—"

"No, no, it's okay," he sat down, reaching into his pocket. "Before you say anything, are you okay with me recording this for my records and for the podcast project?"

"Record me?" she huffed. "Being heard by thousands of people?"

Jared shook his head. "Not if you don't want to. Plus, once I get better at it, I can disguise your voice so no one will be able to recognize you. So if that's what you'd like me to do ..." he let his question trail off, allowing her to lead him where she wanted the conversation to go.

"Yeah," she answered, almost regretfully, "that'd be nice but there aren't many of us here and I'm the only female ranger, so ..."

"Ah," he nodded. "I don't have to use it. Not publicly."

"Can I get back to you on this?"

"Yes," Jared nodded. "Let me know either way. But, you're okay with me recording now?"

She nodded in silent recollection.

"Want to tell me about it?" he prodded.

"It was last week. I was coming in late from a patrol and sort of taking my time." She paused, thinking about something and laughed nervously. "There's a guy who started working here a few weeks ago and ... and ..."

"He's hot?" Jared concluded.

"Yes," McCoy released a nervous laugh, "you could say that. I don't know. I get dumb around him and I said something embarrassing the day before and was trying to avoid him."

He smiled, remembering days all those years ago when he would act like that whenever Maria came around. In a small-yet-more-significant way, he still felt like that about her. "So you took your time coming back from patrol?"

"Stupid, I know. I need to grow up."

"Oh, I wasn't saying that," Jared stressed. "Plus, the last person you need to take relationship advice from is me. Trust me."

McCoy's tone turned more serious, as if resuming business talk would help them both avoid something they didn't want to explore. It was an awkward transition but it met the objective of swerving that danger. "Sorry to hear that. Yeah, so I was coming in late, the sun was already below the horizon but I'm really comfortable out there so it didn't bother me. I've been here for seven years already so I know those woods pretty well. I was walking back to my truck when I heard something. I had no idea what it was. I mean, I've heard stuff like that before, once in a while over the past few years, but it freaked me out this time."

Strange that she'd say it like that. "Why this time?"

She sighed, apprehension brief but evident. "You're going to think I'm crazy."

"I've seen and experienced a lot of stuff other people would lock me up for if I told them. There's nothing you can say that would make me think you're crazy, well, except for telling me you think Bigfoot is a trans-dimensional creature. That is crazy."

McCoy laughed. "No, no. Nothing like that. It's just that, see, we're a small station. Not a lot of turnover and we all know each other pretty well. We talk. A lot. A few months ago we started recognizing each other's daily status reports had some common details," she continued. "Weird noises, like trees being hit or something. And deer mutilations. Lots of them. Bad smells without any obvious reasons. Stuff we're not used to seeing or hearing, so we'd jot down notes. Some of us started noticing the trends in each other's reports. We started reading them like they were the newspapers or something. Then there was weird stuff."

It was his turn to sit forward. "Like what?"

McCoy swallowed, hard. Noticeably. "Footprints. Lots of them. All over the mountain. I know, I know. I swear I'm not a psycho. I wouldn't have thought anything about any of this, but then the other stuff started happening."

It was maddening to try and get details from her. He tried to be patient because there was a lot to unpack there, a lot that was already validating his records and experiences. "You're going to force me to ask you each time, aren't you?"

Her chest swelled. "Stuff like this isn't supposed to happen," she exclaimed, then flopped back in the chair, rocking back and forth, looking up at the ceiling. She rubbed her face. "I'm sorry. I thought if I had a friend send that file then someone would do whatever Bigfoot people do and I'd be left alone. I didn't think one of you would show up here, at my work. I just want it to be taken care of."

The fear of the potential of Sasquatch was a very real thing. He'd dealt with bouts of it himself and he'd been doing this for long enough to forget what it was like to be new to this assault of the senses. "Listen, I can leave if you're uncomfortable but I'm trying to help. I don't mean to ask you to relive anything you don't want to."

McCoy pinched her lip under a row of straight, pearls of teeth. "I know. Sorry," she said before drawing a big breath and getting out of the chair and moving over in front of a side window. A grassy area stood guard between the ranger building and the thick tree line of the Olympic forest that delineated the untamed world from the tamed. Jared watched her. Whatever exuberance that was there when he first met her was now gone. "A couple of us have had stones, like big rocks, thrown at us. One of our trucks had its hood caved in. The ranger who brought it in, Scott, kept the rock. It was as big as a basketball. The hood on his truck was crushed, like five inches! He would have gotten in trouble over it but so much weird stuff has been happening, I guess we're all expecting things like this now. It's crazy. And then, the howls ..."

Jared watched as McCoy toyed with the windows blinds, plucking them one by one as if she were playing a cello, each one popping against the window frame. "We started noticing them, I mean, we started documenting them, about six months ago but we've been hearing them for longer," she continued. "I can't speak for the other rangers, but I figured they were wolves, which is stupid because wolves don't live out here and they don't sound like that. The first few times I heard them ... I've never heard anything so chilling. Then, one time, a few months ago, I heard one howl and then another, in a completely different direction, a few seconds later. There's no way whatever howled like that could have moved the distance it would have needed to in order to pull that off. No joke, I started crying a little." Her fingers continued to pop those blinds.

Jared winced more than once, worried she was going to snap one of them. "You heard a call and response."

She turned but kept a finger on one of the blinds, ready to pop it. "Is that what they're called? Yeah, then. I guess so. I started keeping my weapon close to me after that."

"I don't blame you."

"Are they dangerous?"

"I thought you didn't think they existed?" Jared tried to lighten the mood.

And failed.

"I—" her brow wrinkled and he was only about to add to her worry.

"Yeah, they can be dangerous, very dangerous."

She continued to pluck at the blinds. Jared realized McCoy was lost in thought. He'd gotten what he needed from her so there was no reason to draw out torturing her by asking her to recall everything. So, instead, Jared thanked her for her time. McCoy turned away from the window long enough to give him a brief smile. "You're welcome," was all she said before returning her attention to the outside world and the tree line that stared back at her.

Jared pulled the door closed, careful to not abuse it this time. He didn't want to disturb her and actually felt culpable;

there was a lot going on in her head. The guilt of pursuing answers, answers she'd been willing to provide, was enough to deal with, he didn't need any more weight on his shoulders for disturbing whatever she needed to do to process the impact of those memories.

One thing was obvious; Sasquatch was there, right in the virtual middle of the Olympic National Forest. Roaming, but that was common among most species. What bothered Jared the most were the varying levels of aggression. Curiosity, hunger? That was one thing. But what McCoy described was something entirely different. The Bigfoot in Forks that Frank Hollenbeck saw ran away from him, as did the one on Mount Rainier. The pair that scouted Jared left him undisturbed. And even when he and Lucas were scouted, the rock throwing had been nothing more than a warning. Nothing more. What McCoy reported was tainted with aggressive behavior on the animal's part. But maybe it was McCoy's memory that was tainted with hyperbole based on trauma? It wasn't beyond the scope of possibilities.

Here was someone with no experience with Sasquatch, isolated by thousands of acres of mountainous forest, hearing things she had no foundation to understand. It was easy to see where fear and anxiety would take root and then start forming the narrative around every other experience to follow. He had thousands of hours in these mountains, putting himself in harm's way, and still got rattled. Someone in her position could be forgiven for adding a little dramatic flair to experiences. There was nothing in her presentation that pinged the radar that she was fraudulent. So the question remained: was the Sasquatch population here aggressive or was their territory being invaded more and more by their human cousins and they were done tolerating it? Punching back?

Jared pulled out of the ranger station parking lot and headed deeper into the mountains, quickly moving out of cell phone range, cutting himself off from the world with each mile. Was it the uneasy conversation with McCoy, watching her deteriorate before his eyes, that instigated the morose thought or was it the reality of the situation finally striking him?

That this was it. The end?

He was headed into the mountains and wasn't coming out until he'd found Bigfoot.

Jared grabbed the recorder. It was always good to put voice to his thoughts. There weren't many people who could handle his need to talk about his passion, he had a failed marriage to prove that, and getting his thoughts down was cathartic; it was what spawned the idea to start a podcast about his work in the first place. How many thousands of hours of notes did he have in various files back at the house? The idea had come to him like an unexpected punch to the chops; there were millions of podcasts listeners around the world. Tens of thousands of people interested in the topic of a large, upright primate. But no one reliable was talking about it, being open with their evidence, and sharing all the behind the scenes stuff that polished television shows refused to expose. Initially, he'd wanted to post episodes as he went along but didn't realize how much work podcasting was, work that would keep him chained to his computer at the house. With Maria gone, that was pointless torture.

But then everything started to happen. Pieces fell together. Phone calls from anonymous people. More and more information was passed to him. Word spread. Momentum grew. Threats did too.

Envious people easily became desperate people when they felt threatened. A public podcast that detailed the truth about what it was like to investigate Sasquatch, to find the elusive primate? That would expose the fraudulent behaviors of 'peers' and inform the world about the Sasquatch population, exposing regional authorities as nothing more than fraudsters, and potentially harming commercial interests by educating lawmakers on the natural wonderment that required their protection. His work put too many people, and their money-making careers, in jeopardy.

When he realized that, the decision to build everything first and then release the podcast once it was over was a simple choice. Now, pulling away from the ranger station and leaving Stephanie McCoy to her troubled thoughts, he wondered if he'd done the right thing all along. She represented some of the victims in this, the people who'd fallen subservient to the Sasquatch legend. Employees, friends, coworkers, spouses, neighbors, people who lived in the areas impacted by confirmed sightings and not-so-real claims to such sightings, and the Sasquatch themselves. The tourism industry. The natural environment, protected or otherwise. There were so many victims of ignorance. The lack of reliable information about Sasquatch hurt untold scores, impacted the environment, and allowed bad information to propagate. Each day he delayed releasing the podcast was another day that ignorance and selfishness extended their reach.

And all that damage could be mitigated by accomplishing what he set out to do now: finish this pursuit.

His cell phone rang. No number popped up on his screen, just the ominous word 'UNKNOWN' told him who wanted his attention. "Who the hell is this?" he grumbled, punching the green ACCEPT icon. It could be important and in another few miles he was going to be outside of cell phone range. "Hello?"

The voice on the other end was smooth, rich but unexceptional. "Ah, Jared Strong. So nice to finally get to speak with you."

"Who is this?"

"My name is irrelevant, but you may call me Roger. I was hoping I could catch you before you drove out beyond cell phone range."

"I don't kno—excuse me?" How the hell did he know that?

Roger sounded humored. "My representatives tell me you're out near Whiskey Bend. Just finished visiting the ranger station near there, I hear. Even after you met one of my men earlier. You're either brave or incredibly stupid."

The surge of rage was instantaneous and overwhelming. He was crushing the phone with his hand. "Who the hell are you and what the hell do you want?"

"A meeting, Mr. Strong," the jovial voice laughed. "That's all. I'd like to sit down with you and see if there isn't an amicable solution to this predicament we find ourselves in. I know you're in a hurry to setup up before it gets late, but I'd like to meet you for a quick meal so we can discuss this ... matter. My treat, of course. What do you say?"

23

"Why would I want to meet with you?" Jared snarled into the phone, trying to still navigate the winding road until he could find a portion of the shoulder wide enough to pull over. All the trouble, the assault, the stress, strain, and threats; this was the voice of the person responsible. In a fair world, Jared would be able to reach through the cellular connection and rip this man's throat out.

"It's in your best interest, Jared," Roger said. The cavalier attitude was enough to make Jared want to do harm. "Peter? Maria? That unfortunate thing that happened to your dog? I'm sure you're more than interested in meeting me face-to-face, are you not?"

"Fuck you! Let me find out who you are, I swear."

Almost talking over top of him, Roger answered in a mocking fashion. "You can. I've already offered to meet you. It's that simple."

"I have no idea who you are, who you work for or why I should trust you. The only reason I'm interested in meeting you is so I can rip your head off and shit down your neck." He meant it. Every. Damn. Word. Everything this man had put him and the people he cared about through, Jared was willing to repay ten-fold. For Molly alone, Jared was more than tempted to do violence. He needed to find out who this man was. That was it. There was no taking the higher road. There was no being the better person, turning the other cheek, or any of that shit. In certain circumstances, humankind resorted to its evolutionary infancy and this was that time for Jared. He yanked the steering wheel, pulling onto a gravel patch and slamming to a stop. A cloud of light brown dust wafted past. He didn't notice, he was transfixed on a singular point of rage in his mind's eye. Nothing else existed at the moment.

"Meet me. I'd love to shake hands with the man who found Bigfoot, if you promise not to harm me."

Jared unlocked his fingers from the steering wheel, balling them into a fist, a fist he wanted to shove down this man's throat. "In case your goons didn't inform you, I'm a little preoccupied making the find of the century." It felt good to tease this asshole.

"I can make it worth all your efforts," Roger continued as if nothing Jared had to say was worth his time. "Those years you've scrimped and saved and barely kept your home. The extra hours Maria worked? All those things she gave up because you needed to go on 'just one more expedition'? All the stress and worry of what you're going to do to make a living after this? All of it. Wiped away. You won't have to work again if you don't want to. Neither will she. I'm offering the chance for a very comfortable life."

The words rolled off Jared's tongue like a poisonous mixture he'd accidentally drank. "In exchange for my silence."

"You hand over your work and walk into a comfortable, early retirement," Roger's trained voice remained even, smooth. Exquisitely smooth. "Doesn't that sound better than another thousand nights sleeping on rocks and chasing a monster that might not even exist?"

"You want to know what sounds better?" Jared pointed out the windshield at nothing in particular. "Me kicking your ass if you ever think to harm me or anyone I love. If you send your goons my way, I can't promise I'll send them back to you. Are we clear?"

"You're making a mis—" Roger was saying as Jared pulled the phone away from his ear and punched the red button, cutting off the call.

He made sure he'd disconnected and then immediately called Maria. Regardless of the air temperature outside, the truck seemed to be getting hotter. Jared tried to slow his breathing before she answered but she picked up almost after the second ring.

"Jared? Is everything okay? I thought you were out?"

His throat clenched. His words were rapid, harsh. "I don't know what's going on but I need you to head to your family's camp. Take your parents with you."

The loving, warm tone of her voice was now gone as if it'd never been there. " You're scaring me, Jared. What's going on?"

"I don't have time to explain. You've got to leave. Head to the camp until I can get there."

When she spoke again her voice was icy. "It's those men, isn't it? The men who shot Molly?"

Jared nodded even though she couldn't see him. "I got a call from a man named Roger who doesn't want me to finish. He tried to convince me that giving this up might not be the worst decision I could make. He knows where I've been and where I'm headed now."

"Jesus, Jared! When does it end?"

"Give me two days," he pleaded. Nothing came from the other end of the phone. "Hello? Maria?"

He breathed a sigh of relief when she finally answered. "I heard you."

"Maria, I--"

"It's fine," she said, sounding anything but.

"What?"

"I'll head to the camp," she answered. "I'll take my parents. But, Jared. Two days. Two days! Then I'm going to the police. I'm not kidding. If you won't end this, I will."

"Thank you, babe," he breathed. "I can't tell you how much it means to me to have your support." She hadn't said she was disappearing. She hadn't said she was leaving him for good. She said she would go to the police. Maria was taking care of him. Again. So selfless.

As if reading his thoughts, Maria said, "Jared, I know how much this means to you. What kind of woman, wife, would I be if I refused to stand by you? I know you're close, I hear it in your voice. You've never been like this before. And I know you're ready to walk away and focus on us. I believe in you. And I can't, I won't, ask anything else from you other than your promise that if this is it, if this is the end, that you'll be true to your word that it is time for us."

"I swear it," he promised. "I want us and I want it now. It's hard to even be out here when I just want to be with you."

"I know." The tenderness in her voice was intoxicating. "But you've got one more important job to do. Go finish it."

He nodded, grateful she couldn't see the tears running down his cheeks. "You're right. I'll be east of Whiskey Bend, starting from Wolf Creek. If something happens, that's where they can find me."

"Focus on finding Bigfoot. I love you. Be careful."

And they said goodbye, possibly for the last time.

With that one word, she was gone.

Safe.

Jared held the phone in his hand for another few minutes as he thought about everything that had happened. He'd upped the ante and created a crisis for the people who didn't want him to finish his work. And they'd responded in kind, with the mastermind getting involved. In a way, it could be seen as a compliment, that he was such a threat to them, that his work was so valid they had to deploy their 'Hail Mary' play. One last attack, like an MMA fighter who was getting his ass kicked, knew he was getting his ass kicked, would take one last swing with everything he could, hoping against hope that he would send his opponent crashing to the mat. The man only known as Roger was that knockout punch.

Except that he swung and missed.

Jared put his cell phone back in its cradle, grabbed the recorder, and started the drive deeper into the Olympic Mountains.

24

It was a peaceful night, cool but not cold. The popping firewood was the only sound besides the occasional rustling of nearby tree branches. Jared barely noticed them. He was bundled against the chill, focusing on the dancing flames that kept him warm and any nocturnal friends far, far away.

And he had his thoughts. About Maria and her supportive, almost unconditional love. About the man named Roger who'd done so much to disrupt this investigation and, more importantly, shatter Jared's world. About his friends who'd supported and helped him. And about the mysterious animal he pursued, who evaded all his attempts to be found.

But it wouldn't. Not any longer. Jared was here to make sure of that.

Life had a funny way of altering, of shifting. When you followed your passions you were supposed to be happy and, for the longest time, he was. He was very happy. Fulfilled. For years he popped out of bed and got on with his day, clueless to the misery that so many of his friends suffered through on a daily basis. He never understood the adage, 'thank God it's Friday' more than on a superficial level. What was it like to suffer for five days, focusing on the draw of two days away from work to reconnect with living life? It was a foreign concept to him, a remnant of his schoolboy years that never transferred over into his adult life. He seemed to be the only one who was inoculated against the disease. Even Maria, Peter, and happy-go-lucky Lucas all dreaded their jobs from time to time.

But now, as he stared into the fire, he understood it all too well.

He hated what he did for a living and he hated himself for allowing it to carry on longer than it ever should have. There was no one else to blame. The passion that provided the zest for living was now nothing more than a dismal obligation. If he wanted to be happy again he was going to have to finish this, once and for all. Once it was all behind him he could figure out how to live a responsible and happy life with the woman he loved.

The cost of pursuing Bigfoot didn't register until Maria was settling in at her parent's house after walking out on their marriage. It took a very long time to stop resisting; to recognize his addiction chased her away. Over and over he'd remind himself until he didn't need to. The old dog was able to learn new tricks. As his determination grew stronger, the need to teach himself dissipated, no longer required.

This needed to end before he allowed himself to see another human again. And the world would see a different Jared Strong the next time he made an appearance.

Unless they only ever find my body.

Jared pulled his eyes away from the fire long enough to take in the gorgeous sight of the true power of nature spread out above him in the blackness. Sparkling twinkles of light filled the sky, reminding him this wasn't a dream; he was alive and part of the story of the universe. As much a part of its story as Sasquatch. They had a story to tell too and he could be the one to bring it to the world. He could be the one to enlighten the human race about this wonderful animal. Years from now, decades even, they would mention his name in their conversations. School children in the distant future would argue about the existence of some creature, long-thought to be extinct, and they would cite his work as an example of how to never give up, never quit, if you believed in something. You used good science, strategy, grit and hard work, and you never stopped until you'd convinced yourself you were wrong or you convinced the world that it was. What he was about to begin tomorrow was going to change reality. For Bigfoot. For him.

He wasn't fooling himself about that.

The human race represented all that was wrong with the world, but it also displayed the beautiful power of selflessness, charity, and empathy. The problem? Which one would his species display when they found out that they had a hairy cousin living in the northwest corner of America? Would they accept and protect it, or would they act without regard or, worse, out of fear, and harm the creature or its habitat? The problem with people was that you could never tell which way they'd lean. Plus, people tended to shift in the direction of their own personal, selfish, desires.

Jared swallowed and poked at a log. He hoped that his work wouldn't be to the detriment of a creature that, to this point, was peaceful, wanting nothing to do with their more violent cousins.

It was something he always struggled with. He would never rest if he didn't find the answer to the question. Never. It was time to find out.

Now or never, the firelight seemed to tease.

Jared grabbed the recorder and turned it over and over in his hands. Who knew what tomorrow was going to bring? This might be the last time he sat next to the warm glow of a fire under a crown of celestial kings and queens and enjoyed the self-talk of a life's work. Come tomorrow, nothing might be the same again.

He pressed RECORD. "Using my previous expedition experience and twenty years of data I've collected, I think I found the location that gives me the best chance to find Sasquatch. I'm a few miles east-northeast of Wolf Creek, which is a mile or so east of the trail at Whiskey Bend. I found a comfortable ridge the last time I was out here and that's where I'm camping tonight. In the morning I'll head out. I've got an area narrowed down and I'm confident I'll find something tomorrow, or the day after at the latest. Either way, this is my last expedition. I've lost enough of my life to this damn creature."

That was it. He clicked STOP and packed everything up. The morning would come soon.

*****

The scream echoed through the still air of the night. Jared flipped over, rubbing his eyes and listening.

Nothing. His ears scanned for that sound, nothing else mattered.

Moments passed.

He wasn't going back to sleep now.

Arrrrrrrrrrrrrrrrrrrrrrooooooooooooooooohhhhhhhh!

His visitors were back.

He riffled through the front pocket of his pack and grabbed the recorder, clicking it on. "Dammit. I knew they weren't going to give me any peace tonight."

Another call. A different Sasquatch from a different direction but much, much closer.

The hairs on his forearms stood straight up, for more reasons than the cold night air.

He didn't dare to move, preferring to listen to any clues to the closer Sasquatch's whereabouts. The ruckus from their call chilled him. He swore he felt a vibration! It had to be close and it had to be big.

A branch snapped. No more than twenty feet, Jared estimated. It was here. And it knew he was here. This wasn't a game of curiosity anymore; it was a scouting trip. They were probably as tired of him coming around as he was of doing it. This time they might be in the mood to discourage him from ever coming back.

He didn't want to take any chances testing their disposition. Laying the recorder at the foot of his sleeping bag, Jared reached into the pack and pulled out his pistol. Listening.

Snap. Boom!

An audible footstep. It was close. Too close. "They're coming," he whispered, hoping the recorder would pick up his voice. "At least one of them is."

Thud!

A rock landed a few feet from his tent. He was grateful for their inadequate aim. "They're not happy about me being here. I didn't expect them to be."

The second rock landed much closer.

The bottom corner of his tent ruffled. "Another rock," he whispered, sniffing for a scent of the creature. His nose hairs retreated at the stench. Not as strong as his experience with Lucas, but unmistakable. "Could be the same Sasquatch or a second one. I extinguished the fire before I went to sleep, so the camp is dark, though it's close enough to sunrise for the sky to start brightening. It won't be up for another hour or so. The Sasquatch won't be afraid to explore the camp in this poor light."

Snap! Crack!

"Shit! I can hear him inside the camp now."

Right outside the tent. Closer than twenty feet. Jared swallowed; his clammy hand gripped the pistol. Sliding forward, he reached and carefully unzipped the tent flap. It sounded like the sky was being torn apart. He paused and listened for clues to the Sasquatch's whereabouts. Nothing. He inched the zipper up. When it was high enough for him to slip through, should the need to escape arise, he peaked through the flap. "Oh my God; he's big!" he whispered harshly. There was no science on Sasquatch's hearing abilities. The lumbering giant could be deaf for all he knew or it could hear every single thing he was doing. There was no way to tell and not doing anything was not an option. There was no use in searching for his camera; the night was too dark to get anything decent. "Over seven feet tall. Easily. He's rooting around in ... I think he—"

Then it happened.

Whether Jared's movements or speech set it off, whether it smelled him, or whether it knew Jared was there all along, none of it mattered. The massive creature, covered in matted, brown fur, turned toward the tent and grunted, its eyes narrowed. Jared couldn't breathe. He couldn't speak. It wasn't light enough to make out the finer detail but there was no doubt the monster knew it wasn't alone. It pulled back its lips and snarled before letting loose a growl that came from the depths of the earth.

And it charged.

"Shit!" Jared yelled, no longer worried about not being detected. He instinctively backed into his tent, knowing the flimsy material would do nothing to stop something that big. There was nowhere to run, nowhere to hide. The only escape was through the front flap and that massive beast was charging in that direction. He'd lost the chance to scamper free. The ridge only provided one way out, he'd chosen it for its defensive position and now found himself a prisoner to his own strategy.

Jared lunged for his pack as the thundering footsteps rapidly approached. Only seconds remained before that beast would crash into the tent, ripping it from the stakes and entangling him in a death trap of cotton, nylon, and polyester. Somewhere in his pack he had a hunting knife with a six-inch blade.

The Sasquatch was on top of him. There was no time left. No time to do anything. He'd made one too many trips, invaded their sanctuary one too many times, and now he was going to die for his passion. Knife or camera? That was his only decision now. In about two seconds that monster was going to rip open the tent and beat him to death. He could either find the damn knife, cut a hole in the back of the tent and flee into the woods—getting chased down by the Sasquatch—or he could get a picture or two, some video, and hope that someday a hiker or park ranger would trip across the camera and cement his legacy by showing the world the real reason Jared Strong wasn't part of it anymore. At the very least, if he got a picture or two, then his life's work would live on that way.

But living on in this reality suited him much better. He gave up on the search. He didn't feel like experiencing an avoidable death. He was going to do the only thing he could do. Option C.

The pre-dawn day wasn't old enough yet to cast shadows but Jared didn't need to see the looming shape of the monstrosity. It was there, tussling with the tent. A scream. A male's scream. For a second Jared was sure someone else was here to help him by scaring off the Sasquatch. He almost sighed until the realization slammed into the side of his head that he had screamed. He was the one behind that toe-curling, hair-splitting scream, the sound of a man witnessing the end of his own existence.

Jared whipped the pistol up and tried to steady his arm. It was like watching a first-person point of view shooter video game, the way his arms didn't feel attached, or how he saw the pistol but couldn't feel it pressed against his palms as he attempted to control his wildly shaking arms. But he didn't need to worry about precision; the Bigfoot that stood no more than three feet away from him was everywhere at once, taking up his entire field of narrowed vision. Adrenaline surged through him, the gun dipped, bobbed. He

over-corrected and nearly shot the beast in the head. *No!*
Wound it, you idiot. No head. The trigger was yanked back by
that video game hand. All feeling, all sensation, was focused
on that single point where his skin met steel, where his index
finger curled around the equally-curled metal trigger. He
could feel nothing else. There was nothing else to be aware
of, not even that colossal primate shaking the tent in its own
frustration to get to its distant cousin. Every tangible aspect
of the known universe was focused on that one point of
contact between man and his destructive means.

Jared fired.

The burst filled the world.

His heart skipped. A roar of pain and outrage.

The tent shook. The beast didn't flee as Jared had
hoped.

"Shit! Shit!"

He fired again.

"Fuck!!!"

And again.

Screaming.

And again.

Yelling.

Crying for it to flee.

The Sasquatch roared into the pre-dawn sky and the
tent stopped shaking.

Thundering footfalls quickly faded as the beast crashed
through the underbrush, cracking dead and living branches
alike as it fled. Jared sat on his sleeping bag, pistol still raised
in two shaking arms, aimed at nothing in particular and
finally, after what felt like minutes, began to breathe again.
His heart thumped against his chest cavity. He could hear
nothing over it and the accompanying pulse that thudded in
his neck.

Jared leaned forward to move the flap. The front part of
the tent collapsed from the assault so Jared was actually
thankful he'd unzipped it to inspect the Sasquatch. There

were no guarantees he'd find anything today and staying another night or four was still a very real possibility. He'd need shelter. He couldn't go back into town to buy more gear. The promise had been made and needed to be kept; he was not going back into the world until this was finished.

He was going to chase the demon.

Jared fished around for the recorder and found it knocked into the far corner of the tent, and sighed when he noticed it was still working, still recording.

"He's gone. Jesus Christ, he's gone." His breaths still came in rapid succession, the more he breathed, the less filled his lungs felt. "Oh my God. I can't believe he attacked. I didn't want to shoot. I didn't. I think I can—"

A distant Sasquatch call stopped him.

Listening.

As he opened his mouth the response came.

It was closer than the first call. Weaker. He waited, fascinated by the way these creatures communicated over miles and miles of mountainous terrain.

Much further away, this call had a different intonation. Multiple Sasquatch, relatively close. And after shooting a Sasquatch at close range, he might just have a chance to follow a trail all the way back to its community if it was still as reckless as it had been fleeing his camp.

Jared escaped the tent and started packing. There was no better time than now. The animal was wounded; it didn't matter how big it was. Nothing could be shot that many times at point-blank range and not suffer traumatic, if not fatal, injuries.

Oh God, please don't let anyone find out I killed it. Please.

He hadn't thought about that until now. His survival instinct dictated his actions when he pulled the trigger, but now he was a rational creature again, as rational as human beings can be, and he couldn't stomach the thought that he'd taken a life of something so wondrous.

No, please. God, no!

Never in twenty years of expeditions had Jared ever packed a camp so quickly.

25

The sun was still behind the mountain but its rays extended up and out, brightening the world in a perverse contradiction to his mood.

Jared lunged atop a large boulder, climbing higher and higher up the slope. It was rough going, with steep pitches and soft ground that gave away under the occasional misplaced step. His exhaustion didn't help. The short evening, the pre-dawn visitor, and the adrenaline rush of having to actually shoot the Sasquatch sapped him of any strength he usually had in this type of situation. What he'd seen outside his camp didn't help energize him either.

He used a sapling to pull himself up an outcropping of rock, his thighs burned in exertion and his calves alternated turns cramping up. Jared winced and unslung his pack. He'd record for a few minutes and then keep going. He needed to hydrate anyway. In case something happened. In case he never made it home, he had to have a record of everything. Someone needed to know.

"I'm hiking toward Hurricane Ridge," he recorded. The trees were thick here; a lot of them toppled over and replaced by younger, healthier giants. There were a lot of hiding spots around him, even for an animal as big as Sasquatch. "It's a hell of an incline. I'm exhausted. Especially after what happened this morning. When my adrenaline crashed so did my energy. Any other day I'd turn around and head out but I'm so damn close. To give up now ... I can't."

The mountain mocked him, dared him to push through.

"I couldn't have killed the Sasquatch," he continued after taking a long drink of water. "I haven't come across a body, but he did leave a mess behind that was easy enough to track. Even someone out of Seattle could have followed this path. Tree branches are broken. Saplings are snapped in half. This big boy made no effort to hide."

Keep the brave face, Jared. Keep the brave face. Can't let 'em see you sweat, right? No body meant the Sasquatch was still alive. But the animal was hurt, badly; it had to be. "Man, this trail of blood has stretched for miles. I don't know how much he lost or still can lose, but he hasn't bled out yet. I'm assuming he's headed to a nest. I have no idea what's ... hang on."

The trail continued uphill. Twenty yards ahead there was an open area, no more than two hundred square feet in total. It was free of trees, alive or dead. It was one of the few areas in this part of the forest uncluttered by nature. But that wasn't what drew him to it. The Sasquatch's trail led him straight there and, even from this distance, he could see significant evidence of a struggle for survival.

A large area of matted ferns, twenty feet in diameter, indicated that something had laid on them. Something big, like Sasquatch big. Jared scrambled over to it, immediately noticing the broad leaves covered in dark, red blood that was still drying. Narrower bands of blood trailed down the leaves to the forest floor, indicating that whatever had bled here either stayed for a while or was bleeding heavily. Jared moved some of the fern branches and spotted a footprint— a Sasquatch footprint.

He swallowed down the remorse, scanning the surrounding trees for a large corpse. Or one pissed off Bigfoot. The amount of blood he'd been following for miles should have led him to a body by now, but he'd found nothing. That could only mean the creature was still lumbering on toward its destination. Impressive that it could get this far, at this elevation and against this slope. The resilience of the animal was more than impressive. This was a display of the will to live. No human could have lasted in these circumstances. He was exhausted. This thing was shot and still plugged along.

"Something big was here," Jared recorded. "There's an area in front of me that's probably twenty feet in diameter. Some of the mud has been disturbed and the brush is matted. It almost looks like he laid down. The brush is coated in blood. But there's no body. Nothing at all."

Jared looked up the slope, feeling the discouragement that exhausted hikers felt whenever they thought they'd accomplished something significant only to realize they still had half a mountain to go.

Where is this damn thing?

"What the hell?" he growled. He didn't want the animal to die but the world was going to need something more substantial than audio. Not getting a clear picture was the scourge of Bigfoot hunters for generations and Jared realized that would have been impossible under the circumstances of the pre-dawn visitation he didn't ask for. But now, in the morning light, all he needed was to find the thing resting. That was it. He didn't even need to get close; a few hundred yards would allow him to get enough detail to convince all but the staunchest deniers that the animal exists. That was it—a quick couple of shots, a short video, of an animal so rarely captured, clear and precise, and then the world's appetite for it could return to the fringes so that everyone could be distracted by the latest football standings or what some housewives in some city were doing with their privileged lives.

Just one picture.

Now or never.

"It's possible he got up and ... wait a second. There's something here. Some—" Jared was looking at the far end of the matted clearing. A band of vegetation about three feet wide was flattened by something heavy pressing it down. Jared rushed to the edge for an unobstructed, view.

"What the hell?" He got on his knees, tracing the outline with his fingers the way a person traces their loved one's face while they're sleeping. "It's another set of tracks! Coming from the opposite direction. There's ... God, there are two sets of new tracks. I need to get some shots of this!" He fumbled in his pack to draw out his camera. More tracks! Multiple sets! Opposite direction from the one he'd followed.

It could only mean one thing. A herd.

Jared snapped a dozen pictures and a video, getting as much detail of the tracks and the surroundings as he could. The imprints weren't the sexiest things he'd ever got, the stomped underbrush didn't allow for the best detail, but he didn't need that. This was bigger than getting more visual evidence of tracks. What he needed was evidence of their behaviors. And right now he was getting the type of behavioral evidence he'd longed to find. This would show that Sasquatch weren't solitary creatures. It also supported his theory on communities. This will revolutionize the way investigators and cryptozoologists think! "So there's at least three Sasquatch here," he recorded after he packed his camera again. "That makes sense. It's consistent with my last two expeditions. And the tracks lead back uphill, three sets. But it looks like one, probably the one I've been following, is being supported by the two others. His tracks are less distinct, like a leg is being dragged. Maybe more. He's injured."

Then it dawned on him, erasing all the joy he felt about getting the pictures of the herd tracks. "The world may finally get the corpse they've been clamoring for."

Jared surveyed the mountainside. The path was going to be easy to follow. The two Sasquatch who'd come down the mountain didn't try to hide any trace of their presence. Jared followed it, shocked at what he was seeing. The Sasquatch had—

A howl, not all that distant, reverberated around the forest. It wasn't like the other howls and whistles he'd been hearing over the past weeks around Hurricane Ridge. This was different. Pained. Sorrowful.

He took a deep breath. "Here we go. Time to meet Bigfoot."

*****

This couldn't be real.

Yet it was.

Jared knelt behind a tree that had given up the fight against gravity years ago, laying on its side, top facing downhill. Like many of the felled trees in this part of the world, younger, healthier branches grew out of it, near the root system. They provided decent coverage, but the better coverage came in the form of other flora that stretched out across the face of the mountain. It was dense. Very dense. The perfect hiding spot.

And he needed the perfect place to hide.

Because he was looking at a community of Bigfoot nests.

"I can't believe this," he whispered into the recorder, trying hard to keep his voice low. Excitement coursed through him. Everything shook. "The marked tracks of the three Sasquatch I followed led to a nest. I'm about a hundred yards away but I can see a small community. That's the only way I can describe it. It's under heavy tree coverage and surrounded by thick brush. There's a distinct area that's been rubbed down to bare earth with four different nests built from tree branches. Could there be more of them? I don't know. Each structure is roughly the same build, about five foot high with large openings facing downhill, too the south. Two deer carcasses are off to the east side of this camp. I'm getting as many pictures and video as I can."

Jared snapped a few more, transfixed by what he was seeing, trying to take it all in while also remembering he was here to finish his work. Forget changing the world, he was here for one thing. This was it. This was everything he'd spent the better part of two decades working toward. It was the end of a journey and he was going to enjoy it for all that it was.

He knew he was very lucky to be a witness to this. The first human ever to see Sasquatch in their natural habitat.

"But more remarkable is the—" he stopped when thundering footsteps boomed off to his left. He hadn't expected another Sasquatch! Jared shrunk down, careful to not disturb the flora and draw attention. The new Sasquatch didn't take notice of him. It lumbered into the camp with a small number of strides. Jared controlled his exhale before his breath burst out of him with a cough. "That was close. Another Sasquatch just passed me, about thirty yards away. A massive creature. He's got to be over eight feet tall, and if I had to guess, over seven hundred pounds. Four Sasquatch!

"The one I shot is lying on the ground, close to the nests. Two others are standing near him, one keeps looking around as if it's searching for something, while the other is ... is ... now it's kneeling next to the injured one and it's stroking his arm."

Jared snapped pictures of this display of tenderness. It was all so human. What he would give for the world to witness this. He understood people. The reactions this evidence was going to get when it came out, even if he was able to get a major publication to run it, would elicit exactly what he knew it would elicit. One very predictable human behavior was fear; fear of the unknown; fear of things that were different; fear of anything one could perceive as a threat. Fear was the standard operating procedure for humans. What he was witnessing could change that. Seeing the small cluster of Sasquatch caring for one of their own in a way every single person could identify with, how would that not strengthen humanities' desire to study and understand these creatures, and to respect their autonomy?

"Fascinating!" He switched to video mode. There had to be a recording of this. People needed to see these wonderful creatures in their habitat. They needed to witness the communal spirit as these Sasquatch huddled around their injured one. "It's like it's trying to comfort the one I shot! We know plenty of wild animals display empathy so it's not surprising that Sasquatch would as well. It's just ... I wasn't expecting it, I guess. It's a beautiful thing to see."

The fourth Sasquatch stomped around the group, circling them, its long arms swaying dramatically. Every few seconds it grunted, sharply jerking its head upward. Its antics elicited grunts of their own from the other two Sasquatch tending to the injured one.

"The fourth one has now joined the group," Jared whispered. "It looks agitated. Whatever he's communicating to the others, he doesn't look happy about it."

The fourth Sasquatch circled and circled. Grunts. Growls. It was all so amazing to see but the reality he couldn't escape was that he'd caused this. The beast on the ground was struggling and it was his fault. Its feat of fortitude and strength was still impressive. It had to be at least an eight-mile hike and the animal had lost enough blood to kill a cow. Most of that hike had been accomplished unassisted, which most likely did nothing for the injured Sasquatch but exacerbate its injuries. Its large, round chest rose and fell in quick, slight jerks.

Oh, God.

"The one on the ground ... it's heaving ... it's ... it looks like it's struggling." The other Sasquatch growled, almost in unison. "Oh, no ... it's ... dying."

The animal's chest stopped rising before suddenly heaving. The injured Sasquatch grunted a wet sound from deep in its chest. Everything was a labor for this dying animal. Jared had never been so disgusted with himself in his entire life. Everything he'd screwed up he could fix, or at least try to fix, but this wasn't one of those opportunities. Death couldn't be called back. "This is hard to watch. I can't help but feel for that creature, the suffering it's enduring. I was defending myself but—"

The Sasquatch kneeling next to the injured one lifted its chin, pursing its lips, and howled. Not a call, not a whistle, but a mournful, tragic sound. The single howl rose over the encampment before it was joined by the second Sasquatch. It, too, turned its face toward the sky and let loose a soul-shaking wail. Jared wondered while he watched this display if these animals possessed some transcendent sense. It almost looked like they were turning to the heavens as a desperate attempt to save their loved one. Could this species be that similar to their hairless cousins that they would have developed some sense of something larger than themselves?

Jared watched the injured Sasquatch, waited for the chest to jerk up and shimmy its way back down as the animal exhaled. But nothing happened. He didn't break his gaze to observe the other animals; his full focus was on the Sasquatch he shot, waiting for it to draw another breath. But it didn't.

It wouldn't.

Never again.

It was ...

"He's gone."

The chorus of mourning rang out. This moment wasn't about him but it hurt just the same, like one of those large animals reached into his chest and compacted his heart in their large hands. This was devastating. Twenty years of chasing these animals hadn't prepared him to see this. Throughout his youth and into the early stages of his career it was easy to hate and want to destroy. He'd lost his first dog and, ultimately, his parent's marriage to the Sasquatch and he'd hated the creature all those years ago for what it'd done to him. He'd wanted to kill it, to hurt it as it had done to him. But time changes everyone, life changes, people change, and as he studied this species, as he grew to understand his own, he appreciated that Sasquatch wasn't the type of monster that lived in the mind of a young boy.

The chorus of howls grew. The fist tightened around his heart. Jared swallowed the lump in his throat. "I've killed Bigfoot." Now, even the largest one joined in the song of sorrow. "Somehow I imagined this would feel—they're moving the body. The big one hefted it onto his shoulders. It weighs hundreds of pounds and he lifted it like a duffel bag! What are they doing? Are they...shit!"

The Bigfoot headed in his direction. Jared stood as high as he dared, not wanting to become part of this procession. It was slow going. The Bigfoot could cover much more ground than he could. But he wasn't trying to outrace them; he wanted to get out of the line of their funeral march. He stumbled but caught himself before landing face first and tumbling down the mountainside. There was so much undergrowth that moving anywhere quickly was a risky proposition. He didn't want to get tangled in anything and hurt himself or give them a hint he was here, but they were closing in. He didn't want to think about what would happen if they tripped over him.

He moved as fast as he could, avoiding every branch, every vine, every limb that jutted into his path to slow him down. Somewhere, behind him, he heard a howl that sounded different than the wails of mourning. This one was a warning.

"Shit! Shit!" he cursed, instinct told him he'd been found out. Branches cracked behind him. Jared was afraid to turn, not only because he worried that he'd trip over something in the two seconds it'd take him to get a situation report for himself, but because he was also afraid of what he'd see. Something moved behind him. Something quick. Something large.

The last thing he wanted to hear.

Boom! Boom! Boom!

Up ahead he had about fifteen feet of clear path, so he took the chance of looking over his shoulder. Through the tall branches, he could see a brown monstrosity moving, lumbering but fluid, in the same line he was on. The Sasquatch howled as it ran after him, with increasing speed. There wasn't time or a clear path to see more than the large shape crashing through the underbrush. But he didn't need to see it snarling, he didn't need to see its eyes locked on him to know that he wasn't hidden from it. Jared stood to his full height, crouching was only slowing him down, and sprinted across the mountain. With bears, an effective defensive posture was to run across the face of a mountain. Bears couldn't move laterally very easy and the slope of a mountain worked against them, slowing them down. Jared wasn't sure if the same held true for Sasquatch. As far as he knew he was the first one to ever be chased by one. He was now the test subject. But options were limited. He was in their realm, in their world. This was their landscape so they knew the land better and were physically dominate to him in every single way. He had to try whatever he could to get away.

But standing and running at breakneck speed was still a slow jog for the Sasquatch, which continued to gain on him. The booming footsteps fell quicker, louder. Closer. He was tripping, stumbling, struggling to keep his balance, while the Sasquatch sounded like it was running straight, the mountain terrain and gravity be damned. It carved the path it wanted through the bushes.

Jared zigged to his left, up the hill. His pace slowed to a fast walk. Options narrowed as the Sasquatch closed in. From far behind, howls. Anger mixed with loss. He'd disrespected them. He'd intruded into something he wasn't supposed to be part of.

He turned again, running an even more direct path up the mountain. His thighs burned. His knees threatened to give up on him. Fear propelled him. Nothing more.

And yet the Bigfoot got closer and closer. Jared could feel each time its massive paws slammed into the earth in pursuit.

How long could he fool himself? How long did he think he could outrun and outmaneuver this animal? They'd never been studied; no one knew the lung capacity of a Sasquatch. For all he knew, his pursuer could run twenty or thirty miles before tiring. It didn't matter what other investigators or cryptozoologists thought, they were speculating when they talked about the physical capabilities of these animals. It'd never been measured and studied so their guess was as good as his ... and he was living this experiment.

And he knew.

Boom! Boom! Boom!

Crack!

The steps were slower but they were still closing in on him. Jared could hear the animal grunting behind him. In seconds it would be on top of him.

This was it. This was how it ended.

He dodged to his right at a ninety-degree angle and could feel the air around his head move. The Sasquatch had swiped at him, the powerful swing coming out of nowhere. Jared didn't expect that, hadn't thought the animal was that close.

I'm not getting out of here alive.

The disheartening thought came quick, true, and clear. Even dodging the animal, running uphill or across the mountain, none of it had shaken the Sasquatch off his trail. And he was tiring; he was already exhausted.

The Sasquatch growled and Jared turned to face it. He didn't know why. It was the dumbest thing he could have done if he wanted to get away.

You're not escaping, you know it. This is where it all ends. Now or never.

He almost laughed at the ridiculous reminder he'd played for himself in his head, over and over, trying to convince himself that it was time to end this folly and enjoy a life with the woman who gave him everything he'd ever wanted. Now she wouldn't be able to save him.

The Sasquatch was immense, not as big as the giant who'd carried their dead companion from the camp, but large enough to strike fear into his soul simply by its mere presence. It was a foot taller than him, close to seven feet tall and, judging by its girth, had to weigh close to five hundred pounds. How something that large moved up the mountain with that speed and ease, Jared had no idea. But that wasn't what stunned him. What surprised him was something he noticed when he saw how heavily the animal was breathing. Its breasts heaved from the exertion of chasing him from the camp, bobbing up and down with each breath. This Sasquatch was a female.

Howls came from below them, back toward the camp.

Jared risked a glance back down the mountain to see if either of the two surviving Sasquatch were joining this one. But they were alone. He was the smaller, quicker animal. He'd never be able to outrun her in top speed or distance, but he could avoid her death snare if he stayed aware and mobile.

He stepped to his left, back downhill, and she mirrored his move.

He took a step to the right, hoping she would overcompensate. The animal stood there, watching him and growling, her lips pulled back, exposing her teeth. Not narrow and pointed, but blunt and flat, like a human, but twice the size. He moved in tiny, measured steps while maintaining eye contact with her. There was something in her eyes, an intelligence not seen in a lot of animals. She was aware. Sentient. Aware of him, her, and her community. She lived and she loved and it was obvious she understood that. An immediate and grievous regret, that he'd never be able to tell the world about this majestic creature.

She lunged. He wasn't ready for it. The ground underneath him crumbled when he tried to move, sending him crashing down in an awkward split. There was no time to stand or scramble. "No! No! Please," he begged as she towered over him.

"Please! Don't!"

She reached down. Though her palm was enormous, it was still very relatable with lines of age and wisdom crisscrossing it. As preposterous as it was, he even noticed she had callouses. "I'm sorry!"

Her hand grabbed his chest, his shirt, and straps to his backpack. The power in those five fingers was unquestionable. She squeezed and lifted him off the ground with one arm.

"Noooooo!" he yelled to a world too busy with the distractions of everyday life to care about what was happening in this remote corner of the Olympic Mountains. "Please. I'm sorry. I—"

He thought about the past twenty years of his life as she lifted him and the ground fell away.

He thought about how he'd started this with the fire of hatred burning in his heart, and how it was going to end in remorse and appreciation of their differences and commonalities.

He thought about all the people who'd helped him get to this point and wondered if they would ever get the closure they needed when it became obvious he was lost to them forever.

And he thought about how Maria would mourn for him as these Sasquatch did for their loved one. The loved one he'd robbed them of.

The Sasquatch stared into his eyes when they were face-to-face. Her gaze burned into him. He knew what she'd lost. He began to cry even as she roared into his face, her rank breath gagging him and making his eardrums throb closed against the volume of her pain. His throat sealed, his ears shut down to preserve what they could of his eardrums. And the entire world closed in on that one focal point of connection, where man and beast stared into each other's soul.

26

The arm around his shoulder was warm ... light ... and friendly.

"I still can't believe it," Maria laughed. "Look at these pictures! Jared, you've done it. I'm so happy for you!"

He couldn't believe it either. If fate so decided that he should live for another thousand years, he didn't think he'd even believe it then. It was all too fantastic. Every bit of that experience on the mountain was. *And it's something I'm going to treasure for the rest of my life.*

He laughed. "Trust me, I can't believe it either."

Maria continued flicking through the pictures as they sat together on her parents' couch, like they had all those years ago when they'd started dating. She had seen some of them a few times already but kept flipping through them, fixated on what she was looking at. "What was it like? To walk away from them after being that close?

"Well, I mean, I didn't exactly walk away," his mind drifted back to that mountainside; him and the female Sasquatch, staring at each other, measuring the other's intentions. "I was threatened ... growled at ...the big one started beating its chest. It wasn't exactly a pleasant exchange. But it was more a matter of them letting me go than it was me walking away." Even now, having had hours of hiking and driving to think about it, he couldn't form the correct words. "I guess they knew I wasn't a threat to them but that didn't mean they wanted me around. I didn't belong."

She squeezed his hand with her one free hand. "I'm glad those monsters didn't hurt you."

"That's the thing. They're not monsters," Jared countered. "You should have seen the pain and sorrow they felt at losing one of their own. They were hurting and they still didn't do anything to me when they could have. They could have killed me, yet they let me go. I thought about it the entire hike back. What does that say about them?"

"What do you mean?"

"Those behaviors, that entire experience. Those Sasquatch showed an implausible value for life," Jared felt it, that connection with them, established when he witnessed their mourning. Somewhere, deep within him, he knew it wouldn't last long beyond the moment the female Sasquatch set him back on his feet, took one last look at him, and turned away to rejoin her herd. "How many people would have been driven by rage or hatred or revenge in that same situation? Yet these animals weren't. It was so beautiful."

Maria shook her head, still flipping through picture after picture. "They couldn't have known you were the one who shot. Don't you think you might be giving them a little bit too much credit?"

"Maybe, maybe not," he shrugged, "but that doesn't change the fact that in the middle of their pain they were threatened by an outsider and they responded with understanding and patience and compassion for life, even when they didn't have to. I think there's something to be learned from that."

"I get that," Maria smiled, setting the camera on the coffee table next to a stack of her mother's yellowing Good Housekeeping magazines, and leaning over and wrapping her arms behind Jared's neck. "Come here."

The kiss was light. Tender. Warm. Electric.

He'd never been so glad that her parents spent so much time at their church as he was now.

Maria pulled away but didn't let go. "Yeah, now that's nice," she said, biting her lower lip. "So does this mean I get my husband all to myself?"

Jared locked his arms around her waist and kissed her again before answering. The jolt of passion surged through him and he found himself regretting that he didn't ask Maria to make the three-hour drive home so they could have this moment together there, alone. *Or at least an hourly hotel.* "You better believe it. Want to take bets on how long it'll be before you get sick of me?"

"Not going to happen, mister. Plus, I figure after a month you'll be raring to get back out there and finish all this."

A dark cloud hung over him before he blew it away. There was no place for that in his life. Not anymore. "No. No, I won't."

But Maria's reaction wasn't what he expected. Her brow furrowed and she didn't let go of him but her grip did loosen. "Jared, you're so close. You have so much hard evidence. And you know where they are. You've got everything you need to prove Bigfoot exists. You'll change the world!"

"No," he replied. "I'm done. I'm burning it all. The papers. The casts. The pictures and video."

"But—"

Jared reached up and stroked her cheek, her lovely, soft cheek, with the back of his hand. "I meant what I said, babe. I'm done. And I don't want to play any part in someone else finding them. They'll have to do it completely on their own."

Now he let go of her and leaned against the back of the couch. *God, I'm exhausted.* "Those animals, they're enchanting," he turned to smile at her. There was worry in her eyes, but there was something else there too. Excitement? Hope? "There's nothing to be gained from continuing this. We don't belong there; that's their realm, their small corner of the world. Why not let them have it? This isn't our dominion to invade as we see fit. We share it with millions of other species. Natives understood that even hundreds of years ago, and somewhere along the road that got lost. There's something special about a reclusive species peacefully enjoying their lives in their natural habitat, living off what the land provides and not abusing it for their own gain. They don't intrude on us and they're not aggressive toward us. They just ..."

"Live?" Maria finished for him.

He closed his eyes and smiled, seeing that Sasquatch's face. She wanted to live. She wanted her loved one to live. Tears formed in the outside corners of his eyes. "Exactly." He swallowed back the cry he didn't want her hearing. Throughout this journey, he'd grown a lot but he still had a lot more growing to do. *And now you have the time and focus to do it for yourself ... for her.* He sat forward, grabbing her hands, bobbing them once. "It may be simplistic; it may be me romanticizing what I saw, but I've got an appreciation I never had before. I sort of envy them."

"Yeah, well, you might not have that romantic, simple life, but you've got me."

Jared smiled as Maria let go of his hands and leaned into him, pushing both of them back into the couch, her head on his. He pressed his nose against her hair, taking a deep smell. *God, I love the way she smells.*

"And that's exactly what I want," his eyes closed, smelling. Touching. "Nothing more." Then he paused, feeling like a sarcastic teenager again. "Well, maybe a job."

"Yeah, an actual second paycheck would be nice," she laughed from down on his chest.

"Oh, we've got jokes, do we?" he reached under her arm and tickled her. "Come here."

Maria spun, almost pinning his wrist under her. Maria was now on her back. She squirmed and pinned her arms to her side so he couldn't tickle her, laughing. Jared stopped and took in the sight of her. Happy.

She relaxed when she realized the torture was over, blinked once and, even though the laughing had ceased, her smile hadn't disappeared. "It's good to see that smile again. It's been a long time."

"Yeah," he traced her eyebrow, "it has."

She fidgeted, getting comfortable, and locked her hands together over her stomach. "I can't believe it's all over."

Jared's fingers stopped tracing her face. "Well, almost."

Maria shot up, worry etched on her face in an instant. "What do you mean, 'almost'?"

He had no right to fault her; this was a reaction he'd created. Even though she was responsible for how she reacted to the world around her, that didn't change the fact that he'd constructed this context for her and it was going to take time to undo, a lot of time, but time he now had. "There's one more thing I've got to do."

"But you said—" Maria's happiness began to crumble. He took her hand in his.

"A quick phone call, babe. Nothing more."

She squeezed apprehensively. "Promise?"

He nodded before leaning in and kissing her cheek. "I promise," he whispered. Then he stood up and wiped his now sweaty hands on his pant legs.

Now or never.

"I'll be right back," he pulled his cell phone out of his pocket and stepped outside.

The sun was bright and warm. His heart thumped in his chest as he unlocked the screen and dialed the number that had been left in a voicemail he received after coming out of the mountains. Roger's number. His thumb paused over the SEND button. Could he do this? Would he say something dumb? Now and tomorrow, and the day after, and the day after that. He had to sell it to make this work.

And the sell started with a phone call to the last person on the planet he wanted to talk to.

Jared paced the sidewalk in front of the house where the woman he loved had grown up. Where she sat inside, waiting on him, so they could get on with their lives.

Ring.

Ring.

On the third ring Roger answered. "Ah, Mr. Strong. A pleasant surprise. How can I help you?"

Jared's pulse galloped at the vexing voice on the other end but he forced himself to remain level, calm. "I wanted to let you know that you win. I'm done." Silence greeted his comment. Jared waited.

When Roger spoke again it was in a measured, practiced tone and rhythm of a man who'd made millions by getting other people to do what he wanted them to. This was a man who probably spent the better part of every day perfecting the fabrication that he was. "What do you mean? Are you giving up?"

Jared noted the joy in Roger's voice. He'd let the man have this win if that's what it took. If it meant that this man and his goons would leave him and Maria alone then these next few minutes, this effort, was well worth it. "Yeah," he said. Truthfully.

"You've made me a happy man, Mr. Strong." It was the last thing Jared cared about.

"Yeah, well, anyways. It's all yours." Jared pulled the phone away, his thumb drifting to the END button when he heard Roger's voice, this time with a hint of the loss of control added. Jared smiled. It was working.

"Wait!" Roger rushed. "Don't hang up. Don't you want to talk about our arrangement?"

"There's no arrangement," Jared finally answered. *Stay with it. You've got to sell this.*

"I thought you said—"

"There's nothing to hand over to you that you don't already have and I'm pretty sure you're not the type of man who pays people for nothing. I've got nothing to give you so I don't expect anything from you."

"Mr. Strong, come now. Part of the deal was that you were to hand over any information we didn't already have. You're not reneging on the deal, are you?"

Jared could feel Roger's frustration rising, it was there, in his voice. This made him almost as happy as the prospect of spending the rest of his life, starting at the end of this phone call, with Maria. "See, that's the thing. There's nothing to give you because there's nothing there. I've spent the last twenty years of my life chasing legends."

The lie was effortless. It should; he'd practiced it over and over on the drive to see his wife. This was serious, the moment he delivered on his responsibility to those wonderful animals. It was the moment he repaid his debt to them. He would change the fate of an entire species, at least until humanity overstepped common sense and good stewardship and finally invaded even the deepest reaches of the Olympic range. But by then the human race would be so far beyond help nothing would change anyway. *We're already on the course to self-destruction and there are going to be casualties, a lot of them. But those animals, those beautiful, peaceful beings, I'm going to do my part in giving them as much time as I can.* He was actually quite proud of himself. "A little bit of unsolicited advice?" he offered over the silence. "You'd do well to invest your money somewhere else."

Roger's reply was hot, loaded with venom. "What are you saying?"

"I'm saying Bigfoot doesn't exist."

Epilogue

Four Decades Later

"Jared Strong was a Bigfoot hunter," the widow, Maria Strong, said to the gathered throng of lifelong friends and family. "He was a loving husband and he was a great father." Her elderly voice, a voice that had formed millions of words over her long life, finally cracked under the weight of the moment. She paused to draw a deep breath, taking strength in the angelic faces of her daughter and son, Jared's daughter and son, their spouses, and the six grandchildren they had blessed them with. In those faces, her resolution grew. "And he was a passionate researcher."

She looked around the atrium, amazed that this was because of him. Her heart swelled with prideful joy. His legacy would live on, long after today, long after she was gone. "He would have been honored to have this new wing for scientific research named after him," she smiled through tears she swore she wouldn't cry. "But," she wagged a playful finger at the two hundred elementary school children filling the ample space, "he would also tell you that your journey doesn't stop here. It doesn't stop at the first roadblock or the first challenge you face. It doesn't stop when someone tells you to go no further. You have a responsibility, to the gift you've been given and to the people who will come after you, to keep pushing on, searching and exploring. If he were standing here he would tell you that there are a million questions we don't have answers to and only science can provide them. Each one of you is a torch that will not only eradicate the darkness of ignorance but a torch the rest of us can follow toward enlightenment. Jared would tell you, as surely as I'm standing in front of you, to never let anyone extinguish your flame."

The atrium exploded in applause from excited children and their proud parents. Maria Strong, seventy-five years old, swooned. The excitement of the day, the memory of her husband who had died five years prior, as a grouchy-but-loveable man who finally found his own way through life, was too much for her. As always, her son and daughter were there to support her.

"Come on, Mom," Kessi said, holding Maria's hands, "let's get you home."

"Yeah," Adam smiled at her side, his arm around her waist, "it's been a long day."

They led her to the entrance, the crowd splitting apart to allow them through. Kessi and Adam smiled at the children, reassuring them that Mrs. Strong was okay, she was just tired. Reassured, they went to explore the new research wing of the school the family had paid for, in accordance with Jared's wishes.

At the entrance, Maria squeezed her children's hands and the entire family turned as one to take in the majestic beauty of the domed ceiling, with the large windows that extended the full height of the second level to allow in as much of the Pacific Northwest sun as nature would bless them with.

"Dad would be proud," Kessi whispered.

"I know, honey," Maria agreed, a tear trickling down her cheek.

Adam was there to wipe it away.

"Promise me you'll bring my grandchildren here often," Maria hated sounding like she was begging.

Kessi squeezed her hand and Adam hugged her. "Of course," Adam assured her. "We'll come all the time, I promise."

Maria smiled without taking her eyes off that domed roof ... and that single beam of sunlight that shone through it, striking the opposite wall. *I love you and miss you, Jared Strong*, Maria sniffled.

Adam made to wipe her tears again but she playfully swatted his hand away. "Let's go," she said to her grandchildren. "I'm hungry. How about you all? Looks like you haven't eaten in weeks."

Together, one happy, close family, the Strongs walked out into the day, leaving the Jared R. Strong Memorial Science and Research Center to the hundreds of children exploring it.

The children who were the future of the species.

END

Chapter One of "RIP,"

Subject: Found Book 2

(Available Summer 2019!)

She was being followed.

The night was thick with humidity. Memphis' streets shone ink-black with wetness, the rain long stopped. Streetlights provided a jaded yellow glow that made spots of pavement look as if they were trying to sparkle, but gave up halfway through the effort.

Empty.

The victim's heels clicked in an idiosyncratic rhythm, a sign of the damage done from the club she should have left hours ago.

She tugged at her too-short purple skirt that kept raising up beyond the danger point of her mid-thigh. Inside the club, she felt confident, normal. Acceptable and sexy. Back in the world of adults and business, being dressed like this made her feel open and unlike a proper member of the Southern community. This was Memphis, Tennessee, and here respectable women did not dress this way. This was a big truck country, home of the most audacious outdoorsmen store on the planet; a glass pyramid rising above the cityscape. This was the birthplace of Graceland, of not only Southern hospitality, with a capital S, but also Southern expectations, a place where men were men, and women were taught their roles in subtle and designed ways from before their first words.

One day she would be of Memphis' suffocating conservative culture, her true motivation for spending too much time in clubs, but right now it was the last thing on her mind. The eyes watching her touched her in her most vulnerable places.

***

The person hiding in the alleyway also understood Memphis' culture, and for the briefest moment they wondered if this woman, who's fate was about to change, understood. Stepping outside the place of entertainment on Beale Street would have reminded her that she was a lady, a mother, and cruising the streets of Memphis in search of a taxi in the early morning was unbecoming of all but the dirtiest of women.

In the distance, over by the apartments on Vance Avenue, a dog barked. Its call rose into the early morning as if announcing that even a mangy mutt wanted to draw attention to the fact the woman in purple was a dirty whore. No one answered the animal, only the occasional sound of a car slicing through puddles filled the night, but the victim still hitched her stride and stepped quicker. The heels she wore, tools of a Jezebel, clicked the concrete sidewalk.

Tomorrow, the city of Memphis would wake up to a new world. Tonight, was the overture to the city's violent new beginning. The dirty woman in purple wasn't even First Act quality.

The killer stepped out from the black alley onto Beale Street, the centerpiece of entertainment and irresponsible joy for the city's sinners. They followed Purple Skit—they knew her name, and Memphis soon would too, but it wasn't important now—down Beale Street toward the Robert R.

Church Park, passing the Ida B. Wells historical marker which indicated something significant had once happened in Memphis.

Tonight, another entry would be added to that historical list.

The victim turned down S. 4th St., her pace picking up, enough to give away her fear. This one was smart. Too smart. Too aware. The legacy couldn't fall before it began. The killer grunted quietly, half in satisfaction, the other half parted by frustration and blood lust. Time to control.

The park was near, only a few hundred feet away, and the victim made the fatal mistake of turning toward it. The killer's chest swelled with urgency, accented by excitement. They knew Purple Skirt would stick to her routine; she always did. They had planned on the park serving as the opportunity to strike, and now the moment was almost here.

The victim's steps stretched as much as her too-tight skirt allowed down.

This was perfect. The trap, almost sprung. A few hundred yards deeper into the complete solitude of the park, ensured by the late hour, provided the perfect cover. Emboldened, the killer increased their strides.

The victim clutched her purse to her side. Her heels drummed her panic.

The killer accelerated into a run.

So did the woman, kicking off her sluttish heels, still hindered by the tight purple skirt.

The distance shortened.

The sidewalk curved to the left and so did the victim, heading back toward Beale Street. Past the church.

Past the historical marker for the auditorium.

The killer sprinted. Purple Skirt wouldn't get back to Beale Street.

Twenty feet. So close but still too far, and running out of time.

Ten feet.

Even from behind, the killer heard the victim's exhausted panting.

This was fun.

Five feet. Almost there.

Beale Street loomed. Too many street lamps.

Three feet. Almost time.

Two.

The victim cried. "No!"

The killer grinned.

A foot.

"Please!"

And the killer lunged, laying flat as they flew into the victim.

The woman in the purple skirt was soft and smelled of decaying cigarette smoke. They crashed to the concrete sidewalk, the killer cushioned by then victim. There was a crack. A bone. The victim's. She rolled, trying to escape, but the sprint around the park had exhausted her and she didn't have much fight left. The white marble arch announcing the park's name stood sentinel for this life-and-death struggle. It also marked the edge of the park. They were close to the street, too close. The work had to be done fast. The legacy needed to be cemented.

Yanking the eight inch Wusthof stainless steel blade free, the rubberized handle gripped in a fist of steel rage. The rubber would ensure it wouldn't slip even after the whore's blood flowed.

Down.

The victim screamed as the stainless steal penetrated her flesh.

Down.

Purple Skirt cried hysterically. This would draw attention. A gloved hand over the victim's mouth muffled her cries.

Down.

The third stab took the fight out of the woman. "Whore!" The killer mocked the death of evil.

Down.

"Hey! Knock that shit off!" A voice, a man's, broke the ecstasy. The killer looked up at a burly figure across the sidewalk and down the street. Thirty yards. Only a few seconds to spare.

"Die, dirty girl!"

Down.

Purple Skirt didn't struggle. She didn't cry out. A shrouded whore, bloodied.

The killer jumped to their feet, taking another look at the witness, cursing their bad luck and unfinished work. They weren't going to get the time they wanted with this first one.

But there will be many more.

The park dominated by two churches of different denominations provided a sanctuary. The killer sprinted between them, through trees and down the sidewalk toward Linden Avenue, remotely aware that the witness was huffing his way to the dead woman in the blackened dress.

Blackened to match her soul.

END

Sign up for Paul Sating's newsletter to follow all the news about upcoming novels, like "12 Deaths of Christmas," coming in time for the 2018 holidays, and my audio dramas (fictional podcasts) at http://www.paulsating.com.

Get more stories each month by becoming a Patron! New exclusive fiction each month at https://www.patreon.com/paulsating.

This novel was an adapted work from the first season of the author's audio drama, "Subject: Found." If you'd like to listen to the thrilling, fully-produced drama, you can subscribe at on the website (http://www.paulsating.com), Apple Podcasts, Spotify, iHeartRadio, Stitcher, or wherever you listen to podcasts.

If you enjoyed this book, I would really appreciate getting a review from you.

Reviews not only help other readers find something they might like, but they help me as an author. Your reviews are important to me because they allow me to see what readers like you enjoyed about the book and what I could have done better.

Thank you to each and every one of you who takes the time to leave a review!

Also By Paul Sating

Also in the Subject: Found Series

Book 1: Chasing the Demon

Fiction

12 Deaths of Christmas

The Plant

Nonfiction

Novel Idea to Podcast: How to Sell More Books Through Podcasting

Acknowledgments

This book was a Bucket List item for me, burning in my gut since I was 8. And it wouldn't have been possible without the love, support, and help of the following people.

First and foremost, my incredible wife, Madeline. There is no more powerful force in the universe than you. Thank you for always standing by me, believing in me, and lifting me up when I insisted on kicking myself down.

My daughters, Alex and Nikki, for always watching me and keeping the pressure on, to make sure I set the right example for you, in the best and only way I knew how. I'm the luckiest father on this rock.

Kevin Baker. Because of you, this book exists. It's as simple as it is powerful. Thank you for changing my life! Never doubt that you have.

To every single Patron of my audio dramas. Without your constant support I couldn't have done what I did. I wouldn't have believed that people wanted to hear the stories I had to share had you not been there for me, month after month, sending those encouraging messages, getting excited about what I was excited about, and providing the support I needed to be able to do this in the first place. To Brent Moody, Kevin Baker, Ian Truman-Mason, Alain, Elsa Howarth, James Marlee, Claudia Elvish, Nate Vanilla-Warford, Zane Desjarlais, Genesis Murray, Adam Burke, Cynthia Waddill, Morgan Barber, Dan Foytik, Shelley Perrin, Dohai, Sylvia Lynn, PB Sebastian, Sarah Werner, Philip Flynt, Anthony Dallape, Matthew Eckermann, Brian Tapia, Sandy Smith, Stacey Holbrook, Glen Collins, Raymond

Camper, Cheyenne Bramwell, Patrick Monroe, Robert Chauncey, Sam Mercer, Erin Karper, T Jane, Jon Grilz, and Ryan Bayer, thank you for your never-ceasing, always-awesome support!

To Mom. Thanks for 'hatching' me! We've come a long way and I've enjoyed these steps we've taken together.

My editor, Bryon Quertermous; thank you for patiently indoctrinating me to the professional side of authoring a book. Your angelic patience in helping me navigation adapting 10 scripts into a novel was (and will be) invaluable in my journey forward. I realize now, after having written two more novels in the time this has taken to release to the world, that I did you no favors. Yet you were patient, direct when I needed it, and were invaluable in making this transition a wonderful learning experience.

To Susan Kaye Quinn; there are no words to express how I feel about what you've done to help me grow as a writer. To think of listing the skills, insights, and attributes I've gained over the past year of knowing you would be a monumental undertaking. If the world were full of people like you, who gave before asking, what a wonderful world it would be. Thank you for always giving of yourself to make the lives of others better. You showed me that the impossible was possible.

To all of the wonderful people who took time out of life to help me proof this adaptation and taught me how to spell: Matt Spalding, Natalie Aked, Brent Moody, Elsa Howarth, Patrick Mangano, Derek Brown, Michael Sieber, Claudia Elvidge, Eric Thomas, Nashia Horne, Sandy Smith, Brian Ross, Melissa Bartell, Melissa Taylor, Louis Jackson, Jonathan Tindell, M. Dillon Hickmon, and Alexa Chipman; thank you for helping me launch this the right way. I'm grateful for your selflessness.

And, of course, to the hundreds of thousands of you who have listened to one of my audio dramas and find yourself holding this book in your hands. We may never cross paths, I may never come to know your name behind a download statistic, but my gratitude to you is ever-lasting. You're the ones out there making sure my audio drama stays present. You're the people telling your friends about my shows. You're the ones championing my stories on social media. I hope these stories bring joy to your world in whatever small way they can. Thank you!

About The Author

Paul Sating is an author and audio dramatist, and self-professed coolest dad on the planet, hailing from the Pacific Northwest of the United States. At the end of his military career, he decided to reconnect with his first love (that wouldn't get him in trouble with his wife) and once again picked up the pen. Four years on, he has numerous novels release or in the works and hundreds of thousands of downloads of his fiction & nonfiction podcasts.

When he's not working on stories, you can find him talking to himself in his backyard working on failed landscaping projects or hiking around the gorgeous Olympic Peninsula. He is married to the patient and wonderful, Madeline & has two daughters—thus the reason for his follicle challenges.

Published by Paul Sating Productions
P.O. Box 15166
Tumwater, WA 98511
paulsating.com
Twitter: paulsating
Instagram: @paulsating
Facebook: www.facebook.com/authorpaulsating

68681518R00176